PRAISE FOR LEONARD TOURNEY'S ELIZABETHAN MYSTERIES:

"Vividly evocative of the era and marvelously readable."

People

"Mr. Tourney seems to have a good understanding of his scenery, and his dialogue has a nice unmannered period feel. He gives us just enough of a sixteenth-century culture to establish the appropriate tone."

The New Yorker

"Tourney is a superb writter, skilled in the richness of the Elizabethan use of language."

Tulsa World

Also by Leonard Tourney
Published by Ballantine Books:

THE BARTHOLOMEW FAIR MURDERS
THE PLAYERS' BOY IS DEAD
LOW TREASON
FAMILIAR SPIRITS

OLD SAXON BLOOD

Leonard Tourney

BALLANTINE BOOKS • NEW YORK

Library of Congress Catalog Card Number: 88-1862

ISBN 0-345-35765-5

This edition published by arrangement with St. Martin's Press, Inc.

Printed in Canada

First Ballantine Books Edition: January 1990
Second Printing: December 1990

Thy virgin's girdle now untie
And in thy nuptial bed (love's altar) lie
        A pleasing sacrifice . . .

John Donne, *Epithalamion Made at Lincoln's Inn*

1

BUXTON, DERBYSHIRE. The smoky taproom of the Black Duck Inn. Year of Grace, 1601. Outside, weather fallen out so monstrous wet that the like had not been seen for the month.

Cuthbert Fludd, the aging steward of Thorncombe—and better known as plain "Cuth" to his wife and well-wishers—had thrice told his tale during the long, dreary afternoon and was about to launch another rendition, but none of the men objected. It was a good story the old man told, full of pathos and tragic irony. Just the right sort of story for such an afternoon. And Cuth told it well, told it slowly and with restraint, in a croaking, tearful voice that had a mesmerizing effect on all at the bar sober enough to give an ear. Outside the wind scolded mercilessly, and the panes of glass in the windows rattled like dead men's bones.

The old man's audience was alert to every syllable—like devout Papists at mass. Flattered by the attention, Cuth Fludd wove his tale the longer. From time to time he would pause to let the howling wind and the rattling windows play a frantic chorus before moving on again. The mobile features of his wrinkled countenance showed every emotion; his eyes constantly moved around at the faces of the men, gauging their response. He was saying:

"We knew the master was coming home. He had sent word by post. 'I'm coming,' said he. 'Make ready the castle.' Those were his words, I swear to God. So the women set to work as women will, cleaning the house that was as filthy and foul as a closetool for all the dogs whelping and pissing. The woman lighted fires to dry it out. And that was before this pestilent rain began."

There were murmurs of agreement all along the crowded bar, and someone made a wheezing cough. The steward cleared his eyes of smoke, for the wind was blowing the wrong way and the chimney had no proper draft. The tapster, a burly man in wine-stained apron, came round to fill each half-empty cup and join the listeners. The men all huddled more closely together, like fellows in a conspiracy.

"About noon Edward the hostler comes up from the paddock in his muddy boots to say the master's come. He's seen him riding along the road, says Edward. 'Why, then he's come betimes,' says I. Straightway I went to tell my good wife."

"Who was with him, Cuth?" asked a voice at the end of the bar.

"Only the Irishman. His manservant."

"No Irishwomen this time, heh, Cuth?" inquired another.

The question had an insolent ring the steward did not like. He turned sharply toward the questioner and saw that it was the town blacksmith. In his cups or sober as a judge, no man to fool with. The old man let the remark pass, plodding on like a half-blind nag that had learned the way home by heart.

"Only the Irishman. The master was on Prince, who was limping badly. He had ridden him hard, you see, covering six or seven leagues since dawn. So claimed the master. Filthy with mud, the both of them. Sir John was in a great hurry to get home from that godforsaken land."

"No wonder," said someone. There was general agreement that Ireland was a sinkhole, a terrible place for Englishmen. Of course none of the men had been there; but they knew what they had heard, and that was very bad indeed.

"I went down toward the road to welcome him," Cuth continued, "the sky low and glowering. Some of the women came too. Oh, he was glad to be home again, very glad. You could see it in his face when he greeted us all and asked how we did. When he dismounted he shook my hand, threw his arms around me, and planted a kiss on my cheek. He said that a view of my gnarled scabrous snout was as good to his soul as the thought of supper and enough good English ale to drown in. He had been gone nearly eight months, you see.

"We had heard he had lost a leg. He was fitted with a wooden one. Fixed right below the knee. He hobbled when he walked and the mud gave him trouble but he wouldn't use a crutch, for his manhood's sake."

Cuth paused to wet his throat. He licked his lips and sniffled, wiping away a pendant tear. Then he continued:

"Well, Edward took care of Prince and the Irishman's horse and I helped the Irishman with the master's gear and we followed him up to the house. The hounds were raised to such a pitch of excitement that such a clamor of yelping and howling you've never heard. Why, the pack nearly knocked him over when he came through the door. Believe me, the master was overjoyed to see them too. Called them all by their names, he did. Jack, Digger, Ballfoot, Wolfsleach—he knew the whole pack and they him, though some were sucking at the bitch's dugs when he left.

"I got the dogs out of the way so he could go upstairs. He said he was half dead from the ride and wanted to shift from his clothes and then sleep the afternoon. He ordered supper at five o'clock and was most particular as to what should be served. Said he hadn't had a decent meal since he left England. Then I left the Irishman to see to his needs and went downstairs and began cleaning up after the dogs. There was a fine mess, let me tell you."

"And did he have a good sleep, Cuth?" asked someone.

"Aye, he slept. Or must have. Yet you could not prove it

by me. I was downstairs, he was up. I saw him no more. Until after he was . . . dead."

There was an audible gasp from several of the listeners as the dreadful word was uttered. Cuth paused significantly and made the sign of the cross, which several others, confirmed Protestants too, imitated. Outside the wind still raged, the windows shook. The mere mention of *death* had struck the men to the quick, and each reflected darkly on his own demise, come when God willed.

One in the little group cursed his empty cup, called for more and was promptly hushed by the others, who would brook no interruptions. They knew the tragic conclusion, that a strange death would be the burden of the old man's tale. They leaned forward intently, as though the stiff wind out-of-doors were at their back. The steward turned his long, craggy face upward. He struggled to contain his emotions. His eyes were moist dog eyes.

"Cook had prepared a hearty supper. A feast. A leg of mutton there was, several sorts of fowl, and a hot steaming pie to tickle his palate beyond endurance. Five o'clock came and went, and the master did not come. The table was laid, the supper cooling, the cook in great distress, and my goodwife beside herself for wonder, saying 'If a man is starved, will he not eat?' "

"And where was the Irishman all the while?" asked the blacksmith suspiciously.

"In the hall of the new house waiting his supper. He said the master had commanded that he be not disturbed and said that we should be content to wait his appearance as was he, the Irishman, that is. Yet the master did not come.

"It was I who went up to fetch him then. I climbed the stairs to his chamber. I knocked. No answer came. I knocked and called out his name, reminding him that he had ordered supper at five of the clock and now it was half past. Then I entered and to my wonder he wasn't there. So I went back downstairs. Edward was idling about the kitchen, sniffing at the master's supper and poking his finger in the pie when cook wasn't looking. I told him to help me find the master, for he had not come down and wasn't in his rooms. I was afraid, afraid already. It all seemed passing strange. I knew something was wrong, and my goodwife agreed."

"Tell us how you found him, Cuth. Tell us everything," asked a rawboned, slack-necked cobbler who was standing nearest to the steward and had heard the story four times now from the old man's lips, twice earlier in the day from his wife, and the first time from a scrivener of the town whose shoe he had mended.

The old man took a deep breath and continued.

"It was Edward's idea to let the dogs out of the kennel. It was pouring rain, you see, not like now with all this wind but a steady, blinding rain. Already it was half dark. The dogs got the master's scent right away. They ran across the greensward toward the lake, Edward and I running after. Then we heard them howling, the cunning creatures. When Edward and I got there, we could see the dogs leaping about like they do when their quarry's cornered. They had found him. He was sitting in his boat, drawn up on the shore. He had no hat for his head and was just sitting in that little shallop of his, not caring about the rain. Edward tried to call off the dogs. The creatures were beside themselves, not knowing whether to howl or whine. They were licking the master's face and slobbering all over him. They knocked him over, they did, and so I knew the master wasn't just sitting there because he didn't get himself up again.

"I bent down for a close look. I saw his face. I told him that supper was ready and asked him if he did not wish to come and eat it. He had been very clear on when he wanted supper and what he wanted and it was a great feast the cook had prepared and now it would be cold and ruined.

"His doublet and hose were soaked. His hair was lank on his skull and in his eyes. I told Edward, who was still struggling with the dogs, to let them go hang, for the master needed help. But now the Irishman had come down too. Some of the women had followed and, sensing death, had started that heathen keening of theirs. The Irishman said he had heard the uproar the dogs were making and he wanted to know if anything was wrong. *'Wrong?'* said I. 'The master's drowned dead, that's what's wrong.' Then the Irishman shoved me aside and began to shake the master, rub his hands, try to bring him round again. Black filthy water gushed from his mouth. Dark like blood."

"How did you know he was dead, Cuth?" asked the cobbler in a husky whisper.

"Have I not seen death before?" replied the old steward with a touch of pride. "Death was in every line of his face. I knew it as soon as I touched him, although he was too newly dead to be stiff. He was drowned, drowned dead. Drowned in that lake, the one he had made. And him not even set forth from the shore.

"Then the rain came down stronger and fiercer, and I feared for my own drowning. The Irishman and Edward carried the master back into the house and tried to revive him there. The Irishman said that even if there was no breath, yet the master might be recovered. He said he had seen it done more than once in Ireland. For a full half hour the man stroked the master's limbs, pumped his chest while the black filthy water trickled down the master's beard and ran upon the floor. All the time the Irishman wept and sobbed and cried out Christ's name. Oh, it was a dreadful sight, I tell you, a dreadful sight! And the women would not be silenced for all my goodwife could do. They set up such a moaning and howling after the Irish fashion that you would not believe."

"And him such a brave soldier," said the cobbler. The sentiments were echoed by others in the taproom.

"A very brave soldier," agreed Cuth, who had been the dead man's father's steward as well as his grandfather's and could not have had fewer years than seventy if he had a day.

2

CHELMSFORD, *ESSEX*. Autumn of the year following. House of Matthew Stock, clothier, in High Street.

Matthew Stock was locked in an amorous embrace with his wife of twenty years when the messenger came pounding on the oak door of his shop below their living quarters with the violence of a madman. Matthew cursed softly, climbed out of bed, put on his slippers, nightgown, and cap, and trudged downstairs, candle in hand, mumbling as he descended that ten o'clock on a Sabbath eve was no decent hour to raise a house and swearing to himself that by all that was holy the cause of this disturbance better be murder or mayhem at least and no tippling townsman or pranking prentice disturbing his rest and domestic pleasures.

"Peace! Enough! Spare my door, for God's sake! I'll open, I'll open," Matthew called out irritably as the pounding grew even more peremptory.

Matthew unbolted the door and peered into the darkness. He held the candle aloft, which illuminated a good part of the narrow street and a tall figure wrapped in a heavy cloak. The stranger had a long, serious face, but there was no malevolence in his eye, and Matthew asked him what he wanted at such an hour.

"Are you Matthew Stock, clothier of Chelmsford and constable of the same?" asked the stranger.

Matthew said that he was. "And who might you be, sir?"

The tall man did not identify himself. Seemingly content at having been assured that Matthew was the one he sought, he reached inside the cloak and withdrew what appeared to be a letter and handed it to Matthew. "I am on the Queen's business," he said. "This is for you, Master Stock."

Much impressed, Matthew took the letter and forgot at once about its deliverer, who presently disappeared into the darkness and could be heard a half minute later riding away. By candlelight Matthew could read his own name written in a bold, resolute hand. On the backside of the letter a round seal bearing the royal signet added credence to the messenger's words. Matthew's heart throbbed with excitement.

"What is it, Matthew?"

His wife Joan, a shrewd, practical woman of her husband's years with a pretty oval face and a warm voice, had come upon him unawares, not content to wait upstairs for his return. She saw the signet and at once recognized the letter's origin.

"The royal seal! What can it mean? Might it have something to do with last month's murders in Smithfield?"

She was referring to the Bartholomew Fair murders, the solution to which her husband's quick wit and diligence had provided—and perhaps also to her own not inconsiderable role in saving the Queen's life from the menace of a lunatic Puritan.

"I can't conceive," he said.

"Perhaps Her Majesty thinks to reward you," she said.

"As God wills."

"Well, open it, goose," she said impatiently, thinking it ridiculous that they should speculate in the doorway when this mystery could be quickly solved by reading the letter itself.

Matthew shut the door and shot the bolt. They went into

the kitchen, set the candle in its holder on the board, and sat down. Matthew broke the seal and read the letter aloud.

It was very brief, and probably the labor of one of Her Majesty's secretaries rather than of the Queen herself. In less than a score of words it commanded Matthew—and Joan—to come to the court at Whitehall on the twenty-fourth day of the present month. It said arrangements had been made for their conveyance, and it concluded with expressions of the Queen's good wishes to them both.

It was signed, with elegant simplicity, *Elizabeth R.*

Matthew reread the letter in silence, then handed it to Joan, who examined it herself several times and pinched herself to make sure she was awake.

"Signed by Her Majesty herself!" Joan marveled.

"None other," said Matthew.

"Oh, it must be a reward," Joan said hopefully. "Will she make you a knight, Matthew—and me, thereby, a lady?"

"I would think that some miles beyond our deserts," Matthew said. "We did nothing but what any faithful subject would have done in the same circumstances. I suspect there's something else afoot. I wish I had Sir Robert's counsel now."

"Undoubtedly Sir Robert knows Her Majesty's mind," Joan agreed, perusing the letter for the third time and already contemplating how the document would become a family heirloom, handed down from generation to generation as long as the great Queen's name should be remembered and revered. "Today is the fifteenth. She commands our appearance at court on the twenty-fourth. That hardly gives us much time to make ready."

Matthew looked at his wife. Her face was alive with excitement. She seemed transformed before his eyes. Such was the awesome power of a royal summons, a summons that could command to honor or destruction.

He knew there would be no sleep for them now, not this night. They talked until dawn, never leaving the table, convincing themselves that the Queen's letter and the experience before them was no dream.

Within the next few days a second letter arrived, this causing no less excitement, for it confirmed the substance of the first. It was from Sir Robert Cecil, the Queen's Principal Secretary and Matthew's good friend by reason of honest service to the illustrious knight. It was longer than the Queen's and detailed their means of travel to London—a coach to be provided by Cecil, along with an escort of mounted men for protection against highwaymen and other nuisances of the road. Like the first letter, this made no reference to the cause of the summons, and although both Matthew and Joan were beside themselves with curiosity, they were not surprised to find the letters silent on this important point. It was the royal prerogative to give commands. Of lesser beings explanations might be required, but England's Majesty was to be obeyed unquestionably.

And so the Stocks got ready as best they could amid endless speculation as to what the summons meant. Joan had a new gown made, with a lace bodice and long, flowing sleeves in green and vermilion, and Matthew a new suit, including a handsome velvet doublet with pearl buttons that a gentleman might have envied. Matthew's neighbors and apprentices were equally excited, for somehow the news had spread as such news must in a small town, even though Matthew and Joan had resolved to be discreet about their journey.

The arrival of the coach and the retinue of armed riders on the day indicated did little to satisfy the curiosity of the townsfolk as to why the Stocks were bound for London again and in such style. And despite Matthew's popularity with his neighbors, a good many evinced signs of jealousy at these honors conferred so mysteriously on one of their own—one whom they had known all of his forty years, boy and man, apprentice and master, and now chiefly as prince of Chelmsford's clothiers and constable extraordinary.

A large crowd had gathered around the coach and in front of Matthew's shop. The narrow street was virtually impassable. Of course many in the crowd asked where Matthew was going and why, and to each he answered, "London." But *he* said nothing about the Queen, although the finery of the coach and the presence of the mounted troop gave ample warrant that the excursion was to be no ordinary one.

When the preparations were completed, Matthew turned his keys over to his young son-in-law, Will Ingram. Joan had her own words of counsel to Betty the cook and the several maids of the house on domestic maintenance during their absence, however long it should be. For neither knew that. Nor did they explain to their daughter, Elizabeth, and their son-in-law that the Queen's bidding might also involve some danger. Matthew and Joan had included that possibility within their speculations.

It was a torturous ride, the journey to London. The great square coach rumbled over the rutted road, churning up immense clouds of dust, and even the thick cushions of the seats could not spare them the tedium or discomfort of travel. Mercifully, their journey was broken by a night in a wayside inn, but although their jolly, unctuous host set an excellent table and their chamber was ample, warm, and relatively free of vermin, Matthew and Joan slept restlessly, preoccupied with visions of royal reward or censure. Then, even as the fledgling day began to assert itself against its mighty opposite, they were rousted, clothed, fed, and coached again, moving along a broader road now but one congested with carts, wagons, horses, and poor folk afoot, streaming toward the metropolis like flotsam on a great river destined to empty itself in the sea.

About midday they passed through the city gate and now found themselves on so crowded and narrow a cobbled street that the coach could move only by fits and starts, with the captain of their troop making himself hoarse in commanding and cursing that a way should be made through the throng in the Queen's name.

It took the better part of the afternoon to travel through the city and come to their destination: Whitehall—that glorious palace fronting on the swan-strewn Thames, the greatest jewel among the palaces royal.

* * *

Joan was hardly surprised to find that Whitehall was more like a small city than a mere manor with many rooms and an elegant front and that its maze of galleries, apartments, and chambers had been designed for use as well as show. Upon their arrival, they were provided with a young man and woman in royal livery to attend to their needs, and the Stocks were also directed to their place by a gentleman usher in a black robe and bearing a wand of office, who, having assured himself that these were indeed Matthew and Joan Stock of Chelmsford, dispensed with the courtesy of identifying himself and bore them off with conspicuous dignity and authority. Of the purpose of their visit or of their audience with the Queen the gentleman usher said not a word. Nor did he give any indication when the mystery of their summons would be resolved. It was plain from the expression of his face that he thought they should be content with the quarters assigned, the honor of being lodged in the palace, and the distinction of having conversed, albeit briefly, with the gentleman usher himself.

Then he shut the door on them, leaving the female servant to unpack Joan's things while the male counterpart performed a like service for Matthew.

Meanwhile, Joan walked over to the window and looked out. It was a crisp October day, and above the city fleecy white clouds scudded along. Joan could see across the river to the low marshy ground of the Bankside and beyond to St. Paul's. She could see London Bridge and the solemn square Tower. In midstream of the river a flock of swans cruised in princely dignity, and at the river's bend floated a handsome barge manned by doughty oarsmen doubtless transporting some luminary of the court, perhaps to the very palace where she now was.

How her heart thrilled to it all!

She was about to invite her husband to share her view when her attention was drawn to movement below her.

Beneath her window was the palace garden, an artful arrangement of walks and arbors, flower beds and fountains, all laid out in geometrical perfection. A group of young women, all very elegantly gowned, moved slowly down a path. They were obviously enjoying the fine day, and all seemed involved in a common animated conversation, except for one who, no less comely or finely arrayed, lagged behind.

It was in keeping with Joan's curious nature that she should give her attention to the straggler. Was it lost love, a quarrel with her royal mistress, or some female complaint that caused such untoward melancholy? Joan wondered. While her companions stepped within doors, the girl lingered by a fish pond and stared for a while into its depths. Intrigued, Joan continued to watch. Then, suddenly, the girl looked up at Joan's window and, Joan felt a wave of apprehension—a sudden chill in the marrow—and with that second sight that had been both bane and blessing of her life, she knew it was someone's death the girl contemplated in that solitary stillness.

Joan withdrew from the window, aware of having intruded upon the girl's privacy. Turning, she saw that the servants had gone and Matthew was stretched out on the bed like a gentleman of leisure, his hands behind his head. His eyes were closed but she knew he was not asleep. The satisfaction on his face made her sure of that. He said, "Can this be believed, Joan?"

"Can what be believed?"

"Why, our being here, in Whitehall. And I nothing greater than a clothier of Chelmsford."

"And the constable," she felt compelled to add, for her dignity's sake as well as his.

She was about to tell Matthew of the young woman she had been observing when a knock came at the door. It was not the stern gentleman usher whom she half expected but a more amiable personage she recognized as being in Sir Robert Cecil's household. He announced that supper would be served shortly and that they were to join Sir Robert, who very much desired to speak with them both.

The apartment where they were to sup was in another wing of the rambling edifice, and Joan and Matthew were pleased to be led there by a guide. The chamber had a high ornate ceiling and a bank of mullioned windows along one wall that showed the day in its decline. A table had been laid, at the end of which sat Cecil himself. The Principal Secretary had already commenced eating, for which he at once apologized. "I missed my breakfast. And was nigh unto death for hunger. Pray be seated. Don't stand on ceremony. The food's blessed and cooling apace."

By the settings Joan surmised that she and Matthew would be the knight's only guests. A file of servants now entered bearing meat and drink. As their plates were filled, Joan glanced sideways at Cecil and felt as always the powerful attraction of his personality.

Small and hunchbacked, he somewhat resembled an old child with prominent forehead, long, narrow face, and pointed beard. His eyes were dark and unusually alert, full of a suppressed merriment that could sometimes shift suddenly to black melancholy. He had small white hands, yet rather long fingers, and he ate delicately, picking at his food despite his claim of having been too famished to wait their coming.

She noticed that Matthew did not ask why they were here. Nor did Cecil mention it. Cecil spoke of various matters, deliberately, it seemed, skirting that which was uppermost in her mind. The knight asked them about the suitability of their quarters and whether their journey had been a pleasant one. Matthew complained about the condition of the roads, and Cecil admitted it was a national scandal. But what could be done? Weren't such matters within God's province? As long as roadbeds were earthen, they would be subject to drought and wet, ice and sleet, not to speak of the constant abuse by man, beast, wagon, and, yes, coaches with their great wooden wheels and immense weight. "The Romans built roads of stone," Cecil remarked casually between mouthfuls. He concluded the conversation with a description of some of Whitehall's sights that should not escape their attention, but, of course, Joan's mind was elsewhere. And, strangely, more than once on the young woman she had seen that afternoon in the Queen's garden, the young woman who had meditated upon death.

Then the supper was done and it seemed to Joan that surely Cecil would now reveal the purpose of their coming. Would she return to Chelmsford as Lady Joan, worthy wife of Sir Matthew, or was some less glorious reward in the offing for services rendered? And finally the Queen's Secretary spoke to the question, and she was free from bondage and speculation.

"I know you have been wondering about Her Majesty's summons—what it portends," Cecil began amiably when the servants had cleared the table and the three were alone. Outside night had come. In the several hundred little panes of the mullioned windows as many images were presented of themselves and the room they sat in, illuminated only now by the candles on the table and the fire on the great hearth, which the last retreating servant had taken care to bank high before his departure. "I did not intend to burden you with fears—or with great expectations, but discretion is always advisable in these matters. And talk always better, too, on a full stomach."

Cecil asked them if they had ever heard of Sir John Challoner and when they said never, he told them that this same worthy knight's niece was one of the Maids of Honor and then he began an account of the man himself.

"A soldier of considerable merit, with some four or five Irish expeditions to his credit and a reputation for ferocity. His title—baronet—is hereditary, the family being old Saxon blood. His seat's in Derbyshire—or was, I should say. A castle called Thorncombe. The gentleman is twelve months dead and buried."

Cecil had recited these few facts as though he had been reading Sir John's history from an invisible scroll suspended above the table. Now he paused, and his eyes took on a faraway look as though the same scroll had been removed and replaced with a private vision of the hills and dales of Ireland, the field of battle, the clamor of trumpets. "It is reported he endured every hardship of the camp. Ate raw beef at midnight and lay upon wet corn, drinking water, vinegar, and aqua vitae rather than good ale or wine. In times of greatest extremity he made a meal of horseflesh and once, according to the same report, spent a whole night waist-deep in a ditch surrounded by the bloody corpses of his comrades. He fought bravely against Tyrone, Connor Roe, and other rebel chiefs, and spent so much time in the field that it is said he knew every rock and rill in Munster, and Leinster too. Hacked and hewed the enemy with such fury at the English defeat at Armagh—''

Cecil paused; a servant had entered to inquire whether Sir Robert wanted another stoup of wine. Cecil waved him away with an expression of irritation at the interruption, and when the door was closed again he continued his narrative, promising them that he would presently come to the nub of the matter.

''Late in the summer of last year a musketball penetrated Sir John's leg armor. Gangrene set in below the knee, and a five-shilling-a-week surgeon, newly impressed, no doubt, and resentful thereof, required half-dozen chops with a meat cleaver to remove the rotting member. It was thought best that Sir John retire from the field. Outfitted with a wooden leg, he decamped and returned to his ancestral seat—Thorncombe, as I have already said. It was there it happened.''

''The strange death you spoke of?'' Matthew asked.

''Yes. A drowning. On the day of his homecoming. He had gone out upon a lake next to the castle. In a boat. His servants tried to revive him, but to no avail.''

Joan said, ''Sir John's death seems lamentable but hardly sinister. Many a man has fallen into a river, pond, or lake, never to rise therefrom.''

''True, Joan,'' said Cecil. ''Many have gone to God or the devil in the manner you describe, but few drown and rise of their own strength. The servants found their master sitting bolt upright.''

Joan agreed that altered the case.

Matthew asked if there had been a coroner's verdict.

''There was,'' answered Cecil. ''Death by misadventure.

In want of hard evidence to the contrary. Sir John was dead for a fact; that his death was wrought by another was too much in doubt to pursue."

"Very strange," murmured Matthew.

"I assume this niece you spoke of believes otherwise than what the jury found," Joan said.

"An excellent surmise, Joan. The mouse's nose is in the trap, for Mistress Frances Challoner has complained to the Queen, who has promised to look into the case."

"Which looking my husband is to do," Joan said.

"Right again! The trap is sprung!" Cecil smiled broadly.

"But I have no authority outside my own parish," Matthew protested.

"You'll be Queen's officer—her agent," Cecil said. "It is for that purpose you have been summoned—you and Joan. Now you know the smattering of facts I have and the general character of your mission, the more particular details of which I will leave to Her Majesty to explain when you see her tomorrow."

"Tomorrow?" Matthew asked.

"About nine o'clock. I will bring you to the Presence Chamber myself. The audience will be brief, never fear. Her Majesty has a full schedule during the day and must play host to the Spanish ambassador toward dinner hour, a very slippery fellow indeed. But, pray, don't tell him I said that if you happen to meet him."

Cecil laughed at his own jest and Matthew joined in, but Joan sat still and unsmiling. She thought it very unlikely that she would meet the Spanish ambassador or any other such personage. On the other hand, they were to meet the Queen, and on the next day!

For her that was quite enough excitement. Though she began to wonder if the Spanish ambassador spoke English and what she should say to the slippery gentleman if he addressed her.

Raising a white hand to suppress a yawn, Cecil rose from the table to signal that their interview was over. "Sleep well, the both of you. Some of the beds in the palace are no better than a brothel's—for sure maiming of the backbone, that is. I trust the gentleman usher has done well by you."

Joan assured the Queen's Secretary that their chamber was quite comfortable. Matthew said he had already tried the bed and found it good. Then Cecil bid them good night again, and the gentleman of Cecil's household who had shown them the way to his master's apartment returned to lead them back to their own quarters and wish them a peaceful repose.

It was now past nine o'clock, and since it had been a very long and tiring day, Matthew and Joan prepared for bed without further ado, washing their hands and faces in a silver bowl engraved with the royal arms, and then wiping themselves with towels of such wondrous softness that Matthew swore he had never seen the like. These rituals observed, they dressed in their nightgowns, prayed as was their custom, and then, candles extinguished and kisses exchanged, they succumbed to a sleep that even their anxiety about the morrow could not stay or disturb.

Mistress Frances Challoner was a tall, well-featured young woman of eighteen years with hair the color of flax and skin so compounded of red and white that it put to shame all sunburned beauties of the court. Betrothed to a young man of her own choosing (a great rarity, *that*!), heiress to a castle and lands appurtenant, endowed with an income of a thousand pounds a year in her own right and therefore possessed of such gifts as to cause any other mortal nothing but envy of her lot, she was at that moment engulfed in a gross melancholy of so malevolent a force that even the prospects of marriage to the man she loved could not assuage it.

She had deliberately slowed her pace to let her companions go before her, finding as she did their company irksome like the buzzing of a fly around the face.

They were giggling and chattering, behaving quite indecorously, considering their station as the Queen's Royal Maids and daughters of some of England's most illustrious families. And all these offenses when Mistress Frances was preoccupied with solemn thoughts—of her uncle's murder and of all those other tragedies of her personal history that the murder seemed to aggravate like salt in a wound.

Her father had disappeared in an Irish bog when she was hardly out of her cradle, leaving her his name, a dim recollection of his face, and an embittered widow for her mother. Then, when Mistress Frances was twelve, the mother had died. Her uncle, Sir John Challoner, had been her only close relative, and since he was a bachelor gone off to the wars most of the year, the girl was a virtual orphan. She would have suffered she knew not what fate had the Queen not made her a royal ward. But her uncle, whom she had seen but twice in her life when he had come to London and for whom therefore she had no great affection, had had nevertheless no little value to her as a symbol of the ancient blood that coursed through her veins and separated her from the rout of young women of prominence, some of whose families were relative newcomers to gentility, much less nobility. And so it was not grief for a dead relative that prompted her melancholy, but a sense of injustice done upon her as his heir. Since she was the last of her race, the burden of defending Challoner honor had fallen upon her delicate shoulders, and she was determined to defend that honor in any way she could.

It was the same honor then, coupled with her determination to make Castle Thorncombe the site of her wedding and her future home, that made urgent an explanation of her uncle's drowning. To that end she had appealed to the Queen. The Queen had listened sympathetically and had agreed as to the dubiousness of the facts in the case, which hardly had the color of an accident.

Lifting her head to take the comely young woman in, the Queen had inquired, "Yet, pray, who would want such a man as your uncle was, dead before his time, save his Irish enemies?"

The young woman had reminded her royal mistress of her late uncle's proclivity for Irish refugees as servants. By report, the castle was full of them, beneficiaries of Sir John's charitable impulses. Was it not conceivable that one of them had taken a long-waited revenge? "Certain," Mistress Frances said, "my uncle had one enemy at least—he who killed him. No man falls into water, drowns, and then climbs into his boat again for appearance's sake."

Faced with such cogent reasoning, the Queen had promised to do something. But since the promise nearly a year had passed, Mistress Frances' nuptials approached apace, and the mystery had not been solved. Sir John lay in his tomb unavenged—his suspicious death a blot upon the Challoner escutcheon.

The bride-to-be paused for a moment in the center of the garden, her noisy companions now beyond earshot and offense. She rested near a pool, whose pale, clear water was as smooth as a swath of French silk. Beneath the surface she saw the golden carp, moving furtively in circles. And she thought of the lake in which her uncle had drowned. How and why?

Her meditation was interrupted by a new sense that she was being observed. She looked around her and saw, in a window far above, a woman of pleasant and intent expression. For a moment their eyes met, then the woman in the window disappeared and Mistress Frances moved on. It was late afternoon now. The pale October sun seemed as remote in the heavens as the prospect of happiness.

Aileen Mogaill, the youngest of the Irish maids of Thorncombe, stopped to catch her breath. She had been lugging two full buckets of water from the wellhouse to the castle kitchen, and her arms and shoulders had begun to protest the burden. She sat the buckets down, thinking her rest much deserved, and wiped her brow with her neckcloth. She had been at these labors for the better part of an hour by her reckoning, without so much as a pause to scratch. Besides, she had seen nothing of the hatchet-faced housekeeper who monitored these duties all the afternoon, and she supposed the old woman had gone off to nap in one of the bedchambers, or to growl at her husband. Gray-eyed, ruddy-cheeked, and eminently nubile, Aileen Mogaill looked with dismay at her reflection in one of the buckets. Beneath her white cap, her hair was a fright, tumbling in undisciplined dark curls around her ears. Her small face, distorted in the water, stared back like a gnome's face, mockingly. She looked up at the gloomy pile of the castle itself and felt a sudden chill of apprehension.

The cause of this chill was not her usual complaint, that as the daughter of a prosperous Irish farmer she should be better than a maid, or her general dislike of the castle and of England, or hatred of the housekeeper and the steward, her husband. These were small matters now, matters that had given place to a greater concern. For she had during the past year embarked on a dangerous course; just how dangerous, she had only recently come to understand.

She picked up the buckets and continued toward the castle, still thinking of what she had done. How she had seen on the very afternoon of her late master's death something the full significance of which had only become apparent later, when backstairs gossip had confirmed her suspicions.

And what she had seen was this: her master and another engaged in a furious quarrel while the rain fell, not twenty feet or more from where she stood before hurrying out of the rain into the warmth and dryness of the kitchen. *Then* she had thought nothing about it. It had been a quarrel that had not concerned her. And later no one asked her what she had seen or heard, nor was she disposed to volunteer information.

But time had taught her worldly wisdom—or so she had thought when she had concluded that her knowledge might be turned to gain, and she had spoken thereafter by cunning indirection and subtle hint to that person her knowledge most touched; been understood, and come to terms: her continued silence for a modest supplement to her scanty income.

By such small means Aileen Mogaill had hoped to save enough to secure her freedom and return to Ireland.

But lately she had begun to doubt the wisdom of her bargain. Would not, after all, one who had murdered a knight hesitate for long to murder his maid if it appeared to present advantage?

It was a question well to be asked.

It was a question urgently to be answered.

Aileen had seen lights, heard footfalls, glimpsed shadows in the castle where none should have been at such hours and places. She thought she was being watched, followed. A menace she had felt, a chill to the bone, a premonition of evil, and her prayers and devotions, practiced in the still privacy of her quarters, were insufficient to allay her fear.

How else could these things be explained, she decided, except by her own rash action?

He who sups with the devil must use a long spoon!

She had supped with the devil. She had been foolish. And now God only knew what price she must pay for it.

3

AN unprepossessing pair of birds indeed, these Stocks, thought the Queen of England when she first met them.

It was still early in the morning and chilly in the Presence Chamber despite the great number of attendants, lords temporal and spiritual, and higher gentry gathered there to gape or petition or advise England's Majesty, and whose whisperings had now ceased out of curiosity to learn just who these lesser lights of creation might be who had the honor of presentation before them. Cecil was giving an account of the Stocks' heroism at Bartholomew Fair—not for the Queen's sake, who remembered it well, but for the audience. Eloquently he described the danger to the Queen from the moon-mad, bloody-minded, Bible-thumping Puritan, Gabriel Stubbs—at large and menacing among the stalls and stench of Smithfield.

Had it not been for Matthew and Joan Stock, an enormity of earth-shaking proportions would have befallen.

Cecil finished his narrative and there was a sprinkling of applause, muted by the inevitable envy felt toward ones who had found themselves in the right place at the right time and now were to be rewarded for their good fortune.

The Queen had greeted the Stocks in that ingratiating way she had with the common folk, addressing them as countrymen and friends. They had kissed her bejeweled hand, been favored with the royal smile, and her sour old-woman's breath. Now she commanded them to rise.

"So it is to you that we owe our life," she said. "We are truly grateful."

"England most of all," Cecil added politicly.

The Chelmsford constable's response did not displease her, although it was very brief and made no effort to flatter. "Such is the subject's privilege if the occasion presents itself."

"The occasion did present itself," the Queen replied. "Yet only you—and your good wife—stepped forward to seize it by the forelock."

To this conversation the constable's wife contributed little, and that pleased the Queen well, for she had no patience with garrulous females, especially at court, which she generally kept clear of wives on principle. Joan Stock, however, had a pleasant, honest face and modest regard. She was well-dressed but not above her station. When she had been bidden to rise, she stood without fidgeting. Unlike her husband, whose nervousness was manifest in his sweating face and trembling hands, the wife seemed marvelously composed. And that spoke well for her, too, for although the Queen could not abide presumption or arrogance in a subject, she was ever an admirer of courage and it was this quality of which the simple countrywoman seemed possessed.

"The full extent of our gratitude we have yet to consider," the Queen said. "As for now, another matter of business is at hand in which both of you may be of service."

The Queen paused, and with a little flick of her wrist she beckoned to a slender young woman with pale, serious face, who now came forward from among the Maids of Honor and stood at the Queen's right hand. "This is Mistress Frances Challoner, niece of the late Sir John Challoner of Derbyshire, knight and baronet. Mistress Frances believes her uncle's recent death was foul play, and to our mind such a supposition is not beyond the realm of possibility, despite her good uncle's well-allowed reputation as a soldier. Sir Robert had told us that your endeavors in our behalf are not the first instance of such service; that you are skillful bonesetters to join each part of a mystery and make it whole and plain."

"Your Majesty will find no more diligent servant in such a cause than Matthew Stock," Cecil added.

"More than diligence is wanted," the Queen said. "Intelligence, cunning, the skill to ferret out that which others would fain keep concealed. The world knows how curious we are to be informed when any of our subjects is slain. How much more a knight of the realm, lest the blood of the dead man cry out for vengeance."

Fixing her eye on Matthew the Queen dropped her voice to a husky whisper. "Sir Robert will later acquaint you with the more particular parts of Sir John's death, if he has not already done so. The sum is that we wish to send you both to Derbyshire. Not as open officers but as lawful spies. You will give out among the servants that you are sent by Mistress Frances to act as steward and housekeeper, respectively. And she will write to the present occupiers of those posts to alert them of your coming."

"The present steward is aged and infirm—and I think not competent in his duties," the young heiress added by way of elaboration.

"These servants are ever a closemouthed lot," the Queen said. "To each other belowstairs, they will speak volumes and hand about the private vices of small and great like unwashed linen, but to those in authority they act with vexing discretion. They will need the spur rather than the bridle—and we are averse to torture. Therefore you must find a middle way to the same end. If your spying proves Sir John drowned, as the coroner's jury said, so be it. If otherwise, you will hie yourselves to London again and report the fact and the factor, if possible. Meanwhile, keep Sir Robert informed by letters. He is our agent in this business. But you must act with dispatch. Already we fear the trail's cold, Sir John having been dead all this year."

Matthew Stock said that he would do as was commanded and with a will.

"Your sojourn may last several weeks, perhaps a month," said the Queen.

"If it is a year, Your Majesty, it will be well so it were done to serve," Matthew replied with a bow.

"Excellent. When can you leave for Derbyshire?"

Matthew looked at his wife and she back at him. "Forthwith," he said.

"Good. That pleases us well. Let us then make quick end of a slow proceeding. A month we give you, no more. Now, Sir Robert will instruct you as to your journey north. He will also see that your expenses are taken care of. Your mission accomplished, we will once again consider your reward for Smithfield. As for now, take this purse along with our gratitude for your pains. And may God cover you both with His softest wings."

Matthew and Joan followed Cecil out of the Presence Chamber. They passed the solemn watch of the Gentleman of the Black Rod, the official whose duty it was to allow no one to pass the threshold without permission, made their way through a host of important-looking persons waiting their turn for an audience, and then down the grand staircase. When they were at a relatively private corner of the palace, Joan told Matthew that it was Mistress Frances Challoner she had observed the day before standing alone in the garden. "Just as I supposed in my heart, although how I concluded it was she, I cannot say."

Cecil gave Matthew instructions as to when and how they were to travel and under what guise. By coach as far as Buxton, then by horse and cart to Thorncombe so as to dispel any impression that the Stocks were more than they seemed. Mistress Frances' letter of introduction to the household servants was to be sent ahead by post. Matthew and Joan were to carry additional documents verifying them to be husband

and wife, steward and housekeeper. Even as they spoke, their personal belongings were being prepared for the journey, for Cecil had never doubted that Matthew and Joan would accept the assignment.

Cecil now shook their hands warmly and bid them Godspeed. But with his valediction went a solemn warning. He did hope they understood the mission involved some risk. "If there's a murderer at Thorncombe Castle, he'll not gladly welcome you within the park pale. Be discreet, therefore. You will be steward and housekeeper. Say nothing, do nothing, that will allow it to be thought you are otherwise. And trust no one. If trouble falls in your way, there's precious little I can do at such a remove."

"We are prepared for anything," Matthew said confidently.

"I don't doubt it in the least," Cecil said, smiling broadly. "Again, Godspeed you both and so farewell."

"It was like a dream, the whole of it," Joan exclaimed when they were in their chamber again and waiting for the last of their gear to be removed.

"A dream?"

"The audience with the Queen, goose! Who would have thought that I, Joan Stock of Chelmsford, whose father was a baker and he the noblest of his line, would someday kiss the hand of England's Queen and have her thanks as well!"

"Or such a princely gift," Matthew said, thinking of the purse they had been given. It was made of fine silk, and the contents were enough to keep a gentleman in clean linen for a year or more. If the Queen intended greater rewards, Matthew was confounded to know what they might be. Were they thus to be made rich for doing no more than an honest subject's duty? As grateful as he was for the gift, he was not sure he liked being paid for such service.

"And did you see the gown she wore!" Joan continued in her ecstasy. "How splendid it was! And the emeralds on her bosom!"

"Am I no clothier that I should overlook such treasures,"

Matthew replied, "or fail to appreciate their cost? It's said the Queen loves emeralds."

"Derbyshire?" Joan inquired suddenly, remembering that they were about to embark for the place. "That is near Scotland, isn't it?"

"Almost, I think," replied her better-traveled husband, although his own knowledge of geography was sketchy.

"It will surely be cold then—and wild."

"It will be cold. A hard, inhospitable country, full of moors, hills, ravines."

"And perhaps a murderer," she mused darkly, as the glory of Elizabeth's court faded from her mind and was replaced by more threatening images of desert wastes, solitary keeps, and the stolid, sullen folk who inhabited them.

It had been a long morning for the near-seventy-year-old woman, even if she was Queen. Besides the Chelmsford constable and his wife, she had granted audiences to three peers of the realm, the Lord Bishop of London, a contingent of merchants from Amsterdam, and received the tearful petition of the wife of a man recently drawn and quartered for treason, that the malefactor's bodily parts be removed from the spikes on London Bridge and decently buried and that his estate not fall by way of escheatment to the Crown. She had granted the request. She had gossiped for a half hour with the Spanish ambassador, had a vigorous debate with one of the Privy counselors over a new law then being considered in Parliament. She had chastized one of her ladies in waiting for the low cut of her bodice (why, one could see flesh to the navel and below!), which globular spectacle had so entranced the good aforementioned bishop that he was undoubtedly at home this instant composing sonnets in homage to those twin peaks of mammary perfection.

She was so weary she felt surely God must have added another decade or two to her years. The rheumatism in her right arm plagued her mercilessly. The senseless chatter of her women gave her a headache. Dismissing the women, she told her bodyguard to stand at a distance, and motioned to Cecil to come forward.

"Were the constable and his wife not everything I said?" Cecil asked.

"The man seemed frightened out of his wits," she replied crankily. "That constable of yours stuttered when he spoke. And the woman, she's not dumb, is she?"

Cecil laughed. "Hardly. Joan Stock can talk up a storm when she wills. I've heard her myself. They were nervous. What can Your Majesty expect? But believe me, there are good heads on those shoulders. And honest hearts within."

"I'll take your word, Robin." Yet she was skeptical and made a face to show it. "Words are leaves, the substance consists of deeds—the true fruits of a good tree."

"Pray, give them the month. You'll see."

"The month. I'll give them that, and their expenses, too. Pray I have not given them rope to hang themselves. Who would not stint to murder a knight would hardly spare a country constable with a long nose. I very much fear he is a knight in shabby armor we have conjured up to be Mistress Frances' champion."

"Perhaps," said Cecil. "Yet he may prove like the Knight of the Red Cross in Master Spenser's poem you so much regard. That is, an unlikely fellow who proves a true champion when tested."

She considered this, then said, "Well, I am heartily glad I did not make Matthew Stock a knight for his trouble at Smithfield."

"Saving your life isn't worth a knighthood?"

"His *wife* saved my life. Get your facts straight, Robin. She was not dumb that day, I'll tell you, but gave full voice in my danger."

"And a very good thing too, for which Matthew Stock deserves a knighthood. His actions at Bartholomew Fair were more than yeoman service."

"Knighthoods shouldn't be distributed too generously," she said. "Ruins the breed. Nothing Essex did in Ireland so much angered me as dubbing every fellow he had had a few drinks with, or praised his horse or leg. God's wounds! he vexed me. Besides," she said more calmly, "it would hardly have done to send a knight of the realm into the wilds of Derbyshire to play the part of a household servant—or to have his lady wife tag along as housekeeper. What a monstrous violation of decorum! And yet, if he succeeds in this—"

"If, if, if," he chided, finding his royal mistress in a more pliant mood. "Would Your Majesty be willing to make a small wager that he succeeds?"

"A small wager? How small?"

"Ten crowns."

"Ten! Don't make me laugh, my little man. You'll put a stitch in my side and bring my surgeon running to bleed me again. Ten crowns is a beggar's ransom."

"Marry, fifteen then."

"Minuscule still." She eyed him shrewdly. "Moreover, it shows precious small faith in the constable and his wife. Bet twenty and the wager is done."

"Twenty, then, and to show my faith I'll add twenty more."

"Confident odds—and spoken like a true lover of the game. Gambling was always your *principal* vice, Robin," she said with a throaty laugh and mockery in her eye that made her, for the moment, seem far younger than her years. "Now, to conditions."

"Conditions?"

"Of course, conditions. For what if in a month's time Stock returns with nothing. Which of us loses?"

"Who else but I?" said Cecil. "Since Your Majesty is so ready with her purse, I'll take a broad step out on the plank and wager as follows: first, that the knight was murdered for a fact; second, that Matthew discerns the murderer within the month and returns providing us with the very name and substantial proof of the charge. Be it so, and your twenty crowns are mine to spend as I please. If otherwise, you have my forty."

"Wagered like a true gentleman—or a complete fool." She laughed.

"Time will tell," he said.

"And, mind you, I will have good grounds for any tale of murder he fetches home. I will have grounds, I say, a terra firma of fact and no shifting sands of supposition, or your forty crowns are mine! We princes are wary of our bargains—and our wagers."

"Would Her Majesty be pleased to have her personal secretary notarize the conditions of our agreement, or have it drawn and quartered by an attorney-at-law?" he asked with sly amusement.

She laughed heartily and cried: "Damn all lawyers! If I cannot trust you, Robert Cecil, son of Burleigh whom I loved like a brother, who can a poor old woman trust in these times of villainy and treason? *Thirty days*, Robin. Not an hour more. On that point I will not be moved."

"Thirty days."

"Not a minute more."

"Done!"

She leaned back in her chair, looking pleased that her conditions had been met. She lifted a skeptical eyebrow and said, "Well, my little man, the plot is laid. Let the outcome be as God disposes."

4

MOLL FLUDD peered over her husband's shoulder with restless eyes, suffering the agony of ungratified curiosity and growling her complaints in blistering threats and calumnies that her husband read faster. The object of her interest was a letter—received that very morning and addressed to them both—written on costly vellum and indited with a fine goose quill; and although in her ignorance of learning she could make nothing of its strokes and curlicues, dots and squiggles, its importance had been established in her mind by the fact the letter bore the Challoner seal. That and her husband's present confirmation that its author was none other than the dead master's niece, she who was a Maid of Honor in the Queen's court!

As best as Cuth Fludd could determine, he being the husband in question, the letter's burden was twofold. The first fold being that the young woman was to be married in the castle sometime before winter and that therefore all should be made ready. Further communications on that score were to follow. The second fold, very grievous for Cuth to read aloud, for he knew his wife would receive it badly, was that the new mistress of Thorncombe was to be preceded by two harbingers: a man and wife appointed as steward and housekeeper to stand in Cuth's and Moll's places.

This news, the letter made plain, was not to be received as condemnation, but as word of a richly deserved retirement from the onerous duties their advanced ages could only aggravate. That Moll and Cuth were to enjoy continued maintenance in the household was also promised. The groundskeeper's lodge, a tumbledown structure near the lake, was suggested as a suitable accommodation.

To have all this stuffing brought forth at last, Moll had had to poke her husband in the back as she might have prodded a mule, but now that it was revealed, her irritation at Cuth had not abated. For as he was the conveyer of such ill tidings, she held him in large part to blame for them. Moreover, having no other present—and certain not she who was ultimately responsible, that stringbean of a child, the young puke of the palace, the last drop of the Challoner blood—to blame for the deep insult and apprehension she felt, there was nothing left but to beat upon him, like Judy upon Punch, whose guilt in the matter was further evidenced by his failure to express his resentment as energetically as she.

"Old ponderous fool," she growled with dangerous eyes. "Damn her ladyship's maintenance and freedom of the larder! The groundskeeper's lodge? Or yes, very well and wellaway! Pray, shall we make the rats and other vermin give room to us, for the place has not been tenanted for a generation or more? New steward! New housekeeper! Something more is afoot, I warrant. Something more!"

"Why, what could it be?" her husband asked, looking up from the letter which he still studied, as though new writing should suddenly appear there if he looked away for a moment, writing with even more terrible import. He picked at the thatch of white hair that crowned his long, narrow head and mumbled the words of the letter silently as if praying.

"What be their names again, say you?" Moll asked.

"Says Stock. Says Matthew and Joan Stock."

"*Stock*, is it? As in a wooden stump or block. Godsbody!

I'll wager he's a right blockhead and his wife another and both of them as rightly and fitly named as the Devil."

"Well," drawled her husband, "blockhead or no, he is to be the new steward and his wife the housekeeper. Mistress Frances puts the matter very plainly."

Cuth Fludd had said this quite without thinking how such a capitulation to necessity would affect his wife. She slapped him upon the noggin for his insolence, reproving him too for his lack of respect for her injured merit. He bore his beating with his usual long-suffering, tight-lipped and downcast like a whipped dog.

Her fury spent for the moment, Moll folded her arms on her ample bosom and rocked on the balls of her feet. She stared into the middle distance of the kitchen, contemplating the greater injuries to come—the arrival of the Stocks, her dethronement as reigning female of the house and chief terror of the lower servants, the aggravation of adjusting to a new mistress, surely full of whims and airs and bent on changing the little universe of the castle. These impending developments aroused more anger—and suspicion. And thus her remark to her husband that something indeed was afoot, something more ominous than a change of masters or the appointment of new servants.

"Stocks," she repeated, as much to herself as to her spouse, and making a face as though she had just swallowed a fly. "I like not their names at all—that's their first offense, the names. Surely greater will follow."

"Follow they may," replied Cuth in a philosophical tone of one inured to suffering. "The young mistress who wrote this letter is now mistress of the castle according to England's holy laws and the mighty Court of Chancery. She commands us to accept these newcomers in our place, to relinquish our offices in which we twain have served for forty years or more. That's the sum, as I see it."

His voice broke; his eyes filled with tears.

"Sum indeed," snorted the wife, partly mollified by her husband's expression of grief and half sorry that she had beaten him so roundly. "Sum indeed! I say there's more here than's sounded. Why, all these years we've labored, through several Challoners, and never were we complained of. We knew our duties, and we did them. And never were strangers brought in from outside the shire, save the wild Irish Sir John would bring home from the wars for kindness's sake. Mark me, this does not bode well for Thorncombe. As if enough evil had not already fallen on our heads, what with the master dying as he did."

At that very moment Aileen Mogaill appeared in the doorway, cast a hesitant glance at Moll, and then stepped over the threshold. She was carrying a basket of fresh greens from the kitchen garden. Moll scowled at the girl on general principles but held her tongue until she had gone out again. Of all the crosses she had born in the house the presence of so many heathen Irish was the heaviest. But what was a Christian woman to do? Coddling the Irish had been the master's will, the master's bounty, the master's high-fantastical humor. Surely it had not been her place to deny him.

"When does it say we can expect these Stocks?"

"Within a month—before the winter at the latest," he said.

"Which means they could turn up anytime."

"That's what it means."

"Christ Jesus' Holy Name," mumbled Moll. "We shall have our work cut out for us. Yet I shall accord these Stocks no welcome to the house beyond what I must, nor will I trust them farther than I can throw them, for the thief must expect no thanks from the honest householder, nor the wolf from the sheep he devours. Why, they do take what's rightly ours—our places of long durance!"

Husband and wife contemplated this injustice together. Side by side in a grim parody of comradeship before a common enemy. They were a very curious pair, the Fludds. As physically ill-matched as any two human creatures could be under God's heaven. He so thin and pale and rickety as to be the very image of an early death; she florid and broad—a likely apprentice to the village blacksmith were she forty years younger and of the opposite gender.

For the next few days the letter remained the sole topic of

conversation between them. Nothing was done to prepare the house, nor were any other servants informed of what was to come. Cuth and Moll did their work as usual, as though sheer routine would ward off the terrible changes ahead.

But finally something had to be done, for, as Cuth pointed out to his wife (but very diplomatically!), the promise of continued maintenance in their dotage was something worth securing, and if Mistress Frances arrived to discover that her express commands had been disregarded, the Fludds might well find themselves out in the road.

To such a fate even the groundskeeper's lodge with all its vermin was to be preferred.

And so Moll ordered the Irish servants to ready the late master's chamber for the new mistress of Thorncombe and also to prepare a place in the west ward of the castle for the new steward and his wife. Sir John's armor and trunkful of weaponry, his moldy volumes on war and history, his lank, flea-bitten hounds that had long kenneled themselves on his bed, his five suits of indifferent quality, and a great deal of other assorted stuff were transferred elsewhere to give the chamber a more feminine look. Fresh rushes were laid and the windows were opened to air the place out, which it badly needed because of the dogs. The Irish girls applied themselves to this task with their usual sullen acquiescence. There were six of them in all, including Una the cook. Moll rarely called them by name. When she wanted something done she pointed and blustered, a mode of communication she was convinced was universal. The girls chattered among themselves in Irish and sometimes sang Irish songs. Moll knew the girls did not like her, and she didn't care. To her mind, mutual hostility was the proper relationship between higher servants and lower, English and Irish. As for Cuth, he had no commerce with the serving girls at all. He thought them stupid, and even if he had allowed himself to admire their girlish charms, the brightness of an eye or smooth contour of a calf or forearm, he would have struck the offending member from his own body before he would have allowed his wife to detect his interest.

The preparation of the west ward of Thorncombe was of special concern to Moll, for although she had at last come to accept the need to comply with her young mistress's orders, she was committed to making the newcomers as unwelcome as possible. She had therefore chosen the Stocks' accommodations with that care with which a patient but purposeful spider locates his web.

Moll led the Irish girls down the long corridor that connected the kitchen of the new house with the cavernous banquet hall of the old castle. She climbed the stone stairs to the ward. She came to a massive oak door and selected from the bunch of keys that dangled from her waist one of curious and antique design. This she inserted in the lock; then she pushed the door open.

The chamber exhaled a breath of cold, stagnant air that caused even the dauntless old woman a moment of apprehension. As to the reaction of her fellow servants, Moll could not gauge that, even if she had been less indifferent. But she suspected that the girls, as ignorant of English as they were and isolated from town gossip, would think the chamber simply another of the many in the castle and the house. But Moll knew the story of the chamber in all its horrific fullness.

It was a large, high-ceilinged chamber of oppressive bareness, said to be haunted by the ghost of an earlier Challoner who had been murdered in his bed; indeed, in this very place. One version of the story had the unfortunate victim smothered in his bedclothes. Another claimed that the murder weapon was a large two-handed sword, by which merciless engine the victim's head had been dissociated from his body. But all the variations concurred that the murderer was the dead man's own brother. There was also general agreement as to motive. The murdered man had seduced and violated his own sister!

Why the restless spirit of the dead man should have lingered in his former habitation rather than descended at once to the fires of hell was not explained. The chamber was known as the Black Keep, both because of the legendary crime and to distinguish it from a similar compartment in the tower opposite, called the White Keep.

Moll was unsure as to whether Mistress Frances had heard of the legend. If she had and discovered where Moll had put the Stocks, Moll might be in great trouble. But Moll knew Mistress Frances had never set foot in Thorncombe and inferred from that fact that the young woman knew none of its grisly legends. And even if, by some mischance, rumors had come to the ears of her new mistress, Moll could always point out that the chamber was the most commodious in the castle and readily accessible to the kitchen, the center of servant life, if one did not mind climbing all those steps.

So, justified in her choice, Moll proceeded to direct her assistants to their labors. It was no mean task, the cleaning. The chamber was unspeakably filthy from long disuse. The stone floor was covered with dirt and the moldering remains of rushes a half-century had seen unchanged. A legion of mice and spiders fled at the first wielding of the broom, and broken panes in one of the tall lancet windows admitted drafts of bracing air that might have pleased a monk bent on mortification of the flesh but surely no warm-blooded Englishman concerned for creature comforts.

The room's few furnishings were no enhancement either. A funereal four-poster with tattered hangings like a cannon-blasted vessel occupied one corner. In another stood a tall cabinet which, when opened, exhaled such a miasma that Moll was forced to run to the window for relief. The stone walls boasted remnants of tapestries, but their designs and colors had long ago succumbed to dust, except where a curious observer could detect a martial scene of knights in combat, sieges, castles, sallies, and alarms, reflecting the consuming passion of the baronets of Thorncombe. Above the bed itself hung a rusty two-handed blade that for all Moll knew was the very instrument by which the baronet of the ghostly tale had met his deserved end.

The chamber's only accommodating feature was a large hearth. Moll ordered a fire to be laid, but the chimney proved to be plugged, and the room filled with smoke. The smoke disturbed a previously undetected wasps' nest in the blackened beams of the ceiling and the swarm attacked the women, who went screaming downstairs, the angry wasps in pursuit.

And for all these troubles—the filthy chamber, the loathsome air, the biting wasps—Moll blamed the Stocks and cursed them both aloud and in her heart.

In her tiny cubicle under the eaves, Aileen Mogaill stared forlornly at the painful welts where the wasps had stung her several days before. The cook had given her ointment for the stings, and she had applied it generously each night since.

It had been while applying the ointment that she noticed that the thin copper bracelet with the tiny crucifix that she wore for pure religion's sake was gone. Since earlier that morning she had been aware of its presence while she washed her face and hands, she concluded that she had likely lost it while cleaning the filthy chamber in the Black Keep.

Her heart sank at the thought, for she knew she must return for the bracelet, and waiting until morning light would hardly do, for who knew who might find it in the meanwhile and claim it for her own?

Her bedmate asleep, to judge by the soft snoring beneath the covers, Aileen Mogaill took the candle from her bedside and started out for the Black Keep.

5

EDWARD BASTIAN, the hostler at Thorncombe, had heard of the coming of the Stocks from Michael Conroy, Sir John's Irish manservant, who in turn had had the news by way of threat from Moll Fludd. Conroy, for want of better employment elsewhere, had remained at the castle since his master's drowning, drinking up Sir John's supply of ale and wine and sleeping most of the day. At night he rode into Buxton, won money at cards, and flirted with the local wenches who were charmed by his flaming red hair, his brawn, and his flattering Irish tongue. After more than a year of this, Moll had grown impatient with Conroy's presence; she felt that the advent of the Stocks was an auspicious time to send Conroy packing. She sent her husband to do the job.

Cuth was uncharacteristically blunt. The master was dead, he told Conroy. No servingman was now needed or wanted. And no more Irish—male or female—for there were quite enough underfoot as it was, with their crabby faces and heathen babblings.

But Moll's husband proved an ineffectual ambassador for the mission, and when presented with an order to depart the castle, Conroy took it very badly. Deep in his cups during the interview with the old steward, the well-muscled young Irishman drew his sword and threatened Cuth with emasculation if he so much as showed his wrinkled visage in the upstairs of the house again.

The old steward, his heart pounding with terror at the threat, shuffled off to complain to his wife. He gave her a full report of what had been said and done, and hearing this, Moll, armed with a knobby oaken cudgel she kept in the kitchen for beating off beggars and gypsies, marched upstairs to confront the unruly Conroy.

She found Conroy in the master's parlor and with his great soldier's boots propped up on the master's writing table as if Thorncombe were Conroy's own house. A blue haze of tobacco smoke filled the air. He looked at her insolently. "Well now, what would *you* be wanting?"

"What do *I* want?" Moll returned, already quaking with rage. She held her cudgel firm in her grip, her muscles as tense as catgut. "You impudent varlet! You despicable thing of worthlessness! How dare you treat my young mistress's house as though it were a barracks? You take yourself from this house this very hour, or heaven help, I'll call the servants and they'll turn you out!"

Conroy put his arms to the back of his head and howled with laughter. "The servants? Why, of whom do you speak, old woman? A half-dozen green-sick girls?"

"Then the constable and his men," she replied undauntedly. "You have no rights here. The master is dead. Your duties are done."

The Irishman leaned forward and put his feet on the floor. He regarded her intently, his light eyes large and fixed with contempt. "Shut up, you disreputable old whore. You spawn of a Derbyshire bog not palatable to a toad. Go unman your husband with your bullying and tongue-lashing and leave a real man to his tobacco and drink. Cuth's used to your rantings. You've terrorized the old boy good, you hideous old slattern."

This was not language Moll could readily suffer. She raised

the cudgel above her head and was about to bring it crashing down on her abuser's skull, but Conroy saw the threat and acted quickly. His unsheathed sword lay at his side; he grasped the hilt and thrust the sword toward her so that the point caught Moll's bodice about mid-stomach and then ripped up toward the neck.

Moll gasped and let the cudgel drop to the floor, and, far too amazed at the swiftness of Conroy's attack to be concerned for her modesty, she simply stood there gaping at the damage. Her reddened face now became quite pale. Her heavy, sagging breasts, exposed to the light of day by the Irishman's savage assault, heaved like a blacksmith's bellows.

"It gives me no joy to strike at one of your sex, but a man must defend himself," said Conroy with a glimmer of amusement in his eye and the same insolent smirk that had greeted Moll when she first entered the chamber.

She covered her breasts with her arms, and with rude, brutal anger, she hissed, "You just wait, unruly sir. Just you wait. With a poor woman you will be bold to commit rape and murder. But others are coming. Even now they are on their way. I have it on good authority. From our mistress herself. Mistress Frances. In a letter addressed expressly to ourselves—that is, to my husband and me. A new steward and housekeeper to sustain us in our dotage. We shall see what *they* will tolerate from the likes of you."

She punctuated this mighty threat with an obscene gesture she had observed the local shepherds, a very rude crowd, use to good effect. But the sign only provoked Conroy's derisive laughter. Throwing his head back so that Moll could see his ragged teeth and beyond, the ruddy tunnel of his throat, he said, "Oh God in heaven and all the saints preserve us. I'm so afraid." He invited her to kiss an unmentionable part of his anatomy and then dissolved in a paroxysm of laughter that Moll found even more infuriating.

Yet, threatened still by the pointing sword, she could only stand and suffer the Irishman's crudity. When he recovered, he regarded her coldly and said, "New steward? New housekeeper? Braver warriors than you and your mouse-husband, I warrant?"

"I'll say no more, sir," replied Moll with as much frigid dignity as she could muster, given her half-naked condition and the impending threat of death. "It's true you have the advantage of me now—me a poor weak woman of advanced years at the mercy of a hardened veteran of the wars. But we shall see what time discloses. There are laws, sir. Even in Derbyshire. We are not as you *Irish*." She curled her lips in contempt and paused, as though even to name his race was to condemn it. "You Irish," she continued. "A race of heathen, as well the world knows; but good English souls, we. There are laws, and they are not without their power to evict the unwelcome guest and interloper."

"Damn your laws!" Conroy cried, the sword in his hand shaking a little. "Were I less a man, I would tell you just where you can put those laws you speak of. But I don't care a turd for your laws. And less for the English race. You have the gall to speak of laws? Well now, old woman, tell me if you can, if your law is so good and fine and holy, by what justice was my late master's death declared misadventure and not plainly what it was? Just you tell me that."

He had asked for an answer yet did not seem to expect one, for he provided no time for her reply. He had started to blubber, and she felt less threatened now. A man sodden drunk was a contemptible thing to her, even if he was holding a naked sword at her vulnerable breasts. Conroy turned his face from her toward the goblet from which he had been drinking. With his free hand he picked it up and put it to his lips. The red liquor dribbled down his chin. His slovenliness seemed another deliberate insult to the house and to Moll.

"He was sitting in his shallop. That's how I found him," Conroy recalled, looking at her again. "Out on the lake and him not three or four hours in his own house. Drowned like a rat. We found the body . . . his little boat . . . the lake he delighted in."

"I know all that," Moll interrupted impatiently. She was tired of his raving; his growing incoherence promised to be even more vexing. "I was there, too. I saw the master. There's nothing to be done about it now."

"Nothing to be done?" Conroy cried. "He was murdered in cold blood! Revenge is what's to be done, old woman! And when I find out who's to blame—"

"Drunk as you are now, you're not likely to find your way to the door."

"Drunk or sober, standing or sitting, I'll find out."

"Brave words," she taunted.

The Irishman was suddenly overcome with emotion, and his emotion gave him a kind of eloquence. "The bravest man and soldier I have known, Sir John was. I allow that he was English born and bred. Although he was of such mettle, I would swear to Heaven he was Irish rather, and some English brat put in his place. A changeling . . . good Irish blood transplanted by some malign fairy to test whether such transplantation from Irish sod to this inferior soil would diminish the child's manhood."

"Nonsense," she scoffed. "You speak foolishly. Sir John was of old Saxon blood. He and his race."

Conroy paid no attention to this remark. He continued to ramble, bleary-eyed, but he still held the sword and Moll didn't dare move. She was forced to listen: "Misadventure, indeed! Who but a fool or madman would have viewed his death as such? For did I not once see him swimming in full armor in the river Shannon when it was in full flood and chafing? He came ashore then, dripping wet but breathing as though he had not strained a muscle and the expanse of raging water had been a mere puddle he had been obliged to vault to keep his soles dry. And he had a smile of triumph about his mouth. Well-deserved triumph, too. No, never tell me that such a man falls overboard, drowns in three feet of water, then climbs aboard his boat again to sit there in pouring rain like an idiot in a stupor. Only fools and madmen would believe such a tale."

Moll was about to remind him that Sir John had been weary from his long ride that day, that he had not fully recovered from the amputation, and that, after all, the man had but one good leg, for all his triumphs and heroics. But she didn't bother. Conroy's voice trailed off, became a mumble. His head suddenly fell forward on his chest and he sat motionless. The sword dangled in his hand.

Full of disgust and loathing, Moll saw her opportunity. She inched backward on cat's feet. But the Irishman heard. In an instant he was alert again, the sword aimed with lethal accuracy, the pale cold eyes as hard and threatening as ever. He uttered something in Irish. A terrible curse by the tone of it. With the back of his hand he wiped his moist red lips. He seemed now aware of what he had spoken, the emotions he had revealed, his apparent motive for remaining in the house these twelve months or more since his master died. He started to say something else, then evidently thought better of it. He made a motion with the sword to indicate she should go—and quickly.

"Take your cudgel with you," he said.

"So will I," she replied, not content that he should have the last word. She looked down on Conroy with quiet superiority, but secretly she was much gratified for her release. Although still sensitive to his insults and threats, she had now concluded that he was totally mad, and to Moll, a man who was mad and also a drunkard and an Irishman and made outrageous charges of murder and rude assaults on the bodices of decent women was not only beyond her comprehension but her control too. His maudlin reminiscences had made her even more disdainful. She loathed masculine tears. She herself had had no great affection for Sir John. She was always more content when he was away in Ireland, preoccupied with his soldiery, his cannons, his barricades and counterscarps. She did not believe in Conroy's professions of loyalty to the dead man, nor in his desire for vengeance. She suspected an ulterior motive for his remaining at the castle, where he had no one to serve, no friends, and therefore no business.

Safely exited, she stood in the gallery outside the master's apartment and breathed a sigh of relief, looking heavenward at the same time to acknowledge the divine help in sparing her life. Remembering now how she must look—her florid face sweating, her bodice ruined and gaping, a cudgel in her hand and defeat written upon her face—she boiled with indignation. Her eyes filled with tears of self-pity. Would she not herself be revenged upon Conroy—drunken ruffian who had slandered the English race, taken unlawful possession of the house, and presumed to raise both hand and voice against her?

She stiffened with resolve and, planting a firm hand over her bodice as a temporary repair, she marched directly to the attic chamber she shared with her husband.

She was gratified to find Cuth absent. When he returned she would tell him how she had threatened to brain Conroy if he did not leave, how the Irishman had begged her forgiveness and how she had graciously permitted him to remain where he was—until the new steward and housekeeper should come. She would tell Cuth that if he did not believe her account, he might go to the devil—or to Conroy himself—for confirmation.

That was how Conroy found out about the Stocks. He communicated the news to Edward the hostler, whom he liked, even though Edward was a local and no soldier. The two men were about the same age, well-made in arm, shoulder, and thigh, and they shared a love of horses that often brought Conroy into the stable.

"That old harridan the housekeeper is down on me now, my lad," Conroy said good-naturedly. "I pricked her bodice with a quick parry to her threatening cudgel and saw to my horror such a magnitude of withered duggery that my heart stopped beating for the terror of it."

The two men laughed softly, but Edward more for politeness than pleasure. He did not like Moll Fludd any more than the Irishman did, but he secretly shared some of her offense at Conroy's high-handed manner in the castle.

"She says there's a new steward to come—and a new housekeeper," Conroy said, as though the news were inconsequential.

"Is there?" responded Edward. Edward was saddling Conroy's horse. He paused and looked at the Irishman.

"The Fludds have received some letter from Mistress Frances."

"The old master's niece?"

"She that's heir to Thorncombe," Conroy confirmed.

"She's appointing a new steward? What's to happen to the old folks?"

Conroy shrugged. He assumed they would stay on in some capacity.

"When?"

"Soon, says the Amazon, our lady housekeeper," Conroy remarked jovially. He provided the hostler with an abbreviated account of his interview with Moll. Edward laughed despite himself. It was a soul-satisfying comeuppance for the old battle-ax. No less than she deserved.

"So she says the new steward will throw me out on my ear," Conroy said. He leaned against the horse's stall, watching the hostler cinch up the belly straps, then he followed as Edward led the horse, a piebald, round haunched gelding, out into the paddock. But Edward said nothing to this possibility. He seemed not to care about the new steward.

"A new steward may mean trouble for you, lad," Conroy said.

"How so?"

"Oh, you know very well. What is it that's said, A new broom sweeps clean."

"So goes the proverb," Edward said. "Here's your horse. You should exercise him more often. He's a fine mount."

Conroy shrugged. "Look at it this way: Why should a new mistress be sending a new steward and housekeeper save she were suspicious of how things are run around here?"

"The Fludds are old, the both of them," said Edward.

"A ready answer," replied Conroy. "But so they've been for a good many years. I have it on our late master's authority that he kept the pair only because his grandfather had hired them. It was a matter of family tradition, so to speak. Sir

John could hardly abide Moll Fludd; I'm of the same mind. As for the steward—petty old fool—his wife's drudge. A pestilent excuse for manhood, the old fart."

"If a new steward comes, I'll take orders from him. Same as before," Edward said.

Conroy sighed and shook his head. "You English! Have you no blood in your veins, man?" But when Edward made no response to this question, Conroy brightened. "Look, Ned, come drinking with me tonight. I'm in powerful need of a companion to my labors, and you seem one well-suited to drain a stoup or two." He clasped a friendly hand on the hostler's shoulder.

Edward smiled and shook his head. "Thanks for asking, but I've no stomach for drinking. Besides, my father expects me at home."

At that moment the hostler happened to look toward the castle and noticed a curl of smoke rising above the Black Keep. He commented on it.

"Our lady of the mop and broom has prepared the Black Keep for her replacement," Conroy said, mounting the piebald mount and adjusting himself in the saddle. He patted the horse on the withers, continuing as though he were addressing the horse. "Fancy that, will you? The Black Keep! A fine chamber of horrors for a newcomer to Thorncombe. Can you read the old witch's mind, Ned?"

"She must be mad," said Edward, more to himself than to his companion.

"She's sane, all right, but a nasty, vengeful sanity it is. She may have surrendered her place to the new housekeeper, but she won't do it with a charitable spirit. She's given them the worst quarters in the castle, not barring the servants' cubbyholes in the attic, which are dreadful enough. As for the Keep, Sir John took me on tour once and told me a clever story of it. Seems one of his ancestors had his head removed against his better judgment. By a brother, mind you. Of course there's a tradition of a ghost. Now they say we Irish are superstitious! But the part I like best has to do with the cause of the homicide."

"Yes, I've heard the tale," said Edward, still looking at the tower. "A quarrel over some woman."

"Quarrel for a fact!" exclaimed Conroy with a chuckle. "One of the Challoners niggled his own sister. Got a child upon her body, whereupon a young brother of this Challoner administered a swift, sure justice. But you must give credit to the fatherer. His nether tool was in working order, although they say he was twenty years his sister's senior."

Conroy laughed uproariously and gave his horse a dig with his spurs. Horse and rider pranced around the paddock while Edward watched. Then Conroy came back and looked down at the hostler.

"You mentioned your father," Conroy said. "How is the old man in these days of suffering?"

"Old and infirm," replied Edward. "I've been spending my nights in his cottage. He likes the company and I prefer his to the horses'."

"A wise choice, Ned," said Conroy. "By the way, whatever happened to Brigid O'Donnal, the fresh young thing Sir John brought home time before last? Other than the master's drowning, nothing gave me more sorrow than to find she'd gone. Run off, say the Fludds. Now there was an elegant piece of work, that Brigid. Very plucky, too. I found her myself, you know, on the road. Her town was in flames, all her people dead. A pitiful story, even to one who is not often blamed for having a heart."

"She left months before the master returned," Edward said. "She's probably back in Ireland now."

"Then Ireland is the richer," Conroy said. "Yes, she was a fine piece of work." The Irishman stared off toward the road, contemplating the excellence of female flesh and the distance he was to ride before he could settle down to an evening of drinking, wenching, and card-playing. He again invited the hostler to join him. Again the hostler declined.

"Well, I'll find company enough," said Conroy. He gave the other young man a quick salute and a lecherous wink and rode off in a gay mood, singing as he went. Conroy's clear tenor voice could be heard until he was a tiny figure in the dusk.

Edward went back into the stable. His work was done for the day, and with no master in the house there would be no nocturnal summons for a mount. He shut the stable door and began walking toward his father's cottage. It was about three miles distant, an easy walk for the strapping young man. But Edward was an angry young man too, angry at Conroy and his filthy talk. The Irishman hadn't known how near he'd come to being pulled off his horse and thrashed. That remark about Brigid O'Donnal. A fine piece of work indeed. As though she were horse or whore! The Irishman had made an enemy!

Three quarters of an hour brought Edward to his father's cottage. He opened the door and went inside. In the corner a fire had been laid and before it sat a stooped form. Alerted by the familiar steps and greeting, the old man looked up at his son with vacant eyes and smiled crookedly. Then a woman's voice was heard. It was a soft voice, loving and accented in the Irish way. The woman was seated on a low pallet in one of the corners. In her arms she held a suckling child. Edward could hear the sounds the child made at its mother's breast and they filled him with a tenderness that dispelled his anger.

He went over to the woman and bent down to kiss her. The lips were full and warm, the breath sweet. The child pulled its mouth from the mother's swollen nipple and looked up at Edward with bright eyes. Incomprehensible babbling came from the child's mouth, puckered in the dim light like a little red flower. "He's welcoming his father, don't you see," the woman said softly. "Already he knows you."

6

MATTHEW and Joan traveled by coach the best part of the way north, with a liverled footman provided by Cecil and another square-faced, sober fellow whose duty it seemed to be to guard their bodies from rude assault, although no assaults were threatened. But long before Buxton they said good-bye to the footman and his friend and traded the coach for a countryman's cart. For many hard miles they traveled, passing though country so unlike her native Essex that Joan would have thought she was in a foreign land. The inhabitants, too, seemed passing strange. They appeared to be suspicious of outsiders and spoke with a thick speech, as though they had stones in their mouths. When in one rude hamlet a child begged a penny for her goodness, Joan was only able to decipher what he meant from his supplicating gestures and the obvious fact of his undernourished condition.

Before dark each of their days on the road, they stopped at inns, none of which she found as inviting as the least of those that hosted Essex wayfarers. Matthew grumbled about the hardness of the beds, the damp chill in the air—like winter. And the coarse food, which ill suited his stomach. The driver of the cart was a thickset farmer who wore a woolen cap he'd pulled over most of his head and a heavy outergarment that made him look like a bear. All his discourse was grunts and mumbles, sighs and snorts, from which Joan could detect on rare occasions some affirmation or denial of the simple questions directed to him. She felt she might have had better conversation with a sleeping dog.

And thus, after four days of travail, they came to the village nearest to Thorncombe. It was a mean, lowly place, cursed with an air of unremediable misfortune. There were only a dozen or so dwellings that could be called houses. The rest were mere hovels, without windows or chimneys and half buried in the ground. There was one narrow twisting street, uncobbled and rutted. A stone church without tower to dignify it stood at the town center in a state of scandalous neglect. It was the only public building. Next to the church a churchyard of ancient monuments and memorials was overwhelmed in rank growth of weeds and briers, providing a testament of life's transience to warm the heart of the sternest moralist. It would have been as futile to inquire who occupied the pulpit of the church on Sundays as to speculate as to the number of worshipers. The village church would not see the meanest of curates in twelvemonth, and there would not be a dozen of the village's dour, impoverished inhabitants who would complain of the loss.

There was an inn in the village, aptly named the Sheepcote, for it was as filthy as one. Of need, the Stocks lodged there, it being too late in the day to continue. They were served a middling supper by a dour innkeeper who was also cook and scullion and then were shown to a small, windowless room—hardly more than a closet—and to a bed that might have served as an instrument of torture to the most obdurate of malefactors. It was short and hard, a scattering of straw upon roughhewn boards, and the sheets were smelly and crawling with vermin. Joan's consolation was that these quarters were cheap and the house was silent during the night, for they were the inn's only guests, their driver having had the wisdom to bed down with his horse in the stable.

The next morning, they dressed themselves shivering from the cold and damp, then went into the kitchen to warm themselves by the fire. But they took no breakfast there. Instead, they bought boiled eggs and milk from a street vendor, Joan having sworn not to taste another morsel in so unsavory a place. "Even the direst poverty cannot excuse such squalor," she pronounced as they rode out of town.

A heavy morning mist shrouded the valley, and Joan experienced the eerie sensation of passing from one world into the next, of leaving behind the familiar shape of things and moving into a realm of shadows and illusions. They made a slow ascent up an escarpment of rocks and deep ravines until they came to a range of long hills with gentle slopes covered by low, scraggly bushes and totally devoid of occupants except for an occasional prowling fox or darting hare, circling hawks, and—at greater distance—flocks of sheep browsing on the hillsides like patches of old snow.

Toward midmorning the driver brought the cart to a halt. They were now at the crest of a hill, overlooking a broad valley. Joan, aroused from the torpor of travel, first thought the pause was another concession to the driver's horse, of which there had been a great many already that morning, for it seemed they had been traveling for hours, yet could not have made more than six or seven miles. But the driver lifted his hand and pointed into the distance. "There 'tis," he said. "The castle."

Joan looked. She could see a crescent-shaped lake, a little wood on its shore, and, in the midst of the wood, a stone edifice, two square towers thrusting up through the foliage. The morning mist had passed away. Castle Thorncombe was no dream after all. "Thanks be to God," she said to the driver. "At last we're here."

She begged him to proceed, for both she and Matthew were so weary from travel they had been reduced to a miserable silence the entire morning. The driver grunted and brought his switch down hard on his horse's rump. The cart gave a jolt and moved forward.

There was a road through the trees which they now took,

past a dense wilderness of tree, shrub, and fern, making in its furious verdure little more than a pair of wheel ruts of the road. Overhead the long, drooping branches met and intertwined, obscuring the sun and creating an obdurate gloom, like that of an old garden run riot. But although the woods were thick, they were not deep. Within minutes the cart emerged from the tunnel of overhanging branches to a rising lawn or greensward. For the first time Joan saw Thorncombe in its fullness.

Now she could see that the ancient seat of the Challoners was not one house but two very unlike structures yoked by an architect with more mischief in his heart than sense of harmony. One structure was the hoary Norman keeps of gray stone with their threatening battlements and air of decay and ancient violence. Attached at a right angle was a newer building of modern design, resembling in its form, although not in its condition, some of the finer houses of the Essex gentry. The new house had a great many windows, downstairs and up, a low-pitched roof bristling with chimneys, and a handsome clock tower. Joan was cheered by the sight of the chimneys. They promised warmth, at least.

But she did not like the look of the stone remnant of baronial pomp, or the way it was attached to the new house, as though it were a grim, unspeakable past that could not be denied, or a corpse bound hideously to a living soul for some punishment's sake. She knew those austere battlements had not been made for vain show but for resolute defense, and she wondered how many dead men's bones lay unmarked beneath the greensward that swelled so gracefully to meet the castle's walls.

The road took them around the castle to a cobbled courtyard. In passage, Joan had a good view of the lake and the hills on its farther side. She saw that there was an island, and some sort of tower thereon, and then her attention was drawn to the castle's outbuildings—a rambling wooden structure she assumed was the stable, an adjacent horse paddock, a small barn of stone and timber with a high-pitched roof, and a scattering of other sheds and privies.

A strapping young man in his twenties, clad in coarse frieze jerkin, patched hose, and galoshes that came nearly to his knees, advanced from the stable. Square-jawed and clear-eyed, the young man identified himself as the castle hostler and said his name was Edward Bastian. Meanwhile out of the castle itself had come a train of servants, led by an elderly couple whom Joan guessed to be the steward and his wife the housekeeper.

"The old couple must be the Fludds," Matthew whispered, giving voice to Joan's own supposition.

Matthew gave the driver of the cart a little money, and, with a doleful glance at the castle and mumbled thanks, the driver used his switch again and the horse moved obediently forward, turned, and then headed in the direction they had come.

Whether the driver's quicker pace was to be attributed to a lighter load, or to the driver's enthusiasm to get clear of the castle as soon as possible, Joan could not tell. But she could see now that the cart's departure had apparently been a signal to the Fludds that they should come forward, however unpleasant a duty such an overture should be. Arm in arm they descended the several stone steps of the porch and began to move toward Joan and Matthew. Behind them came a clutch of female servants.

"We are the Fludds, Cuth and Moll," announced the female member with a kind of defiance when they were still a good twenty feet from Joan. "Cuth," remarked the man of the family redundantly. The old man made a jerky little motion with his head, something between a bow and a muscle spasm, that Joan took as a gesture of greeting. But the movement—and perhaps its significance—was detected by Moll, who gave her husband an interdictory poke in the ribs for his indiscretion.

Joan took in this little drama and formed an instant dislike for the old housekeeper. She did not approve of prideful servants, nor did she care for domineering wives. Moll Fludd was clearly both.

"We are Joan and Matthew Stock," Matthew announced

with a tone of voice he used when he was determined to be pleasant under conditions to the contrary. "Come from London at the command of Mistress Frances Challoner to serve as—"

"All that we know," Moll interrupted. "As our replacements. In our dotage. Very well, Matthew Stock and wife. We have ever done as we were told and we will do it still. We are not twain who must be driven to pasture like dumb beasts."

With great ceremony, the old woman drew a collection of keys she wore at her waist and surrendered them to Joan. Her husband, equipped with a like badge of authority, proffered his to Matthew. Cuth said, "There are also ledgers, kept with great care by me." The old man's voice broke with emotion, tears glistened in his eyes. "These you shall find in very good order in the steward's office, giving the particulars of all the servants and providing other such matters that—"

"I warrant the new steward knows what he shall find and what not, Cuth," said Moll, cutting her husband off in mid-sentence and looking sternly at Matthew as though he were to blame for any rudeness she had offered.

"I trust all will be in good order," Matthew said.

Moll now turned her attention to the four female servants in her charge. She counted their number twice over and then said, "What, where's the pretty one—Aileen what's-her-name?"

Her companions professed not to know and Moll was highly displeased. "Foolish girl—I'll whip her smartly for this insolence. Here now, don't stand there gawking. The rest of you take these folks' baggage to their quarters at once. You know where it is." Then she turned to Joan again and said, "It's nigh unto one o'clock. You will probably want dinner. The cook is a woman—Irish, like all of the female servants saving myself, who am true English born. She speaks very little English, and the rest are hardly richer in learning. Her name is Una, and as for her skill in cookery, well, what can be said of one born in so savage a land?"

These disparaging comments were evidently ignored by the other servants, who obediently distributed the burden of the various chests and bags in proportion to their respective strengths and went filing into the house.

"We aren't used to fine food," remarked Joan, largely because the departure of the other servants had created an awkward silence and also out of sympathy for the defamed Una, who Joan was sure was not so bad a cook as Moll Fludd claimed.

"Not used to fine food?" asked Moll with a sudden and clearly pretended expression of amazement. "Why, I would have thought your long sojourn in the great houses of the high and mighty of London would have made standard servants' fare as great an abomination to your tongues as swine's flesh to a Jew."

"As my wife has said, we are not used to dainty cates, nor do we require them," Matthew answered severely. "Where we have served, we have always conducted ourselves as servants, not as masters. We have shared with our fellows and gladly."

"Oh, was it so," returned Moll with contempt. "Well, I suppose that is to your credit. Follow me, then, if you will. First, you shall both feed to your content, then see your chamber, which I pray you find to your liking. Tomorrow, or the next day, is soon enough, I trust, for a tour of the house and grounds."

"Tomorrow will be soon enough," Matthew said.

Moll faced about and started off toward the porch, leaving her husband and Joan and Matthew to follow. The door led directly to the kitchen, a large, airy room with smoke-blackened ceiling and aromatic with herbs, a recent stew, and burning wood. Against one wall was the hearth, a dark cavity of generous dimensions in which sat three sturdy-looking kettles and a huge caldron. On both sides of the hearth hung pans and other implements—knives, ladles, tongs, pincers, spoons, and spatulas. In the middle of the room was a long trencher table and benches.

"A very ample kitchen, is it not?" Moll asked Joan when

they had all come indoors. "In the old days the Challoners feasted monks and others of their ilk here. Grand meals, they were, if local legend can be believed. They gluttonized very well, those folks—gluttonized while our local sheepherders and farmers starved for want of a tithe of the same."

Moll looked at Joan suspiciously and asked, "You aren't Papists, are you?"

Joan answered negatively, and this seemed to please Moll. During this conversation a buxom, dark-haired woman of about Joan's age came into the kitchen carrying a bowlful of apples. She saw Joan and Matthew and stopped. Then she looked at Moll.

"This is Una, our cook," Moll remarked by way of her earlier assessment of the woman's cooking. She said to Una, "These are the new steward and housekeeper. You are to follow Mistress Stock's orders as diligently as you followed mine."

Una nodded at Joan and then at Matthew. She continued with her work. Moll looked after her and shook her head. "These Irish," she said under her breath. "Well then, there's bread and some cheese and a little mutton from yesternight's supper," Moll continued casually, glancing around the kitchen. "You may eat where and when you like. I wouldn't trouble Una but with the simplest of instructions, however. It was her master's whim to have her cook. I suppose the wishes of the dead must be honored. God knows, there's no one else."

"Some cheese will do very well," Matthew said.

"And perhaps something to drink?" Joan added.

"The larder and pantry are through there," said Moll, indicating with a nod the narrow passage through which Una had recently come. "While you feed, I'll see that those idiot servants have found the right chamber and that it has been properly prepared. I'll return shortly. Wait here until I do. The castle has many rooms. It would be a shame were you to become lost on your first day."

When Moll left, Joan and Matthew sat down at the table. Una came presently with cups and plates and a half-loaf of brown bread and a slab of cold beef smeared with rich mustard. The woman smiled pleasantly but said nothing, and to Joan it seemed she was relieved to have Moll out of the kitchen.

Although neither Matthew nor Joan was very hungry, they both ate what was before them. While they ate, Joan studied the cook, who was busy at a little worktable by the window chopping up the apples with a meat cleaver she wielded with considerable skill. Indeed, she chopped the apples so neatly and quickly, Joan was half afraid she would slice a finger or two in the process. As she worked, the Irishwoman hummed to herself. Although her hair was dark and graying a little around the forehead, her eyes were a deep blue and her complexion freckled like that of many of her countrywomen. Lines around her eyes and across her brow betrayed her age, as did the thickening at her waist and buttocks. Joan guessed the woman was about forty. But Una had a strong, determined chin and a shapely nose. The bones of her cheek were pronounced and her lips had a sensuous fullness that Joan was sure must have made her attractive to men in her younger years.

"A cold welcome indeed," Matthew said.

Joan turned away from Una and looked at her husband. "Very cold," she said.

"Hardly surprising," he said, keeping his voice low. "We are intruders. We knew there'd be no cheering upon our arrival."

"Yet I thought not to find the former housekeeper so resolute an enemy."

"The cook, Una, seems friendly," said Matthew.

"She has no love for Moll, that's for sure," Joan observed.

"Nor Moll for her. A very friendly house this. It's a wonder they don't all kill each other in their sleep. I could never abide such a wrangling of serpent tongues under my roof," said Matthew.

"Nor I," she answered.

They finished their meal and then sat talking for a while

in low voices about their journey and their first impressions of Thorncombe. They agreed that if it had not been for their promise to the Queen, they would have cheerfully set out for Chelmsford on foot, rather than spend a night in the forbidding castle.

"That woman is taking her good time seeing to our chamber," Matthew said after a while when the former housekeeper had not returned.

"She is truly," answered Joan. "Perhaps she's forgotten about us. Let's look around."

"She told us to remain here," said Matthew.

"We shall be very naughty then," remarked Joan dryly, "and disobey her ladyship's orders. What, are we not now steward and housekeeper of Thorncombe? That woman is insufferable, and we shall presently have to remind her of her place and our authority."

Joan led the way from the kitchen down the corridor to another door which, when opened, revealed a chamber of such vast size that Joan surmised at once it was the great hall of the old castle. The hall was very dusty and unfurnished, like the inside of an empty barn. The floors and walls were stone; the high ceiling a crisscross of sturdy beams, roughhewn and blackened from equally ancient fires. At one end were a huge hearth and dais. High on each flanking wall were banks of clerestory windows, and at the end opposite the dais was an arched passage leading to a chapel.

The chapel apparently was no longer used for religious purposes. The crucifix that had hung upon the wall and whose traces yet could be seen had been removed; and a faintly discernible mural of some pious theme had been desecrated—as the rotten rags of popery—by the charcoal of torches.

Matthew and Joan were examining the chapel when they heard Moll come up behind them.

"I thought I told you to stay in the kitchen," Moll said crankily.

Joan faced the woman and said, "So you told us. We chose not to be kept waiting longer. Our new duties give us rights of passage in this house. And so we left the kitchen and proceeded to this place and find it in very poor condition indeed."

Moll glared at Joan. "It's the banqueting hall, a scurvy place, I admit, but the master gave no instructions that it should be otherwise. Sir John lived in the new house. He never ventured here. He didn't like the old castle."

"I heard him say as much. 'I hate the old castle,' said he, many times."

This was the voice of Moll's husband, who had come up behind her and was now peering with unveiled hostility at the Stocks over his wife's shoulder.

"It's still a disgrace," Joan replied undauntedly. "And it must be cleaned and repaired."

"Surely you would not have these Papist images restored?" the old woman asked, aghast.

"Of course not," Joan said. "The place is no longer a sanctuary. It's a gentlewoman's home, and part of it should not resemble a barn in its filth. Why, look you, is that not a nest of bats there in the rafters?"

Joan pointed upward to the high ceiling where indeed there was a little community of bats occupying one corner.

"I never noticed them before," Moll said defensively.

Joan persisted in her attack. "And this chapel! Look at those walls! The images thereon shall not be restored, but must the walls look as though they bore witness still to some drunken riot of Puritan fanatics—drunken with zeal?"

"Drunken with zeal—?"

"Yes, drunken," Joan went on, sensing now that she had the old woman in full retreat. "Order the Irish girls in with soap and pails and clean this disgraceful mess. It smells like a stable in here too!"

For a moment Moll seemed too thunderstruck to speak, then, assuming a new dignity, she went on, "I have no authority to order anyone. You have been given the keys to the house. And you may do with them as pleases you—and with the servants as well. As for my husband and I, our duties are now few but plain. We are in retirement. Honorable retirement. The letter we received from the new mistress grants us room and board in the groundskeeper's lodge. In token of our long and satisfactory service, I might add, for not once in forty-seven years did the masters of Thorncombe complain of my supervision. And I assure you that neither Sir John nor his father nor his father before him ever ordered me to keep the banqueting hall in such fine condition as you order. For all of me, this hideous old relic could burn to the ground tomorrow and I should gladly warm my feet by the fire. Now my husband and I will go our way. Since you found your ways hither without a guide, I suppose you may have equal success finding your chamber."

With these good wishes, Moll turned, indicated with a nod to her husband that he should follow her, and the two of them marched off toward the kitchen.

"Detestable, unruly woman," Joan remarked in a heat when they were alone again.

"A disgrace to her sex!" exclaimed Matthew.

And then both of them laughed despite themselves, for the Fludds had looked very droll in their attitudes of high dudgeon.

"But how shall we find this chamber to which our chests have been hauled?" Joan asked when their laughter had subsided.

"It's not that large of a house, surely," Matthew replied, looking about him with confidence.

They left the chapel and hall the way they had come and found Una in the kitchen. Joan asked her where her and Matthew's chamber could be found, and it was only the woman's puzzled expression as response that recalled for Joan Moll's comment about the inability of the female servants to speak English, at least very well. She next tried communicating by gestures and had some success. Una smiled pleasantly, said something in Irish, and then beckoned Joan and Matthew to follow. She led the way back through the banqueting hall and then up one of two winding staircases. They climbed what seemed a great distance until they arrived at a landing off which were several doors. Here the Irishwoman paused, pointed to the door, and nodded her head several times vigorously as one completely incapable of speech might have done, and then, making the sign of the cross over her aproned bosom, she hurried downstairs.

Matthew opened the door.

It was with some relief that Joan saw first her chest and then Matthew's placed next to a large bed. But the chamber itself, once Joan had entered and taken it in, had a distinctly unwelcoming appearance. The room was clean but no fire had been laid in the hearth, and the broken panes in one of the several windows let in a stream of cold air. The inhospitable effect was aggravated by Joan's weariness and a throbbing headache.

Matthew walked over and sat down on the bed. He bounced on it a few times and pronounced it adequate. Joan inspected the bed linen. It was clean. But she could tell by her husband's expression that their chamber was as unappealing to him as it was to her.

"Well," he said with a sign of resignation. "We won't lack for space."

"Indeed," Joan said. "Large it is, but I would have been glad for something less austere. Why, look, I'll wager Moll's quarters in the groundskeeper's lodge are more comfortable. Wouldn't you have thought that terrible woman would have directed a fire to have been laid and some rushes upon the floor? How I hate to tread of a cold morning on stone."

"You unpack," Matthew suggested. "I'll go below to find someone to fetch wood for a fire. And there's also the matter of supper."

"Supper!" Joan exclaimed, not hungry at all. "After the day's travel I'm ready for bed, and you talk about eating again!"

Matthew laughed and said he would return soon.

She urged him to be true to his word. She didn't want to go looking for him, much less to stay there by herself.

Soon she could no longer hear the echoing of his boots. Solitary for now, a lethargy settled upon her and her headache become more clamorous. She looked at her traveling chest and considered unpacking. But she could not bring herself to begin. She sat on the bed. Homesickness for Chelmsford, her own chamber, her daughter and her little grandson conspired with her growing melancholy. Why had she consented to come? Could the Queen not have found others to see to this matter?

She tried to shake off her melancholy by humming a merry tune, but unlike Matthew, she had no pleasing voice and her effort only made things worse. The impression the vast chamber made on her mind was too strong. A chamber designed to repel invaders, or to keep a traitor close prisoner. A fine night's sleep she would have in such quarters. And what dreams should be inspired by the cold stone she dreaded to think.

Surely their assignment to the tower had been deliberate on Moll's part, perniciously conceived. The old woman's remark about the burning castle, about roasting her feet by its flames, had made her motives clear. It was a palpable effort to intimidate them—worse than cold welcome or no welcome at all.

Which, despite the physical discomfort of the moment, brought Joan's mind around to another point. Just why had Moll done it? Was the old woman merely jealous of her replacement? Or was her hostility rooted in suspicion that the Stocks had come to Thorncombe to uncover something that Moll and her husband were at pains to keep concealed? Murder, for example.

She sought relief from her aching head by lying on the bed for a while. She had no idea when Matthew would return, and she thought a nap might put all in order again.

She must have slept an hour at least, for when she awoke the chamber was growing dark and as yet Matthew had not returned. Alarmed, she got up and walked toward the windows, feeling a flush of unhealth along her throat and an insidious ache in her joints too pervasive to be only the consequence of the long, torturous cart ride. Through the tall, narrow apertures, she could see in the distance the purple shapes of hills like a reclining figure, raw against the fading light. It struck upon her brain that what she saw there across the lake was a woman disrobed and turned upon her side with her head resting on her arm. She saw the roll of hip, the sloping flanks, the smooth contours of knee and calf, and the image fixed in her imagination and gave her some momentary relief from her anxiety. Then she dropped her eyes and saw in the middle distance the expanse of water, still and dark. She felt a sudden chill and wondered if it was another symptom. Or was it a premonition?

Matthew. In God's name, where was he?

She was about to go in search of him when her attention was drawn to a large wardrobe standing in one corner of the chamber. Curious, she walked over and opened it.

It was empty except for a long, tattered garment hanging in one corner like a dead man on a gibbet. There was also an unpleasant odor.

She looked far back into the shadowy recess, and her heart leapt into her throat. Something, someone lurked there, motionless and silent.

Without thinking of the dangers to herself, she yanked open the door to admit more light and saw the thing was a slight female form sitting against the wall with her thin white-stockinged legs pulled up protectively to her chest. Clutched to the bosom like a suckling child was a dead cat.

And where the girl's head should have been—oh dreadful to see—was a mass of bloody pulp.

7

JOAN pressed both hands over her mouth to stifle the scream welling up within her. As though empowered by a will not her own, she staggered back toward the open window, turned, and took great gulps of the cold air while endeavoring to contain her nausea.

Through eyes misty with shock she looked at the purple hills that moments earlier had resembled a reclining woman. Now the hills were a dark mass, draped in funeral dusk like a corpse upon a catafalque.

How long had it been since Matthew went to find wood?

It seemed a hundred years. But never had his familiar footfalls or call—heard now over the pounding of her heart, the clamor of her headache—been so welcome. She had not moved from the window since her awful discovery. She wanted Matthew both to console her and to deny what she had seen in the wardrobe. Had it been a palpable horror, or the figment of a disordered mind?

Matthew entered, followed by the young hostler, his arms loaded with faggots. Matthew began to explain his delay in returning when he noticed Joan's face. He asked her what was wrong.

She could not bring herself to speak but pointed toward the wardrobe, the door of which had remained ajar.

"God in heaven," Matthew gasped when he had seen for himself, and in anguished countenance resolved Joan's doubts that what she had seen was real.

Peering over Matthew's shoulder, Edward let his burden drop, and in a dry, wheezing voice declared that the body was that of one of the maids.

The one not present at muster, Joan thought. The one Moll had called Aileen and threatened to beat for her insolence.

Matthew ordered Edward to go fetch the Fludds and to say nothing to them or any other person about the gruesome discovery. He pushed the wardrobe door shut and went over to where Joan stood. Putting his arm around her shoulders and drawing her to him, he said, "Sir John's drowning may have been murder or misadventure, but this poor creature's death could only have been murder. What possessed devil would so mutilate a mere child as this girl obviously was, or prop her up with a dead cat as though she were giving it suck?"

Joan had no answer for her husband's question. With the wardrobe shut and Matthew holding her, the ghastly vision now seemed less real, as though it had been a dream. The question lingering in her mind was unspeakable: Where was the rest of the hapless girl—the poor severed head? Was it concealed somewhere in the chamber, or beneath the bed, waiting for her, Joan, to discover it at some awful moment to come?

Then she heard voices outside the chamber and presently Edward reappeared with a brace of candles in hand and the Fludds at his heels. Moll was complaining about the sudden, unexplained summons, the steep steps that were a torment to her bones, Edward's sweating pallor and perverse refusal to say just what was wanted and why such urgency. Was it not nigh time decent folks were abed?

Matthew asked Moll and her husband to look into the wardrobe.

"Wherefore?" snapped Moll. "Is the chamber not satisfactory?"

"It is not," answered Matthew coldly. Again he ordered them to look in the wardrobe.

Moll snorted with discontent and, her husband following, marched toward the wardrobe and looked in, Edward holding the candles high so that the interior was fully illuminated.

For a moment there was no response from either Moll or Cuth; then Moll let out a great bellow of grief and rage: "O God in heaven preserve us all," she cried. "It's Nebuchadnezzar. It's my dear, sweet cat that I loved before all the world."

"And, more important, a human soul, treacherously used," Matthew said.

"It's Aileen Mogaill," Cuth said in a shaking voice. "Why, we thought she had run away, like the others before her."

The old man tried to comfort his wife, but she would have no comfort. She kept lamenting the cat's death.

Matthew said something about going for the local constable, and Moll suddenly stopped her blubbering and turned her face toward him. "Oh, I wouldn't do that," she said. "It will do little good for the girl and surely great harm to them that's living."

"Why great harm?" Joan asked before Matthew could.

"John Andrewes—him that's constable for the year—is a right blockhead, *that's* the harm. He'll come when called, gawk, say tut-tut and wellaway, and make nothing of this horror but to scratch the fleas in his beard and summon the coroner, who's his match as a numbskull."

"Numbskull or not, he must be summoned," Matthew said. "So goes the law."

"So may the law go for me," Moll answered sharply. "But it's more than law you'll have when this gets out."

"Why, what do you mean?" Joan asked.

"Marry, I mean nothing less than there'll be not a servant left in the castle, that's what. All will fly, believe me. The Irish wenches, the lot, and you'll have none come from the village or Buxton to take their places. A fine wedding the young mistress will have then, she and her bridegroom, alone in the castle."

"But this girl within the wardrobe has been *murdered*," Matthew protested.

"She came here of herself, she did," Moll said, as though the victim had somehow been responsible for her own tragedy. "She should have known better than to haunt the Keep without companions."

Joan exchanged a puzzled glance with Matthew. There was obviously more to Moll's concern than met the eye.

"It's the curse, the Challoner curse," Cuth pronounced, casting a knowing look toward his wife.

"Shut up, you old fool," Moll said.

Ignoring this kindly admonition, Cuth commenced to stumble through an account of a decapitated baronet of Thorncombe, with sufficient competence to send a shiver down Joan's spine as he told his tale. Joan looked around the chamber when he was done. A fit chamber of horrors, this, with a notable history of monstrous acts, yet she did not believe for a moment Aileen Mogaill had been beheaded by a ghost. This was mortal mischief, she was sure; nestling the dead cat in the girl's arms was the bizarre humor of a sick mind, not the work of a tormented spirit.

"Man, ghost, or devil, the constable *must* be summoned," Matthew insisted.

"Well, summon whom you please," Moll said. "But if you do, you might well not unpack your gear, for it will be even as I have said. When this act is proclaimed, no servant will darken these doors. You will have the place to yourselves, and right welcome to it, and the mistress can marry elsewhere."

Moll stood, her arms akimbo, staring at Matthew as though to allow the full implication of her warning to settle, then she turned to Cuth and said, "Come, husband. We've had our say. Let them agree who will."

The old couple marched out, and Matthew sent Edward to find something to cover the girl's body. When Matthew and

Joan were alone, Joan said, "Moll's right, you know. Nothing can be more injurious to our efforts here than the news of this fresh and most blatant homicide. It will surely have just such an effect as this wicked old woman prophesied."

"Surely you don't believe this was the work of a ghost?" Matthew said.

"No, I don't," Joan said. "It may well be the work of the same hand that killed Sir John—although why he should have chosen to slaughter an innocent child is beyond reason."

"Well, there's no help for it. The law is plain."

"The law is plain, but our course may vary and achieve the ends of justice after all," Joan said. "What if we follow Moll's advice?"

"What?" Matthew said incredulously. "Say nothing?"

"For the present, at least. Until evidence of both this and Sir John's murder is brought to light."

Matthew went over to the bed and sat down; his face took on the expression it had when he was deep in some perplexing problem. Joan understood her husband's dilemma. A man of rigorous probity, zealous to a fault for law and order, he could not easily depart from the prescribed path, and particularly one first recommended by someone he disliked.

"It's not, after all, as though her murderer will go unlooked to," Joan reasoned. "You are the Queen's agent by her express command. It is only the outward trappings of official inquiry that will be postponed. You, as Queen's officer, will investigate secretly—and with such subterfuge, we'll not alarm the castle or put to flight our suspects at the very time we need them close at hand."

"And to those who know the truth—the Fludds and Edward Bastian—we will seem to have acted only out of policy."

"A more subtle policy than they suppose," she added, putting the capstone on her argument. "And there'll be no meddlesome local constables to muddy the waters."

Matthew thought some more. He stood and paced the chamber a few times, glanced toward the wardrobe, and shook his head. Then he stopped and looked at Joan.

"So be it," he said. "We'll go find the Fludds and tell them we have decided to follow their counsel. Then we'll see to the burial of Aileen Mogaill in some private place until time and circumstances make the cause of these horrors plain. Meanwhile the other servants can continue to believe the girl fled. If Moll speaks true, the fiction will be readily credited."

"All well and good," Joan said, smiling faintly, although her headache had returned with a vengeance. "As for this chamber, I'll not spend the night here, nor in the tower, either, but in the new house if I must lie all night upon the floor, which I would fain do soon. I am weary and sick of heart, and my head pounds to let the poor brain free."

"You *do* look ill," Matthew said with sudden concern. "I'll lead you to other quarters, then Edward and I will see to the poor wench that's dead. She'll have a decent grave, with pious words said above it, though no priest nor public mourning. Meanwhile I pray this sickness of yours has no more grievous cause than horror at finding Aileen Mogaill's body and exhaustion from the long journey."

8

NEXT morning, the rain fell remorselessly, and Moll's grief passed the understanding of her husband, who stood slightly behind her, a supportive hand on her elbow. He knew she could think only of the dead cat, the worthy Nebuchadnezzar, while he tried vainly to think of everything but the human remains in the wardrobe. They both looked down at the cat, stiff in its little shroud of dirty cloth. Edward had brought the body round early to the lodge. The hostler looked grief-stricken too, although for cat, maid, or both, Cuth Fludd couldn't tell.

"A poor, innocent creature, Nebuchadnezzar was," Moll said, sobbing softly. "Would to God I had an account of his end."

"Well," said Cuth in an effort to console his wife, "maybe the cat died of apoplexy. He was very old."

Moll turned slowly, wiped a tear from her red cheeks, and regarded her husband with contempt. "Just died? Of old age? Apoplexy, say you? Why, you old fool, he was in his prime."

Moll knelt down slowly, as she might have done before a religious relic, and examined the body, tenderly touching the fur, stroking the animal's side. Then she gasped and said: "No Challoner ghost did this. Look here, he's been strangled, strangled dead!"

Both Cuth and Edward joined in the inspection and were forced to confirm Moll's finding. The cat had been strangled, no doubt about it.

Moll rose and began propounding several theories of the murder with a completeness of thought suggesting she had already been considering such a possibility: that Aileen Mogaill was the perpetrator, or one of the other servants, taking their resentment of her, Moll, out on a poor dumb animal. Or perhaps it was the blackguard Irishman who had treated her with such rudeness. Finally, Moll's speculations brought her to Joan Stock as a culprit.

"I'll warrant the Stock woman killed him," she said. "Out of pure spite."

Edward said he thought that unlikely. He said the cat had obviously been dead for several days, if stench were any clue. Certainly that should exclude Joan Stock and her husband from Moll's list of suspects.

But Moll made a face to suggest that any effort to absolve the newcomers of responsibility was unwelcome. Terrible in her new spirit of vengeance, she said, "I hate them both, and more particularly the woman. Come, Cuth. Help me bury our darling as befits his character as a good cat. And damned be she who strangled him."

Cuth began to scoop up the cat but Moll said, "Not in that filthy rag, you dolt! Fetch clean linen from the sideboard and bring it straightway."

Cuth went to do as he was ordered and Edward said, "I'm truly sorry I brought your cat to you, Moll. I should have buried it myself."

"No," Moll said. "You did the right thing. The decent thing. When one's beloved is taken by violence as in this case, it must be known. How else can justice be served? I'm only a bitter woman—made more bitter still by life's misfortunes. But even I know *that*. No, murder will out, or so they say."

All this Moll declared with great dignity, tears streaming down her cheeks and her fist clutched to her bosom in a gesture of determination. Cuth reappeared. He was carrying a piece of cloth of appropriate quality. Moll inspected it and said it would serve; she handed it to Edward, who placed the cat upon it and wrapped it up again.

The three of them stepped out into the rain and walked toward the woods. The trees provided some shelter from the drizzle. Edward found a suitable spot for the burial in a little clearing where the earth was soft. Having no shovel, he dug the grave with his hands, raking up the moist earth with his fingers. He took the body from Moll, who had carried it to the burial place, and gently laid it into the hole.

The grave Edward had dug was not quite deep enough and he had to dig it deeper. Then the fit was perfect. Edward covered the body while above him Moll said, "May she howl in hell a thousand nights who did this."

The curse was the cat's epitaph.

After the burial Moll went off to the castle kitchen to find some sweet to console her grief, while Cuth returned to the lodge and stoked the fire to dry his bones. He had got drenched there in the woods, bound as he had been to observe decorum at Nebuchadnezzar's funeral, but the worse was the image of cruel murder and mayhem the cat's burial had brought to his mind. Somewhere in the same woods Aileen Mogaill was buried. Cuth was thankful he had been given no part in that gruesome interment.

He drew his stool up toward the flames. How good the heat felt. Wet weather was not good for his old body, nor was his recent change in habitations. He was used to his quarters in the new house, having dwelt there a score of years or more in perfect felicity (his relationship with Moll was another matter altogether). The lodge was not only tumble-down, but the suffering he endured from aches in his joints and the hacking cough the proximity of water aggravated was almost as painful a cross as the humiliation of his forced retirement.

Feeling better now, he thought of Nebuchadnezzar—this time without an accompanying image of Aileen Mogaill. Cuth had always hated the cat, hated its outlandish, heathen name, given it by Moll from the days of her religious phase, the only remnant of which now was her virulent anti-papistry. She had heard the name Nebuchadnezzar in a sermon, liked it, and was wont to explain the name was that of one of the Twelve Apostles of Our Lord. A very pious cat.

But the truth was that Cuth had strangled it himself. He had stumbled out of bed the first night in the lodge, disoriented by the unfamiliar surrounding. In desperate need of the chamber pot, he had stepped on the creature's tail, heard a snarl, felt a painful retaliatory nip into the thin flesh of his ankle. With a dexterity that amazed him in recalling it, Cuth had reached down, seized his assailant by the scruff of the neck, and dispatched it without a thought of the consequence. The miracle was that his wife had not been awakened by the sounds of combat.

By morning light he realized what he had done. Feeling no remorse, only regret that he should now have to dispose of the evidence of his wrongdoing, he pulled the limp body from beneath the bed and stole out of the lodge, intending a hasty burial somewhere in the woods. It was only after he had covered the body with a thin layer of dirt and old leaves and had returned to the lodge that he realized what an opportunity lay before him. So the day before the arrival of the new steward and housekeeper, he had exhumed Nebuchadnezzar from his shallow grave and concealed him in the wardrobe. He knew that his wife had finished her work there. It was all she spoke of—how she hated the Keep and how she wished the Stocks what joy they'd find there. Soon, Cuth knew, the cat would be all maggoty and reeking—and a fine welcome he should give the interlopers.

That Moll now held the Stocks responsible for the cat's murder was a measure of luck he had not bargained for.

Nor, for that matter, the terrible thing that had happened to the girl, the very thought of which caused such turbulence in his gut that he wished to heaven his wife were present to distract him from it. When he had taken the cat to the wardrobe, the wardrobe had been empty. Of that he could swear upon a dozen Bibles if he was required. The murder of Aileen Mogaill must have been done thereafter, he supposed—in the dead of night. And by some old Challoner offended by the girl's solitary trespass. Was not the beheading of the victim clear evidence of a malign spirit?

Cuth knew all the old stories of the castle—and he believed a goodly share of them as much as he believed in the existence of God, witches, devils, and other supernatural forces in his world.

But what Cuth could not fathom was this: surely Aileen Mogaill had not been the first servant to wander into the Black Keep alone. Why this sudden fury of a ghost content for all the years of Cuth's service to claim no more than a rumored existence?

He was still pondering these perplexing matters an hour later when a knocking snatched him from his meditations. At first he thought it was his wife, kicking at the door because her arms would be full. He responded accordingly—with great haste, to open before she began a clamorous complaint.

But it was not Moll. It was Edward, standing there in the rain with as little concern for the drizzle as if it had been the sunniest day in July.

Cuth asked Edward what he wanted.

"Only a little talk with you, friend. A privy talk, if you please."

"A privy talk?" Cuth replied, eyeing the hostler suspiciously and feeling greatly bereft of his wife's presence. "About what?"

"Your good wife's cat, that's what," Edward said, coming inside without invitation.

Cuth knew something was wrong, and he found himself trembling a little. He shut the door against the rain and turned toward his uninvited guest, waiting to hear what Edward's visit was all about.

"I've been thinking, thinking of murder," Edward said slowly.

Cuth thought he meant Aileen Mogaill and said, "Why, the ghost did it, killed the girl and the cat as well. Or it was that Stock woman who killed the cat, as my wife supposes."

Edward laughed mirthlessly, his face taut. "I know nothing of ghosts. When I see one, I'll believe it, not before. I did take a close look at your wife's cat, though. I found pieces of dirt in its fur, yea, in the nostrils. Your wife's inspection of her darling wasn't very thorough."

"Whereby you conclude what?"

"Why, someone killed the cat, buried him, and then dug him up again—carried him to the Black Keep as an afterthought. The cat was stone cold before the Stocks arrived, before Aileen Mogaill was dead. Any fool can see that. Besides, why would they have killed the cat and left him to rot in their own wardrobe? I doubt neither knew the cat was Moll's. But someone hated the Stocks, hated them before setting eyes on them, and that was Moll—and you."

"You're not saying my wife killed her own cat?" Cuth exclaimed, as much amused as astonished at the accusation.

"Of course not," Edward said. "Moll would never hurt a hair of that cat. But the case is not the same with you. You'd strangle the cat soon enough because you could never abide the thing and then conceal it in the wardrobe to annoy the Stocks—and perhaps even make them guilty."

"So you reason," Cuth responded with ineffectual sarcasm after he had paused for a moment to take in all that Edward had said. His trembling was worse now; it had begun to affect his voice, and Cuth was sure Edward could detect it as well. He would have demanded that the hostler leave his premises had he not been driven with such a desire to know what Edward intended to do with his terrible knowledge.

"Your wife will reason likewise when I lay out the facts," the hostler continued with easy assurance. "It'll be as plain as your scabby nose. When she finds out it was you who deprived her of her darling, it'll go hard with you."

"You can tell her what you please. She'll believe *me*," Cuth said, wishing it were true but already feeling his fate cast.

Edward laughed. "There's more, you know."

"More?"

"Maybe if you strangled the cat, you dispatched Aileen thereafter. Now there's something for a curious man to ponder, for I would as soon believe you did the deed as believe in some moldy ghost fetched forth from old servants' tales."

"Killed the girl!" Cuth explained, really alarmed now. "Why, I never did such a thing." He felt the blood drain from his face and his whole body quiver as though he had been struck with the palsy. "I confess I strangled the cat. I confess it, but before God, I had not jot or tittle to do with Aileen Mogaill, not since she came to Thorncombe. I never so much as looked her way."

Transfixed between insult and terror, Cuth felt hot tears run down his cheeks, and he was ashamed to weep before his accuser. Edward looked on, a grim smile on his lips and a skeptical expression in his eyes.

"Will you say aught to my wife about the cat?" Cuth brought himself to ask, having decided he had no alternative but to throw himself upon the hostler's mercy.

For a few moments Edward made no response. He looked as though he were trying to make up his mind, weighing the advantages of silence against those of revelation. Finally, he said, "Maybe yes, maybe no. The same goes for my suspicions about you and Aileen Mogaill."

"For Christ's sake, man—"

"Make no appeals to Christ, you whited sepulcher," Edward said, all smiles gone. "You are a self-confessed liar, for you looked upon two corpses and played a mighty hypocrite agog at your own villainy. So it will be thought since you killed the one creature, you probably killed the other too."

"Not if you say nothing," Cuth pleaded, his pride totally gone now.

"Not if I say nothing," answered Edward, suddenly friendly again.

"Oh, what must I do?" Cuth begged.

9

THAT same morning, Matthew's worst fears about Joan's symptoms were confirmed. It was now plain that she had been stricken with a fever, ague, God knew what—aggravated to the quick by the ordeal of travel, the discovery of a dead woman in her wardrobe, and the commencement of the steady drizzle that seemed to permeate the stone walls of the castle and make all within damp, soggy, and joyless. Joan burned and shivered by turns, like a lover in an old sonnet, while Matthew, concerned that no physician was available to bleed, purge, or pronounce upon his wife's urine, resorted to the few remedies he had learned at home—herbs, compresses, and earnest prayers for Joan's delivery from evil.

Joan was bedridden for three days, convalescing for another, sleeping upon rushes in the parlor of the new house where she and Matthew had established a temporary hospital. During this time Matthew played a good nurse, for he dared not trust Joan's health or safety to another soul, given the evidence of homicidal madness in the castle. Was there *anyone* beyond suspicion?

Their investigation of Sir John's and Aileen Mogaill's

murders was postponed, therefore, and even the normal course of their respective duties as housekeeper and steward suffered a necessary neglect, waiting upon Joan's recovery.

But recover she did, even in the absence of a physician and his leeches, and Matthew took the first dry day thereafter to ride into Buxton, where he contrived to converse with the foreman of the coroner's jury that had sat in Sir John's case. The foreman, a lanky, talkative fellow named Broomfield, revealed that the verdict of death by misadventure had been reached for want of compelling evidence to the contrary. Matthew also learned that the suspicion that Sir John had been murdered was widespread. Matthew only needed to identify himself as the new steward of Thorncombe and he was deluged by volunteered information and gossip, local legends, and petty slanders. It was difficult for him to discern which was which, but he left town with the impression that, if but half of what he had heard was true, Thorncombe was a very sinister place indeed.

The evening of the same day he spent a good six to eight hours poring over the former steward's ledgers—not that he supposed he would discover in their yellowed, dog-eared pages evidence of Sir John's murder, but because it was the thing a new steward was expected to do and he wanted to be perfect in his guise. Besides, as a merchant he was full of natural curiosity as to the estate's income and expenditures.

For all his faults, Cuth had been a meticulous record-keeper, or so Matthew inferred from the ledgers. The whole sad story was there: a tale of declining income offset by a reduction in servants, the sale of livestock, the pawn of plate and furnishings, and then, too, sudden and unexplained infusions of capital from unidentified sources. Matthew took careful note of all these details, although as yet they formed no meaningful pattern nor any clear relation to Sir John's death. For one thing, the ledgers did not give evidence of who, despite his heir, of course, might have benefited from the murder.

Joan had discounted Frances Challoner as a suspect even before they left London. The pleasant young woman simply did not look the sort to commission a murder, which is what she would have had to do at such a remove. Moreover, it seemed unlikely to Joan that Frances Challoner would have sufficient motive to kill her uncle to secure land and chattels that would fall to her anyway in the course of time.

"A jealous neighbor, then? Perhaps a disgruntled servant?" Matthew suggested.

"If you are thinking of Moll," Joan said, "I will readily grant that the woman has the disposition. Whether she had cause is another question."

The problem with all these deliberations was that, because of Joan's illness, they had hardly begun to investigate matters or persons at the castle. And a good third of their allotted month was nearly gone, if one counted the days of travel from London to Derbyshire, as Matthew was convinced the Queen had.

"Tomorrow, I intend to rise from my bed of affliction and go about my duties, ready or not," Joan declared with grim determination. She was as frustrated as her husband by the delay in beginning their real work at Thorncombe.

"And so you shall," Matthew said. "But only if you're able. The Queen's business is important, but I'll not sacrifice your health."

She was pleased by his concern and told him so, kissing him heartily on the lips and calling him sweetheart and other pet names she had for him, and they spent a pleasant hour in such amorous discourse, wherein she proved to the satisfaction of them both that she was a whole woman again.

Later, Matthew said, "The sun has dried things out now. Tomorrow Edward will accompany me on a visit to the tenants' farms. There aren't many left—no more than half a dozen. We may visit the neighbor, too. Stafford's his name. Wouldn't hurt to introduce myself to him. I also want Edward to show me the exact place where Sir John drowned."

She warned him against making his interest in the death too obvious. He told her he would be discreet.

"You'll be gone all day, then," she said.

"Very likely."

"Well, see that you don't lose your way in this wilderness. See that the hostler provides you with a good mount and no uppity stallion to break your neck with and—"

She stopped when she saw the suppressed laughter in his eyes. Realizing that she was mothering him unconscionably, she flushed with embarrassment. Would she make her good man into another Cuth Fludd with all her admonishments, and herself a something worse thereby? She knew Matthew was an able horseman. Never had he become lost that she remembered, nor had he ever been thrown. She remembered, too, that Edward would be a more than adequate guide through the neighborhood. She took Matthew's hand and held it in a firm grasp. "Forgive me," she said softly. "I didn't mean to treat you as a child."

With a good-natured laugh he bent and kissed her on the cheek. Then they walked downstairs and through the kitchen to the rear porch of the house.

"You take care," he said to her. "I would sooner face the menace of these lonely wastes than the dark passages of Thorncombe, where madmen lurk to do harm of nights. Are you sure you're well enough to be up and about?"

She assured him she was. Over his shoulder, she saw Edward coming across the courtyard with a broad stride. Matthew turned away from her to the young hostler and greeted him.

Then Joan watched as the two men went off toward the stable. She envied her husband a little for his day's adventure, and yet she realized, too, that he was right. She had an adventure of her own, and she had exaggerated her recovery. In fact, she felt weakened by her long sojourn in bed and she still had the sniffles. Besides, she thought in one last effort to expunge the demon of self-pity, why should she envy Matthew's tour of smelly barns and tenants' hovels?

As she turned to go into the house again, she thought of Moll. Had the old woman's resentment and hostility not so poisoned their relationship, Joan would have had her predecessor for a guide to her new duties. But Joan would not want Moll for a guide now, nor did she suppose the old woman would offer her services. Joan's illness had prevented a confrontation over the dead cat. It had also prevented any questions about Aileen Mogaill's relations with the other servants. The decision to keep her murder a secret had made it seem, at four days' remove, that the murder had never happened at all, that its hapless victim really had vanished into thin air.

Joan found Una in the kitchen. The woman wore her usual expression of friendly accommodation and Joan felt a surge of fellow feeling for the Irishwoman. Although a foreigner and ignorant of the English tongue, Una seemed to be without guile. Even more to the point, she was no sourpuss, which was a welcome relief to Joan, whose natural inclination was to be friendly to all she met, save for knaves and fools, whom she did not suffer readily.

She decided to ask Una to be her companion on her explorations of the castle. The problem was *how* to ask. At first, Joan put her request into simple English accompanied by such sign language that seemed, to Joan, to express her intent. To which the cook responded with an affable smile and an obvious failure to comprehend. Then Joan grasped Una's arm and made gestures indicating the various regions of the house. This strategy proved more effective. Understanding shone in the Irishwoman's eyes and she nodded her head vigorously and pointed to the passage leading to the deeper recesses of Thorncombe.

"Then let us begin," Joan said.

Her husband had, since their arrival at Thorncombe, strolled curiously through the chambers of the new house and the castle and given her some report of his findings, so what Joan now saw in person was no surprise to her. The downstairs of the new house consisted of a spacious hall, an adjoining parlor or withdrawing room, a grand staircase, a dining room—in addition, of course, to these smaller rooms occupied by the household servants in the course of their duties: the kitchen, pantry, buttery, and steward's office. All the larger rooms of the ground floor were sparsely furnished, as was befitting a master who had spent only a few months of the year in residence and had no wife or child to maintain and no interest in entertaining the local gentry. The Challoner hounds had been sold at their master's death, so that there was little sign now of canine damage, although there was a slight lingering odor. Joan noticed a layer of dust here and there, but nothing that could not be remedied in short order once she had organized the maids.

Access to the upper floor of the house would have been most convenient by the grand staircase, and in her capacity as head housekeeper she might have properly ascended by this route, especially in the absence of the mistress of the house. But to set an example for her companion, Joan ascended the back staircase, wedged between the steward's tiny office and the buttery and so narrow as to require the two women to climb single file.

The stairs led to a long gallery that afforded a fine view of the woods and lake. The interior wall opposite was hung with family portraits—a grim line of baronets, most in armor, with each portrait marked with the Challoner crest, a chevron surmounted by a boar's head. Between the portraits were doors, which upon inspection proved to give access to mostly unfurnished bedchambers. One, however, opened to a suite of chambers, which Joan surmised both by their size and superior furnishings had been Sir John's. Her supposition was immediately confirmed by Una, who seemed afraid to enter the apartment and muttered her late master's name beneath her breath.

Joan did not compel Una to follow her into the apartment. She did not think to find evidence of Sir John's murder there, but she did feel she might sense something in the chambers that would give her a better idea of the dead man's character. Her sensitivity, she believed, would be the greater if she was alone. But as she began to inspect the apartment, she recognized that changes had been made since Sir John's death. The austere masculinity she was sure had characterized the room during the baronet's occupation had been modified. Its wall hangings and embroidered coverlet, the tall cheval glass, and handsome turkey carpet of brilliant floral design suggested a feminine presence. Or at least the anticipation of such a presence.

As she was admiring these furnishings and allowing herself a little vanity of studying her own reflection in the cheval glass—noting with some alarm her residual pallor—she heard an unfamiliar masculine voice coming from the gallery. Going to see who it was, she found Una conversing in Irish with a ruddy-complexioned young man of about thirty, dressed in canvas doublet with silk buttons and wearing a knife and sword. The man was broad-shouldered and thick-waisted. His calves, bulging beneath the cotton hose, were muscular, but his shanks were somewhat out of proportion to the rest of his body. His hands were large and hairy. He had the straight nose, large lips, and square jaw that many women would have found attractive.

On seeing Joan, Una and the man ceased conversing, and the man introduced himself, in English, as Michael Conroy. At the same time he made a graceful bow to Joan, as though she were a gentlewoman.

"You must be our new housekeeper," Michael Conroy said. "I had heard you had fallen foul of some fever since you arrived here. I'm pleased to see you so recovered."

She thanked him for his courtesy, wary of a certain flirtatious quality in the young man's eye and not about to be flattered into a premature approval of his presence in the house. She had heard about Sir John's manservant from Matthew, who had spoken to him briefly the second day at Thorncombe, but had reported being unable to determine why he remained in the house, his master dead and buried. She decided to exert her authority and ask him outright what he did to pass his time.

"Why, I wait upon Mistress Frances Challoner," he said, lifting his eyes in surprise at the question and speaking in the same well-modulated voice as before. "I was her uncle's personal servant. I am therefore a piece of his estate, which, upon my good master's death, fell to his heir." His pale handsome eyes flashed winningly.

"Are you?" Joan returned, not bothering to disguise the

cynicism in her voice, for she was not sure whether what Conroy had said had any merit in law or was merely the witty retort of an obnoxious idler.

"Indeed," he said, and he looked to Una for support, but the Irishwoman was standing quietly staring at Joan. "It was Sir John's express wish that I continue in the employ of the family."

"As a manservant?"

"As . . . whatever pleases my mistress."

"And you are under her orders?"

"I am."

"Do you have letters in hand declaring as much?" Joan asked.

Conroy paused and flashed another broad smile. He stroked his chin. "Well, I *had* such a letter."

"But you do not have it *now*?" she said.

"No. I've misplaced it."

Joan decided it would be best to keep the upper hand in her catechism. She suspected Conroy was up to no good, and she did not like at all his masculine arrogance. "That's very convenient for you—your misplacing it," she said. "And, pray, how do you spend your time in the interval?"

"The interval?" Conroy asked, not quite as pleasantly as before.

"Between your master's death, before which you had clearly defined duties, and your mistress's coming, which may be a month or more from now."

"Ah, yes," he said. "Well, I read . . . I care for Sir John's papers."

"His papers? What papers?"

"His diary, his letters," Conroy answered. The old smile returned. But Joan suspected the Irishman was a varlet of the first order. She could read the insolence in his eyes. Had she not seen it often before—in saucy tradesmen and apprentices and city constables contemptuous of honest country people such as herself?

"His papers record his experiences in Ireland," Conroy

continued, more boldly. "Sir John was a famous soldier. His papers have importance as . . . historical documents."

But Joan was not to be cowed by learned phrases, especially not from the lips of a smooth-talking Irishman. "Historical documents indeed!" she said. "I think, sir, you are no antiquary or scholar but do little else here but be idle, which you might as well accomplish in the stable, if your legs will bear you the distance."

At this remark, Conroy's countenance changed utterly. His brow furrowed and he seemed to grow taller before her. "I am Mistress Frances Challoner's servant," he declared coldly. "As are you, Mistress Stock. It is her command that sends me packing, or bids me stay, not yours."

Joan was about to tell Conroy just what authority she had been given when she was prevented by Una, who put a hand on Conroy's arm and said something in Irish to pacify him. For a moment Conroy continued to glare threateningly at Joan, then his anger seemed to subside. He stepped back from her and put his hands behind his back and rocked on the balls of his feet. "Very well, very well," he said. "I suppose Edward will share a bed with me—or put me in with one of the horses. But I warn you, my mistress will not be pleased to find out how I have been used."

"If she is not pleased, then I will suffer her displeasure," Joan said, keeping her voice steady. "In the meantime, collect your gear and move from the house. There's much to be done here to make things ready for Mistress Frances Challoner, and it will not do to have you under foot."

Joan left Una and Conroy standing in the gallery while she went back into the master's apartment, not so much because she had not seen enough there but because she wanted to terminate a discussion that had become increasingly heated and dangerous. She thanked God for Una's timely intercession, but wondered what the woman had said to mollify Conroy.

She went over to the cheval glass and looked at her reflection. At least the confrontation with Conroy had brought some color to her cheeks.

She looked around the chambers some more but found nothing that could be called a clue—either to Sir John's death or to his maid's. When she returned to the gallery she found Una waiting. Conroy, Joan was happy to see, had gone. She told Una she was ready to continue their excursion and Una looked pleased to be going. Yet suddenly, and unaccountably, Joan felt less secure in Una's company than before. Was it only because Una had exchanged words with Conroy in a language unknown to Joan, or was there something more sinister that Joan sensed?

Still rankled somewhat over her quarrel with Conroy, she now tried to focus her thoughts on the matter at hand, for she could not forget the ulterior motive of her tour. At least she had had a glimpse of Conroy's violent nature—and could easily add him to her list of suspects. Indeed, Conroy was now the chief! He had a blackguard's smirk, the slippery manner of a backstairs villain, and that his sword was quite capable of Aileen's murder was well within the circumference of belief.

Joan would have liked to question Una and the other female servants about their master's drowning, but the language barrier permitted only the most rudimentary communication and she hesitated to arouse suspicion. She did hope Matthew would learn something from Edward Bastian, who had become a co-conspirator in the hushing up of Aileen Mogaill's murder and whose amiable deportment gave promise of further shared confidences.

Una now led the way to the end of the gallery, where a little door opened to a steep flight of narrow stairs. They climbed and came to a low-ceilinged attic, where there were many small chambers furnished with straw pallets and other simple furnishings. One chamber, detached somewhat from the rest, had a good-size bed. Joan asked if this had been the Fludds' quarters before their removal to the lodge, and Una, evidently understanding the question, nodded her assent.

Joan looked around the chamber and decided that this should now be hers and Matthew's. The small downstairs parlor that she and Matthew had occupied during her convalescence had been adequate as a temporary refuge from the horrors of the Black Keep but lacked the privacy and security required for longer habitation.

Joan made Una understand her intention of occupying the chamber forthwith, and the cook went off to secure help in transporting the Stocks' things.

While Una was gone, Joan inspected the chamber carefully. She was gratified to find no dead cats or even innocent relics of the Fludds' recent occupancy, but she understood now, seeing how light, airy, and accessible these quarters were, the malignity that explained her and Matthew's assignment to the Black Keep, and a new wave of resentment swept over her. She thought, too, about Michael Conroy and his impudence. She dearly hoped she would have no further trouble with the rogue and realized how right her husband had been when he had said there was more danger in Thorncombe's passages than in the wastes of Derbyshire.

Then Una returned and said something in Irish that Joan interpreted to mean her orders had been carried out and soon her belongings would be transferred to these new rooms. She smiled in approval, but she indicated to Una that their tour had not finished. There were still parts of the old castle Joan had not seen which she felt came within her responsibility.

Since, like the second story of the new house, the attic afforded no passage to the castle, Joan and Una were forced to retrace their steps. Joan led the way and the two women returned to the kitchen and from there passed through the cavernous banqueting hall. There was a cellar with stone walls and low vaulted ceiling that occupied their attention in between. Like many a chamber of Thorncombe it was empty, and its rough walls oozed with moisture. The place was dark and dank like most cellars and had no particular interest to Joan. Their visit was therefore brief and Joan indicated that she wanted to visit the White Keep without further ado.

Each of Thorncombe's keeps had its own staircase, located to the left and right of the dais and hearth, and extending upward and outward in a graceful arc. The two women climbed the stairs to the left of the dais and came to a landing. Joan could see that the arrangement of chambers in the White Keep was identical to that in the Black. A large bedchamber and several smaller rooms were separated by a narrow corridor at the end of which was a tall, unglazed window. The large White Keep chamber proved to be a repository of trash—boxes and old casks, discarded furniture, much of it broken—an arsonist's delight. Joan found moldering in one corner an old arras with faded scenes of castles and ships and a battered chest full of rusting weaponry, chain mail, and old tools some stonemason had left behind years earlier. The windows afforded the same view as those in her former quarters.

While Joan was conducting this inspection, Una remained in the corridor. When Joan had concluded, she noticed the anxious expression of her companion and suggested they take a quick look at what remained and then go downstairs. Una seemed to understand this communication and smiled gratefully. The first of the remaining rooms was empty. There was little evidence that the room had ever been occupied. The second room, however, was a mystery. The door was equipped with a lock, but Joan found no key in her collection that would fit.

She was puzzled. Why should this room be locked when the others weren't?

She was contemplating this question when she heard something stirring on the other side of the door. She wasn't sure if it was a footstep or the rustle of a gown. Then she heard what sounded very much like a muffled cough. She looked at Una and knew that the Irishwoman had heard the noise as well. Una's eyes were large with fear.

Joan rapped sharply on the door. "I know there's someone there," she called. "Open at once."

But Joan's commands had no effect, and although she

heard no more movement within the room, she had the absolute conviction that someone was there.

When subsequent knocking met with equal failure, she ordered Una to remain by the door while she went to find Moll. Una seemed very reluctant. "Stay here," Joan ordered with gestures unmistakably to that effect.

10

MATTHEW looked for Edward in the stable but the young hostler wasn't there. The stable door gaped wide, admitting a generous swath of sunlight into the dusty, horsey interior. The horses were standing in the paddock, and the broken harness draped on the workbench with the mending tools at hand suggested that Edward had been about his business earlier that morning, had been interrupted, and would presently return.

Matthew was content to wait, glad for a chance to look around on his own.

The stable, pleasantly redolent with the smell of beast, straw, leather, and horse dung, was old but in good repair, with a sound roof and sturdy timbered walls. It had been constructed to house a veritable herd of animals but provided for only a small number now. Most of the stalls appeared to be unused; several had been converted to storage of hay. In the back of the stable was a small room outfitted with a pallet where, Matthew presumed, Edward slept.

While he waited, Matthew examined the hostler's tools, an orderly array of knives, auls, mallets, and pikes. The knives were sharp and arranged according to size. The tools Edward had been using to mend the harness were placed at right angles like a table setting at a feast. The bench itself was smooth and brushed clean of scraps and dirt. There were a small forge and bellows, a blacksmith's tongs and hammer.

Then a shadow fell across the sunlit doorway and Matthew looked up to see Edward standing there. "Good day to you, Edward."

For a moment Edward said nothing. He seemed startled, and Matthew wondered if he had offended the hostler by invading his domain while Edward was absent. But what should he have done? And after all, he was the steward of the house. He asked if Edward would keep him company on his rounds. Edward, relaxing, it seemed to Matthew, said he would.

"I looked around the stables while you were out. All seems in good order. I want to visit the tenants. I have a list from Cuth's ledger."

Matthew reached in his pocket and pulled out a crumpled sheet of paper on which he had written the names. "I see one of the tenants is named Bastian. Would that be one of your kin?"

"My father," Edward answered. "He occupies a mean cottage on a small parcel of land—it's hardly worth a visit."

"Perhaps not, but I will want to meet your father all the same," Matthew said.

The two men walked out into the paddock. "We'll ride," Edward said, eyeing the horses. "It's four or five miles to the farthest tenant."

"I want to call upon Master Stafford as well."

"Yes, sir. His property lies to the north of here, but he'll give us a cold welcome."

"Cold, why?"

"An old grudge—a dispute over the lake and the dam that made it." Edward walked over to one of the horses, a bay gelding with a fine-shaped head. He patted it on the withers and whispered something in its ear.

Matthew came up behind the hostler and said, "You know, I think I'd like to take a look at the lake before we ride."

Edward turned sharply; his eyes were puzzled. "The lake? Why, there's nothing to see there that can't be seen from the house."

"I know, but I feel obliged to see everything."

Edward shrugged and patted the horse on the rump; it trotted off. He walked back through the stable door with Matthew.

Matthew followed the hostler around the stable to where a path led through he woods. They walked a hundred yards or so through dense foliage until the lake came into view. Matthew stood on a high, slippery bank overlooking the water, which even on a fair day had a strangely leaden hue. He noticed an unpleasant smell and asked Edward about it.

"The water," Edward said. "Most pestilent and unhealthy it is, yet no one is sure why. Sir John made the lake, you know, not nature. That is, he caused the lake to be made. Before his time there was a good running stream and marsh. Sir John had been south and had seen some great house there—Kenilworth, I think."

"Ah," said Matthew. "The castle of the mighty Earl of Leicester."

"The same," Edward said. "That castle, I have heard tell, had a moat, a very fine broad one. Sir John wanted the same. He hired a French engineer to build an earthwork dam against the stream that coursed through the valley. A hillock called hereabout, 'the thorn,' became the island you see yonder."

"And the little pile of stones upon it?" Matthew asked, casting an eye across the water.

"A replica of Thorncombe's towers—or at least one of them. A pure novelty, for it has no practical use, being hardly large enough for a tall man to stand upright."

"You've been on the island then?"

"In my youth. There's nothing more to see than what you see at this distance, I assure you."

"But the water is foul," Matthew said.

"It is indeed," Edward said with an ironical laugh. "As the waters rose they found something strange and malignant in the ground they covered. Instead of being deep and clear and sweet as the natural lakes of the region, Sir John's was warm, murky, and foul-smelling. Some of the neighbors said it was God's judgment for Sir John's presumption. Lakes were God's work, not man's—or so they said. Some more charitable said the smell was caused by seepage from old lead mines. They counseled Sir John to seek some learned man conversant with the properties of stones and rocks—they thought the water might be a cure like St. Ann's in Buxton. But the lake proved to have no such virtue. Sir John stocked the lake with fish but they all died; the jackdaws are its only denizens."

"You know a good deal about your late master's history," Matthew remarked, turning from his inspection of the lake to his young companion.

"These things happened almost before my time. My father told me of them, for he too was a servant in the castle and knew Sir John, his brother that died in the Irish wars, and the father before them."

"I have heard Sir John drowned in this very lake," Matthew said. "On the day of his homecoming."

"You've heard true, then," said Edward. The hostler pointed to a spot on the lakeshore. "We found him down there—Cuth and I—where the shore curves inward."

Matthew could see the place, a stretch of rock and pebbles, and started to walk in its direction. He climbed down the bank. The odor of the water, reminding him of something he had once smelled in an alchemist's den in the final stages of distillation, seemed not so strong as before. The shore itself was littered with dead branches.

"Is the water deep then?" Matthew asked Edward, who had followed him down from the bank.

"Some of it is, some isn't," Edward answered, picking up a smooth stone and flinging it out across the water. "There were old lead mines and potholes in the valley before the lake was made. The water covered them. But most of it is shallow, not more than four or five feet, I should judge."

"Sir John couldn't swim?"

"Oh, he could," said Edward. "He could wade as familiarly through rivers as a water spaniel, or so the Irish manservant tells the tale. But he lost his leg, you see, in Ireland. He came home with a wooden one and was not yet recovered fully from the surgeon's knife."

"He was in a weakened condition, then?" Matthew asked, turning to look at the hostler, whose expression suggested he was genuinely pained by these recollections.

"He had ridden a long day the day of his death," Edward said.

"That's strange that he should choose to go out on the water on such a day, in such a condition. Was the weather fair?"

"The weather was miserable," said Edward. "An unseasonable tempest."

"The stranger, then," Matthew said. "Why should a soldier, convalescing from surgery and weary from a long, exhausting ride, choose to go boating on the lake? And in a tempest?"

Edward seemed to think about this. Shrugging, he said, "We don't know what time he set out. The weather wasn't so bad earlier. The tempest came of a sudden, as I remember. For his other reasons, I did not think it was my place to inquire."

Edward's tone suggested that the question was equally impertinent on Matthew's part. Matthew decided to change subjects. "I see no shallop or other craft now."

Edward looked up and down the shoreline and agreed. He said he didn't know where the shallop was. Its care had been the charge of Sir John's manservant. Edward said he himself was no sailor and water made him queasy.

Matthew decided he had seen enough of the lake. He was satisfied that even if he had been at liberty to search the scene of Sir John's drowning in private, he would have discovered nothing more than what was in plain view. It had been over a year since the drowning. There had likely never been evidence of foul play, and had there been, it would long earlier have been removed by weather or will of him who had done the deed. But there remained another question he wanted to put to the hostler, a question that had been bothering Matthew since the night they had discovered Aileen Mogaill's body and Edward had helped Matthew bury it.

"It was a dreadful thing that happened to the girl," Matthew said offhandedly, as though he had introduced the subject only to while away the time it took to climb back up the bank and walk through the woods to the paddock again.

"It was, in truth," Edward answered solemnly.

"Who did it, do you think? Was it the Challoner ghost, as Cuth affirms?"

Edward scoffed at the idea. "Cuth is a fool. His wife's another."

"Who, then?"

Edward stopped; he had been leading the way back. He said, "Live men wield swords more often than the spirits of dead folks do, I warrant. But I'd as lief believe some tramp or roving bedlamite made the keep his bed for the night and did murder for lust and madness's sake than in a ghost's revenge. I tell you it wouldn't be the first time the old castle has had uninvited guests. In summer the roads are full of vagabonds. I sometimes have found them sleeping in the stable or in the field. I've given them something to eat and sent them on their way—before Moll spots them. She's hard on peddlers, she is. Whacks them with her cudgel she does. A very hard woman."

"Aileen was killed by a passing stranger, you think?"

"Why, it's an explanation good as any other. What think you, Master Stock?"

"Why, I agree it's an explanation as good as any other," Matthew answered, because he could think of nothing else to say and because it suddenly occurred to him that the hostler's theory could be sound.

* * *

Matthew waited by the paddock fence while Edward got the horses. Soon Edward was returning, leading a bay gelding and sorrel mare. Matthew watched while the hostler saddled both. Meanwhile the young man talked casually of horses, about which he obviously knew a great deal. He did have something to say about the castle's tenants, too. "It's always bad when the master is an absentee landlord, as Sir John so often was." Edward said the tenants were an uncouth, unruly lot. He warned Matthew that the survey of the estate might not be a pleasant one.

Edward's words turned out to be true. The next several hours he took Matthew to a series of habitations that were little better than hovels, where the denizens spoke such a thickly accented local dialect as to be virtually incomprehensible, and where there was little welcome for the new steward. The tenants seemed indeed an ignorant and complaining brood; they regarded Matthew with suspicion and whispered among themselves. Matthew left them behind in relief that his position as steward was a temporary guise.

But then he remembered they had not yet visited the cottage of Edward's father. He reminded Edward of the fact.

"My father's cottage is no better than the others you've seen," Edward said.

Matthew detected the hostler's reluctance, but was not content to let the visit pass. He might feel compelled to disguise his curiosity about Sir John's drowning, but he was certainly under no obligation to do likewise with one of the tenant's cottages. "We can spare the time, Edward. Lead on."

"Very well," Edward said, "if it is your pleasure."

Matthew assured him it was.

They traveled along the road for some way, passing several of the tenant cottages they had already visited, and Matthew realized that Edward had deliberately avoided the byroad which would have brought them to the cottage sooner.

"My father is not well," Edward said. "He's like a child sometimes, at others like his old self. Half blind too. Death will come as a blessing to him, but that's in God's hands."

"So there's just your father and you at the cottage?" Matthew asked.

"We two. When he fell ill and could no longer take care of himself, I moved from the stable to the cottage to become his companion and nurse. So I have done these twelve months."

"It's a fortunate father who has so dutiful a son," Matthew remarked approvingly.

Despite the hostler's disparaging comments about his father's cottage, the habitation that now came into view suggested a higher level of existence than those Matthew had previously visited that day. It was situated in a little clump of trees and had a roof of new thatch and a chimney from which a thin curl of smoke could be seen. The yard was girded by a sturdy picket fence in good repair, and inside the compound and before the front door an assortment of ducks, geese, and chickens was hunting and pecking, while at the side of the cottage there was a neatly tended kitchen garden and a shed.

Edward said he would ride ahead and announce their coming. "We rarely have visitors to the cottage, and your sudden appearance may startle my father."

Matthew was about to protest that he hardly thought himself a presence that should alarm an aging invalid, when Edward put his words into action and went galloping toward the cottage, leaving Matthew to follow at leisure.

At Edward's advance, a large dog of indeterminate breed crept from beneath bushes growing near the cottage door and commenced a clamorous greeting, straining against the rope to which he was tethered. Edward dismounted, tied his horse to the fence, and bounded into the cottage. By the time Matthew had reached the fence, Edward reappeared in the doorway, smiling and beckoning Matthew to come in.

Although several inches below mean height, Matthew had to duck his head to clear the lintel before stepping down on a hard earthen floor. The interior of the cottage was a single room at the far end of which was a hearth of ragged stone with a good fire going. Beside it was a battered cupboard, heavy with pots and crocks and other implements of rural housekeeping. There was a square oak table that might seat four with luck, a bench, several stools, two pallets, one larger than the other, and a large chest. Although it was a humble dwelling and the furnishings no better than to be expected, everything was neat and orderly. Certainly, there was not the squalor Matthew associated with the houses of old invalids and frisky young bachelors. Flowers from the kitchen garden had been gathered and placed in a vase on the square table, a touch that reminded Matthew of something his wife might have done.

But of greatest interest to Matthew was not the furnishings of the cottage but its human occupant. On a stool near the hearth, his palms outstretched toward the fire as though he were trying to keep the heat it generated at a distance, sat an old man of fifty-five or sixty with thinning gray hair and scraggly beard, and an expression—Matthew noticed as the aged face turned in his direction—suggesting not so much deficiency of sight as indifference to what he looked upon. Edward's father, for Matthew supposed this to be he, was broad-shouldered and sinewy like the son and he wore the garments of a rustic, except on his feet were slippers rather than boots or shoes. His complexion was darker than Edward's and his nose had once been broken, for it veered toward the left part of the face, where there was a noticeable tic. It was in the vacancy of his stare that Matthew recognized the true nature of the old man's decrepitude. It was clear now why Edward felt obligated to look after his father: the elder Bastian was a man living in a body beyond the mind's strength to govern it, an unfortunate adjunct of age Matthew had observed in many of his fellow townsmen.

"Master Stock, this is my father, Hugh Bastian."

Matthew said something about being pleased to meet the old man, but Hugh Bastian turned his face back toward the fire.

"My father speaks little now," Edward said apologetically. "Please don't think him disrespectful or rude."

Matthew assured Edward that he had taken no offense at

his father's mute response. He complimented the hostler on the cottage's condition. Edward made a motion to leave.

But Matthew was not finished with his inspection. He walked a little farther into the room, taking as much in as he could, sensing that Edward was trying to hurry him out, and not sure why.

He saw that the fire that warmed the old man had been banked high. The faggots had only begun to burn. Who had laid the fire? The decrepit old man? The strong hostler, who only a few moments earlier had raced for the cottage and leapt off his horse to run indoors so that his father would not be alarmed by a stranger's appearance? One of them would not have had the strength, the other lacked the time. Here was a mystery.

Matthew said good-bye to the elder Bastian and was following Edward out the door when he noticed a cerecloth hanging on a wall. He thought perhaps a recess was behind it and would have gone boldly over to see for himself had he not thought the action would offend the hostler. He decided to leave his curiosity unsatisfied, and continued on into the yard.

His emerging from the cottage sparked another burst of canine fury. Matthew jumped backward in alarm, crying out to Edward for help. Edward ordered the dog to be silent. "I'm sorry," he said. "Since you're an honest man, the beast will have his fun."

The dog kept barking despite Edward's reprimands. The two men walked hurriedly across the yard. Matthew felt better when he was on the other side of the fence. He turned back and looked at the dog and the cottage. It was then that, for all the dog's uproar, Matthew heard the cry of an infant. The small plaintive note was almost lost in the noise of the animal, but Matthew was sure that it was a human cry he had heard and that it had come from inside the cottage.

When the two men were mounted again, Matthew said, "Strange, but while your dog railed, I thought I heard a child within."

Matthew noticed that at the remark Edward's face tightened. But then the hostler grinned broadly and said, "A child? Why, there's no child here, sir, unless you count the youngest of the servants, who may be no more than twelve or thirteen."

"None?"

"Well, in the tenants' cottages. The Stokes have children, as you saw, and the Robinsons."

Matthew remembered the grim and grimy little faces of the children of the two families. He supposed the women of the cottages had infants as well, somewhere within the dismal dwellings he had not inclined nor been invited to enter. But the sound Matthew had heard had issued from the Bastian cottage.

Edward led the way to the road again without there being any other mention of the child. The hostler seemed nervous, however, and this strengthened Matthew's conviction that Edward was hiding something—or someone. But who—the person who had laid the fire? The person whose child had cried?

As he rode he wondered if he should not have looked behind the cloth. What would he have found there? He reasoned that an infant concealed in the cottage strongly implied the existence of a mother, and perhaps her presence. Was Edward wived then? Encumbered with child? And what if he was? Even in Derbyshire there was no law against marriage and parenthood. And even if the child was a bastard, still, where was the purpose? Edward was no gentleman or scholar with a reputation to protect; only a hostler whose personal morals were expected to be no higher than his calling.

Matthew resolved not to dispute with Edward over the matter. What would a confrontation produce? Vigorous denials? Open hostility? And yet Matthew knew what he had heard, and he suspected Edward had heard the cry as well.

When they came up to the junction of the roads, Edward broke his silence and said, "I'll take you to Stafford's now. It's about five miles."

Matthew nodded his approval, and Edward turned his horse

off the road and started out across a stretch of damp ground until they came to a horse trail. This they followed for about half an hour until they reached a road. They traveled it, not talking further.

It was past noon now. Matthew was hungry, but since there was no prospect of satisfying his hunger, he suppressed the rumble in his stomach. Presently he noticed a great mound of earth that in the smoothness of contour did not seem the work of nature. The mound was off of the road some distance. He asked Edward about it.

"That's a barrow, as we call them hereabouts," Edward explained, pausing to view the sight. "The ancients buried their dead in them."

"The ancients?"

"The old ones. Those who lived here at first. Before the Saxons, before the Romans, even. We're riding upon an old Roman road, you know. If you look sharp, you can still see the stones. But the Roman and the Saxon were newcomers to this ground. The barrow-builders were first, and that is one of their tombs."

Interested, Matthew asked if there were many barrows in the neighborhood.

"A good many," replied Edward, warming to his office as guide. "Some have been dug up. Bones, weapons, spears, arrowheads—sometimes rings and bracelets have been found. And pots of lead, which the Romans used to mine here. They say a cobbler of Buxton discovered in one barrow an immense treasure of gold, but died before he could recover it. When his wife went to where the treasure was supposed to be, she found naught but a pot of lead. They who are familiar with such matters say the treasure was cursed—as was he who disturbs the ancient bones, wherefore the man died."

"It's a wicked thing to disturb the dead, even if they are long gone to dust," Matthew reflected, although he was unsure as to how much credence to place in stories of curses and buried treasures.

Beyond the barrow were hills and there sheep could be seen as well as the lone figure of a sheepherder.

"Those are Stafford's sheep," Edward said, moving forward again. He talked over his shoulder as he rode. "The old barons of Thorncombe kept large herds, but Sir John had no interest in sheep. He called them filthy, stinking creatures God made in error, too dull-witted to live. He let the herd decline and sold off the rest. First and last he was a soldier. He cared for little more."

Matthew listened with interest. He looked up at the hills and thought it was a sad thing that the herd had been sold. He asked Edward to tell him more about Stafford.

Edward pointed ahead of them. "Yonder you can see a little ravine and wooden bridge. When we cross, we'll be on Stafford's land."

Matthew saw the ravine and the bridge—and at a greater distance he now could see a sprawling manor house.

"There's Stafford Hall," Edward continued. "The ravine's the cause of the trouble—or the stream that made it. When Sir John damned the stream to make the lake, Stafford was left only a trickle. It's been a bone of contention between the families for years."

"Could the law not settle the dispute?" asked Matthew as the two men passed over the bridge and he looked down at the little trickle of water at the bottom of the ravine.

"The law could if it *would*," said Edward. "But the lawyers have been wrangling forever, with little hope of a resolution satisfying to either party."

"Then Sir John did have enemies—the Staffords—contrary to common report," Matthew said.

"Report?" exclaimed Edward, vehemently. "*Report* is a most vile slanderer of good men and resolute defender of hypocrites. So say I of *report*. In fact, Sir John was not well liked in the neighborhood. The gentry found him cold and contemptuous of them because his blood was old Saxon blood and theirs wasn't. The common rout feared him with a superstitious dread. He was a hard-visaged man, you know. Some without tact would have called him ugly as sin."

Matthew was about to ask more about this fear of the baronet when his attention was drawn to two horsemen approaching them at a fast gallop. "That's Stafford and his man now," Edward said, raising his hand in salute.

Stafford and his servant reined their horses in and came forward slowly. Stafford was a stout man of about thirty-five with a square face and shaggy brows and beard. His servant was a rawboned fellow in a buff jerkin and big boots. He had close-set eyes, a sharp nose, and long jaw.

"Wide of your master's property, are you not?" Stafford said after introductions had been made. "My line commences at the ravine."

"Well I know, sir," said Edward. "Our new steward wanted to pay his respects."

"Oh, did he?" asked Stafford, regarding Matthew with a contemptuous expression. "I thought this person in your company was certainly a lawyer by his suit, come to serve some document or writ."

"I am the steward at Thorncombe," Matthew reiterated.

"A new steward? Well then, Cuth Fludd gone to heaven?"

"Cuth lives and in reasonably good health for his years," Edward said.

"I am appointed by the new mistress," Matthew inserted.

"Oh yes, Mistress Frances," Stafford said, "a winsome child, if I remember her right. I do get to London now and again, although my present appearance may mark me a country squire and no more. How came you to have been appointed at such a distance? Could not your mistress have found some competent fellow in the neighborhood, or is that beneath the proud Challoners?"

"Undoubtedly there were those in Derbyshire who were qualified—more qualified than I—but it was hardly my place to question my mistress's choice, only to serve as directed. My wife accompanied me and is the new housekeeper."

Stafford nodded and scratched his beard. He looked at his servant and then back at Matthew. "You're a married man, are you? You have the look."

"By which remark, I presume, sir, that you are not married," Matthew said, impatient with the man's sarcasm.

"Oh, but there is a Mistress Stafford. Isn't there, Wylkin?"

Stafford hoisted himself in his saddle and addressed this question to his servant, whose hard eyes remained fixed on Matthew.

"There is a Mistress Stafford, my master's wife," Wylkin said flatly.

Matthew gathered from this exchange that there was something about Mistress Stafford that created tension between master and servant, but at the moment he was more concerned to hold his own with Stafford than speculate about the man's domestic infelicities, if that was what they were.

"I don't speak by way of criticism," Stafford said, "but commiseration. Undoubtedly, your companion will satisfy your curiosity on your way back to the castle, servants being what they are. Isn't that right, Bastian? You will fill this good man's ears with gossip, won't you—as soon as my back is turned?"

Matthew looked at Edward to see how he was taking this obvious provocation and was gratified to see the hostler showed no signs of wilting before the quarrelsome gentleman, despite the great gulf in their stations in life.

"You accuse me unjustly, Master Stafford," Edward replied calmly. "The affairs of Stafford Hall are none of my business, and therefore I make them no part of my conversation—with fellow servants or with my masters."

"Why, you're a true pillar of virtue, aren't you, Bastian?" Stafford said with heavy irony. "Wylkin, give Edward Bastian a coin or two from your purse to reward him for his virtue. It's the least we can do to advance the cause of discretion in the world."

Smirking, Wylkin reached into his belt and found his purse. He brought forth a penny and flung it into the dirt. Edward didn't look at the coin.

"Pick it up, Bastian, like a good fellow. It's your reward. Why wait for heaven?"

Wylkin said, "Go ahead, Edward. Don't be shy. We well know your need—not to mention your father's."

It was a vicious gibe, and Matthew noticed the hostler's face go livid with suppressed rage. Stafford saw it too, and the response his servant's words had provoked prodded him to even greater injury.

"I said," Stafford repeated slowly and emphatically, "*pick up the penny like a good faithful dog.*"

It was a calculated insult, designed to humiliate Edward before Matthew's eyes. Matthew felt embarrassed for the hostler and angry at Stafford for the insult, which was an insult to him as well.

In all this time Edward refused to budge, nor did he even look at the ground. He stared at Stafford with open hostility. The silence lengthened and grew pregnant with impending violence. Of the four men, only Wylkin was armed. He wore a knife of a good eight inches at his belt. But if menacing looks could kill, the field would have been a slaughterhouse. Realizing the danger of the moment, Matthew dismounted and picked up the penny himself.

"If my friend has no need of your alms, perhaps there's poor in the parish who will bless you for your charity," he said, looking up at Stafford. Then he remounted and said, "Come, Edward. We've kept Master Stafford and his man too long in the sun. We still have something to see of Thorncombe before the day's done."

Matthew's gesture apparently so surprised Stafford that the man could find no quick response, although it was evident from his glare that his hostility had shifted from the hostler to Matthew.

Matthew turned his horse and headed back the way they had come. He did not look behind to see if Edward followed. He prayed he would; Matthew wanted no violent confrontation. The exchange of words had been sharp enough.

Matthew was relieved when in a few moments he heard Edward hurrying to catch up. In the greater distance he heard Stafford's voice. "Don't cross me, Stock. No inhabitant of Thorncombe is friend to Thomas Stafford. Take care where and when you walk."

The threat echoed across the ravine and settled into Matthew's heart. He rode on as though he hadn't heard, nor was he willing to give Stafford the satisfaction.

Edward came up alongside. "Devils incarnate the both. Would to God I had been armed."

"Thanks to God you were not," Matthew said. "Wylkin looks the sort who would kill his own mother."

"He doubtless did. And Stafford's another."

They crossed the bridge and Matthew felt relieved to be on Challoner land again. They rode on in a strained silence for about two miles, passing the barrow and coming to the first of the tenants' cottages, where the tenants' children came out to watch them pass. Matthew waved. The children waved back. Edward seemed to have settled into a black mood. To ease it, Matthew asked him about Stafford's wife.

A smile spread slowly on the hostler's face at the question. He laughed bitterly and said, "Since I am damned and bribed for a gossip, I might as well earn my reputation. The truth is that Stafford and his wife are ever at each other's throats. And rumor has it that she's cuckolded him with Wylkin."

"Ha!" said Matthew. "Wylkin *has* the look. It's a rare villain that does not show it in his face. It's a wonder that Stafford doesn't kill Wylkin, or at least send him packing."

"Well," said Edward, "possibly the gossip is false. Or perhaps Stafford finds Wylkin too useful to discharge or murder."

"In either case, I do not like the man," Matthew declared. "Nor his master."

"Stafford is hardly worth a curse," said Edward with even greater bitterness, "though he be a gentleman born and bred and own a fine house and tell his servants where to go and when."

When she could no longer hear the voices, she stepped out from behind the cerecloth where she had concealed herself and her child during the new steward's visit. What a start Edward had given her with his madcap arrival, bursting into the cottage of such suddenness that she had nearly dropped her child, who had cried out in alarm. Edward had told her she must hide herself and the baby, too, and she had done as she was told. She had stood as mum as death behind the cloth, clutching the child to her breast protectively and praying that it would not betray them.

Eventually, inevitably since it had capacity for fear but not prudence, the child, alarmed by the dog's furor, had betrayed their presence, but by then Edward and the steward were gone.

Edward's father was still seated on his stool, watching the fire intently as though something of great pith and moment were being enacted in the conflagration of faggots and small branches. Then he swiveled toward her, his mouth agape and his eyes pale and lusterless as a dead man's.

The movement frightened her a little by its suddenness, yet she knew the old man's mind was gone now, sunk into a second infancy and awaiting ultimate dissolution in a half-life between dream and sleep. She felt an aching pity for him, and for herself, and for her child. Indeed, she pitied the whole human race at that moment, fated as it was to follow such a torturous course.

The child began to cry, declaring its need for nourishment, and she quickly unfastened her bodice and pressed her nipple into the child's mouth, feeling, as always when she gazed upon the little face, an intolerable burden of grief, in which despair, love, and resentment at fate were perniciously mixed. "It's all right now," she said, in her heart not sure that it was. "The strange man's gone."

As though in response to her words, a heavy sigh from the old man—like an amen from fellow worshipers—seemed to agree with her somber reflections. Then he grinned a toothless grin, as though her words had somehow been meant for him as well as for the suckling, and she felt afraid again—for herself and for her child—without quite knowing why.

11

STAFFORD and Wylkin had ridden a half mile toward Stafford Hall when the stout gentleman pulled up on his horse and signaled to his servant he should do likewise. Both men were overtaken by a cloud of gagging dust.

Stafford said, "This Matthew Stock may be only the steward, but he's no fool. His plain, simple mug's a guise for mischief, mark me." Stafford stroked his beard in the way of those whose thoughts are running well ahead of their words. He eyed his servant narrowly, waiting for a response.

"A guise, sir?" asked Wylkin, not slow to follow but curious to hear Stafford's opinion of the steward.

The horses had been made nervous by the sound of human voices raised in anger; they kept stomping and shifting as the men talked.

Stafford said, "It's as certain as death that Stock's appointment means the young heiress intends to stick her long nose into matters at the castle."

"As well she might," said Wylkin. "Now that she's mistress."

Stafford glanced sideways toward the ravine and bridge,

then looked back at Wylkin. "I don't mean into those matters that should naturally concern her, but rather those that concern me."

"Do you think she's suspicious about her uncle's death?"

"Why shouldn't she be—if she knows the facts and her noggin is more than a prop for her golden locks," said Stafford. "Of course there's a chance she doesn't care one way or the other. A rich uncle dead is better than a poor one living. If you're his heir, which she is. For all I know, she may have hired someone to drown him. Stranger things have happened, although few are spoken of in church. How much love could she have for a bachelor uncle she knew largely by his letters, which couldn't have been very frequent? What worries me is that she may want more than the castle and the land."

"You mean—"

Stafford nodded. "She might know, or at least suspect, and have sent Stock and his wife as spies to discover that her uncle fetched more treasure home from Ireland than an occasional wench for his lust's sake."

"What shall be done then?" Wylkin asked eagerly, for the manservant had a colorful past as a soldier and highwayman and was ever ready for employment.

"A very good question, Jack—and quickly answered. Hie you over to the castle and have words with that confederate of yours. Make her a party to our plans only in so far as to make her companion of your watch of the Stocks. If the new steward appears to be a spy as I suspect, we'll rid ourselves of him straightway."

"So he won't be any trouble to us," said Wylkin, drawing his finger across his throat to suggest the method of Matthew Stock's disposal.

"Oh, you *are* passing eager, Jack." Stafford grinned with approval. He reached over and placed a hand on the pommel of Wylkin's knife. "If it comes to that, you'll have your orders. An obvious murder would only confirm what doubt already exists about Sir John's drowning. Be subtle, therefore. I know you have it in your heart to be so. Scare him off, if you can. We'll kill him if we must."

"And what of the Irishman?"

"Conroy's a stone in my shoe. Continue to watch him. It is unthinkable that he wasn't privy to his master's secret. Why else would he remain at Thorncombe, Sir John dead? Quickly, now, about your work."

Stafford watched as Wylkin galloped off, feeling a surge of satisfaction. Wylkin pleased him at the moment, for the man was totally unscrupulous and fearless—qualities in which Stafford, for all his bravado, knew he was deficient. Not that he pursued his present intrigue with any reluctance. His long quarrel with the Challoners extended to his father's time and was like a raw and open cancer. Any treachery seemed justified. And if the law's delay continued to deprive him of a free-flowing stream, he could at least enjoy the Irish booty he believed on good report and reasonable surmise was concealed somewhere at Thorncombe.

When he had heard the news of his old enemy's death, Stafford had been much gratified. He had also been hopeful that it might be his opportunity to secure the estate for himself. For why should the young slip of a girl want to worry herself about the gloomy pile of the old castle and the troubles that went with tenants when she could continue to enjoy the social delights of the metropolis? He had envisioned himself as master of Thorncombe—at leisure to dig for treasure in perfect privacy.

But the assignment of the new steward suggested that his vision was not to be fulfilled.

With respect to his treasure-digging, his wife had suggested he turn informer and receive the thanks and reward of the Queen. The trouble with his wife's proposal—in addition to its having no stomach in it—was that it would have been too easy for the living Sir John to deny his wrongdoing. And not much more difficult for Frances Challoner to deny it on her deceased uncle's behalf. Was Sir John not an honorable soldier of well-allowed reputation? Without satisfactory proof—and what proof was satisfactory other than the hoard itself?—his accusation would appear the grossest slander and fall upon his own head. And thus his present intent to work by stealth and subversion until such an hour as the gold was found and in hand. But this purpose was made more difficult of fulfillment because of Stock—and also because of Conroy. For if Sir John had been murdered, as Stafford devoutly suspected, he believed the motive was the treasure. Which meant, to Stafford's way of thinking, that someone else in the neighborhood was capable of deviousness and violence, knew of the Challoner hoard, and was as bound and determined as he to have it.

But as much as Stafford worried about competition in his search, he found solace in the hope that he would be the first to the gold and receive, at long last, just compensation for the numerous injuries he and his family had suffered from the arrogance and pride of the Challoner.

Sometimes at night he would wake in a cold, quicksilver sweat and fear that it was all a dream, this Irish hoard of Thorncombe. His wife, at such times, more sanguine than he, assured him that his fears were the work of too much meat the night before, or of the damned spirit of melancholy that afflicts the soul between midnight and dawn, or, of a sickly irresolution and close cousin to cowardice.

To bolster his confidence and prick him on, husband and wife would pass the time speculating about the treasure—both as to quality and to quantity. Stafford would imagine a half-dozen chests or more, brimming with silver plate and cup, thousands of gold sovereigns, and twenty thousand coins of inferior denomination. His wife imagined jewels—emeralds, rubies, diamonds as big as the Pope's nose, necklaces, crosses and other religious relics, each worth a prince's ransom, and God only knew what other fine stuff snatched from the barbarous hands of Irish Catholics and brought to the Protestant haven of Thorncombe to be ensconced there, dedicated to the private use of a soldier of good repute.

And in such mutual recitals, the Staffords nourished their hopes, and Thomas Stafford's mind to larceny became as razor sharp as his manservant's knife.

12

UNA'S ignorance of the Queen's English did not prevent her from expressing her unease about being left to guard the locked door. As a concession, Joan promised to make haste in securing a key. She would find Moll, she thought. Surely the cranky old woman had kept an extra set.

She rushed down the stairs at great risk to life and limb, tore through the kitchen, and covered the greensward like a dog chasing a rat, despite her tight bodice and flapping farthingale and other female garb made to shackle a fleet foot.

As she approached the lodge, she heard from within the clamor of domestic discord. She knocked; the wrangling ceased, and Moll's face appeared.

"Mistress Stock? It's you, is it? Rumor had you sick unto death. You seem well enough now, though sweating like a horse."

Joan ignored the rudeness of this salutation. It was clear that her visit had interrupted a debate of some magnitude and that her appearance on the scene was offensive in being an interruption and in being a call where she was not wanted. Moll's face was a veritable map of conflicting passions and discontents. Although it was late in the morning, she was still dressed in an ungirdled nightgown and her feet were bare. Capless, her steel-gray hair was a fright. Behind the old woman, her husband's mumbling could be heard. The last word for once, Joan supposed, in whatever issue had ignited such hot debate.

Joan explained her need coolly. She was still out of breath from her race, but exerted herself to maintain control.

"Why, that room hasn't been used in years. It has no lock," Moll said.

"It *has* a lock. There's someone inside!"

"Someone inside? Well, demand that he come forth—that's the way to do it. Don't trouble me about keys. I gave you all I had."

"If he had come forth at my beckoning, I would not have risked my life to come to you for a key," Joan responded crossly. "I can't believe there are no keys to these rooms."

"Believe what you like, dispute the rest," Moll said, thrusting her face forward aggressively. "I gave what keys I had, and that's *that*. Besides, why would you want admittance to the room anyway? It hasn't been used for years. If there's anything there, it's old foul trash from before the Flood."

"*Why* I want to enter is no concern of yours," Joan returned sharply. "It is sufficient that I have warrant to enter such rooms as I see fit."

"No one disputes your right," Moll shot back with equal vehemence. "Such a right I enjoyed for forty years. Yet I cannot give over what I never had. I have not set eyes on the insides of the White Keep since our late master's brother went off to Ireland and never came home again. If you want in, you must break down the door."

"And so I shall if I must," Joan said.

"Then for Jesus' sake do what you must," said Moll. "And let us be. The care of the castle is no longer my concern. Good day to you."

Moll slammed the door shut in Joan's face, leaving her quivering with rage. Joan said something found more often on the lips of London alewives than her own and stamped her foot in irritation. She had come to Thorncombe to discover a murderer; now she wasn't sure she wouldn't do murder herself before she departed. She had already selected her victim, and she prayed God would forgive the thought even as He understood the justness of her rage.

She turned and marched toward the stable to find Edward and an ax, determined that the door to the locked room should fall, if not by key, then by main force. She was halfway to her destination, feeling the resurgent fever in her cheeks, when she remembered that Edward would be with Matthew.

For a moment she saw the pair in her mind's eye. Horseback. Riding down a quiet road. Coming to a tenant's tidy cottage. Receiving a gracious welcome from humble folk.

She stopped to catch her breath. No, Edward would not be there when she needed him, nor would Matthew. A very fine day it was turning out to be, she thought with disgust. She would be lucky if she didn't fall ill again.

Then she remembered Una, who would be maintaining her solitary and frightening vigil outside the locked door, and began to feel both fear and guilt. Who knew what horror or dastardly knave was her prisoner? She gathered her skirts and rushed back to the house, climbed the stairs, and found Una. The Irishwoman showed no sign of distress. By Una's gesture and very broken English, Joan determined that no one had escaped the room during her absence, but that neither had Una heard any more noises. Joan tried knocking again and commanding, but these efforts were no more successful than before and she began to feel very foolish. Was it possible there was no one within at all? Or could it have been a rat she heard?

Concluding there was no more to be done—at least for now—she thanked Una for her company, and the two women went back to the kitchen. It was all nearly too much for Joan—the frustration of dealing with these folks of alien speech, the locked doors, the recalcitrant, impudent servants such as Moll Fludd. She decided to go out-of-doors again, but to walk, not run.

The sun was high in the sky. The air was mild and clear. From the woods she could hear the twitter of birds. Restless with confinement in the castle and still fuming over her injured dignity, Joan set her course for the woods, where she hoped to find nothing more offensive than a thornbush or anthill. She needed to collect herself, to regain the control lost in these broils with Moll and Conroy. The woods were deep and serene and she longed to escape the grim walls of Thorncombe.

The trees of the wood grew in such closeness as to make almost a wall of greenery except where paths had been made, and even these were narrow and enclosed with bramble and fern. She followed one path that took her toward the lake and in no time she stood upon its shore, contemplating the broad expanse and the little humpbacked island at its center.

She had smelled the fetid water almost before it came into view. She looked up at the sky. A cloud drew itself across the noontime sun. A flock of high-flying birds headed south. Beyond the lake were the hills she had seen from the window in the Black Keep. They were only hills now, nothing more.

She looked at the island. It was like an enormous turtle with only its shell above water. And on its back, a risky purchase, was a stone replica of one of Thorncombe's ancient towers. She wondered who had built the tower and why.

She scanned the shoreline before her. Sedge grew to the water's line and possibly went beyond it—except in one place, where a pebble-strewn stretch would have afforded a landing. Knowing it must be the place where Sir John had been found, she pulled up her skirts and made her way down the bank. A cloud of buzzing insects followed her, but she beat them away, determined not to retreat until she had seen all there was to see. The peace she had sought in the verdant wood could wait. For the moment she was driven by an intense curiosity to examine the place where murder had occurred, even though she thought it very unlikely she would find any trace of the murderer.

She stood in the midst of the little beach and looked again

over the water. The cloud had passed and the sun shone clearly as before. The lake now seemed neither sinister nor treacherous. She reviewed the facts of the baronet's death, imagining how this same scene must have looked in a heavy rain and where the shallop must have been. She came to no conclusions and was somewhat depressed by the seemingly complete absence of any sign whatsoever that anything of note had occurred on the spot.

It was not as though she expected the murderer to have returned to the scene, or that a monument should be raised to the event. But even the shallop was gone, and no footprints other than her own were evident where she trod. Never had she felt with such force the absolute indifference of the natural world to human tragedy.

Deciding there was nothing more to see, she started back the way she had come and had gone a little way when her shoe became stuck in the mud. She bent over to release it and stumbled forward awkwardly. She cried out and fell upon her knees in the midst of a clump of grass. As she was struggling to regain solid footing she noticed an object at a little distance that by its sharp right angle and color did not belong there. Curious, she forgot about her muddy shoe and skirts and moved with difficulty toward it. Then she bent over and brought it up from where it was half-submerged.

It was a brass-bound chest of middle size and very well made but filthy with mud. She dragged it from the sedge to firmer ground. Kneeling, she opened it and saw that the chest was empty except for a little brackish water at the bottom and a large black beetle swimming desperately therein. She tipped the chest onto its side, liberating the beetle, then contemplated her find in more careful detail.

She reasoned the chest was too artfully wrought and sound of construction to have been discarded wantonly. Nor did it seem to have been deliberately concealed where she had found it, half-buried in water and mud. This conclusion, she believed, was all the more reasonable for the chest's having been found empty. Which left the question: How did the chest come to be where it was? And how long had it lain there?

As to the second question, Joan found it impossible to say. The wood showed signs of deterioration and the brass was badly tarnished. Given its exposure to water, rain, and sun, it might have been half-submerged for a month, or perhaps a year. She thought it unlikely that it had been exposed to the elements for a longer duration. She was thus able to associate her discovery in *time* at least with the death of Sir John Challoner.

The question of how the chest came to be where it was required even more desperate conjecture. She speculated, however, that the chest might have been discarded in the lake and drifted ashore like an abandoned vessel. Empty of heavy contents, the chest would have been buoyant. Once it had undoubtedly contained something of value. But what?

She felt around the smooth sides of its interior, feeling undulations where the thinner sheets of rosewood had begun to warp. As she did so, she was suddenly seized by a melancholy of such profundity that further examination of the chest was impossible.

Her vision blurred, and she seemed to sink into a moist, hideous darkness. She felt there was water all around her, above and below; and all along her nether parts she felt the grip of ruthless hands pulling her deeper into the watery abyss. She would have screamed but she had no breath. She tried to struggle but she found herself paralyzed, her body a rebel to her brain. More agonizing to her than the thought of imminent suffocation was the horror she felt of the water itself. For somehow she knew all that element was alive with slimy, eyeless creatures with soft, gaping mouths—sucking and writhing.

She knew she was about to die, and yet she could not utter a prayer.

Then the vision passed as suddenly as it had come, and she found herself as before, on dry ground. She got up to her knees, her heart pounding. Looking out over the torpid water, she felt a seizure of dread. In her mouth was the foul taste of the lake water. Her head swam with nausea. Fearing she would lose consciousness again, she got herself into a sitting position, her legs folded beneath her. She covered her eyes with her hands and she kneaded the insides of her cheeks to make spittle. She spat over and over in an effort to get rid of the horrible taste. She was sweating terribly too; the front of her gown, filthy from her fall, clung to her. She took a handkerchief from her waist and wiped her face and neck.

Joan realized what had happened but not why. She knew the darkness that had enveloped her had been one of her glimmerings, triggered by her contact with the chest. She had had such experiences all of her life—strange, often prophetic seizures wherein not only the vision but the sensation of peril was opened to her. Sometimes her glimmerings would come upon her with such force she would remain in bed a half-day to recover. Not in her power to evoke, nor to deny, they came when *they* would. Ignorant of any scriptural warrant for such experiences, Joan still trusted they were not of the devil. Her husband, tolerant and optimistic in such matters, assured her they were from heaven, although he professed not to be so great a theologian that he could square them with the teaching of Christians. Matthew had learned to respect her glimmerings, to accept their reality—and their authority.

Now it was clear to Joan that she had just had a vision of death. Was it a premonition of a death to come, or a confirmation of murder done?

For the next hour or more, Joan sat motionless. She could not bring herself to look at the chest she had found, much less touch it again.

It was dusk before Joan's strength returned and she began to consider the urgency of returning to the castle. She would have no difficulty explaining the condition of her gown, if explanations were required, for the simple truth would serve—that she had gone abroad to take the air, stumbled, fallen, injured herself and sullied the gown. Of her discovery of the chest and the attendant vision she resolved to say nothing, except to Matthew.

She managed to stand. Her legs were numb from the awkward position in which she had been sitting at such length. She moved along the path carefully and entered the wood, picking up her stride now that the lake was behind her, her thoughts full of Matthew and what he might say of her experiences.

A sudden awareness that she was not alone amid the gloomy trees brought her to a halt. Ahead she saw a figure moving across her path. The familiar white cap and apron told her it was one of the castle's female servants.

Joan could not imagine what would bring a servant into the woods at such an hour and became at once suspicious. She decided to follow.

She stayed far enough behind to keep her own pursuit a secret. The maid moved swiftly, purposefully, along the path and Joan's curiosity grew stronger; she had forgotten about her vision now, caught up in a more soluble mystery.

Then ahead, she saw another figure come out from behind a tree and she quickly concealed herself.

She realized now it was a lovers' tryst she witnessed, for there was a man and a woman meeting secretly, a quick embrace, an exchange of words she could not hear. More curious than ever, Joan crept closer, and when she was within twenty feet and dared not venture nearer, she stopped and listened.

The man spoke English and so did the woman, although the woman's English was imprinted with a strong Irish accent. As yet, Joan could not see the woman's face, but she could see the man. He was tall, in his late thirties or older perhaps, with a sinewy body, hawklike face, and cruel, sensual mouth. Then the woman turned and Joan saw that it was Una.

It was not what a man and maid might do in solitude that caused this reaction in Joan, but Una's deception. Una had spoken English—and been understood! But all along she had made Joan think otherwise. Joan felt an anger within her, felt betrayed—betrayed as she had felt when, coming into the gallery earlier that day, she had found Conroy and Una conversing conspiratorily in their native language. Joan listened. Yes, it was English for a fact, for from time to time a familiar word or phrase would carry across the middle distance between them and her.

She watched, fascinated but puzzled by the deception she had uncovered. The man swept the cap from Una's head and the long, dark hair of the Irishwoman tumbled down her back. With spreading smile along the cruel mouth, he slipped her bodice from her upper body with a deftness of one removing a glove and began to caress her, moving his hands swiftly and lightly over her breasts. Then they both lay down and Joan could only hear the woman's laughter and then the man's, more whispers, and all was quiet for about a quarter of an hour.

Joan was deeply embarrassed and ashamed of her role as witness to these amorous proceedings. She did not feel comfortable as a spy, despite her royal license, and never so uncomfortable as now, hidden and gaping at another woman's pleasure like a dog-faced wench who never hopes to enjoy the same herself. She would have slunk off and left the lovers to their pleasures had she not been so outraged by Una's pretense—and as a consequence so convinced that what she was observing was not merely a backstairs alliance but a conspiracy that it was her duty to fathom.

Was it not reasonable to assume that this same conspiracy involved, in some sinister way, the deaths of Sir John and Aileen Mogaill?

Listening, Joan heard the voices come again, muted and intimate in the dusk. The two stood; Una dressed, the man bare-chested. Joan heard their farewells, saw them embrace again and kiss. Then Joan realized Una's departure would bring her close to where Joan was concealed and she buried herself even deeper in the bush that had been her hiding place.

She heard the steps come very near and a crackle of dried leaves underfoot and a twig broken in passage. Una seemed to stop for a moment before continuing. Joan held her breath and waited, fearful of discovery. After a few moments, to her relief, she heard Una singing at a greater distance.

It was an Irish song Una sung, low and plaintive and very beautiful in the gathering gloom. Joan waited until she could no longer hear the strains, then she looked up and saw that Una's lover had disappeared too.

13

JACK WYLKIN thought Una was a little long in the tooth for one of his inches. She must have been very near his own age by his reckoning, and he had been baptized a Christian soul thirty-six years ago that very month. He knew this for a fact because he had seen the register wherein the event was recorded, and the clerk had pointed out the name; thus Wylkin knew his own age and surmised Una's and found her wanting in that respect. Also, she was an unmarried female, whereas he much preferred the conquest of married women, so as to experience the gratification of cuckolding the husbands.

On the other hand, he reflected generously, Una's broad beam and bountiful bosoms pleased him, not being the sort of man averse to a little extra flesh about the bone. Her skin was satin-smooth and white, her eye wanton as he might wish. She was diffident, peevish, and her Irish brogue irritated him, but the truth was he enjoyed her body, her unrestrained passion, her moans of pleasure, and certain tricks of lovemaking that a Parisian courtesan might have envied. In sum, he might have been sneaking over to Thorncombe to enjoy her even if she had not provided him with information by which he aimed to make himself very rich.

In return for this information and subsequent reports of the goings-on at the castle, Wylkin had promised to marry Una. It had been an easy promise to make. The wedded state had no more meaning for him than a dog's bark or a clap of thunder. That she believed in his promises he approved; and he approved as well that they slipped so easily and readily from his lips. Wylkin was born without a conscience, as some men are born without arms and legs. Moreover, he was a confirmed disciple of Machiavelli, whose doctrine he knew by common report, Wylkin himself being unable to read or write.

Una did not know where Sir John's treasure was concealed, only that it was concealed, and that it was Catholic wealth appropriated in the Queen's name, but neither delivered to its royal owner nor reported to her.

"Is it in the house, do you think?" Wylkin had asked Una for the hundredth time.

But as often as he asked, she shook her head doubtfully. Had she not looked, at every opportunity, in those rooms of Thorncombe to which she had access? Had she not even pried behind the wainscoting in the master's chamber? Had she not made a friend of Conroy—to make sure he knew no more than she? She had told him nothing of treasure; he had mentioned nothing to her. But she believed he knew, and had told Wylkin what she suspected.

"It's buried, then?" he prompted her.

"Perhaps, buried."

"A barrowful of rich treasure." The thought pleasing him, he squeezed her affectionately and promised her a rich jewel when the treasure was his.

"*Then* you will marry me," she said.

"Then I will marry you," he replied.

More than once he thought of forcing an answer out of her, for he was skillful in that art, but he liked her too much for that. And he was pretty convinced that her ignorance of the booty's whereabouts was unfeigned.

What Una *did* know and had conveyed to Wylkin consisted of gossip, conjecture, and just enough personal observation to make the story credible to one whose greed disposed him to believe. Ironically, her story had slipped out by a chance remark of his. During one of their early meetings he had commented idly that it was a poor house that must subsist on a soldier's pay, referring to what he supposed was Sir John's modest income as a commander. Whereupon Una had said, "But surely, Sir John is a very rich gentleman indeed."

She thought, in her simplicity, that everyone knew. How Sir John Challoner had burned churches and houses of the Catholic gentry, sparing only those willing to ransom their lives and property with hard cash, jewelry, or plate. How he had accumulated a small fortune by these methods and brought it home to Thorncombe, where it supposedly had been stuffed in some secret place. In Ireland, Una had been a servant in a house spared only by a bribe of several hundred pounds and thus had firsthand knowledge.

But everyone had not known, and as Wylkin had explored her story he realized she knew what Sir John Challoner had been at great pains to keep concealed. And for good reason. The Queen had little patience with officers who misused their authority for private gain.

It had been fifteen years since Sir John had brought Una from Ireland to serve in his house. Her people in Ireland all dead, she had been alone and desperate, and although she had been warned by a priest to beware the charity of the English, and accused by the same priest of betraying her own people and, yes, the Holy Faith as well, she'd gone with Sir John. She felt no loyalty to her native ground, nor to the Church. She believed a religion that would let her suffer could hardly demand her allegiance.

And so she'd come to Thorncombe, had progressed in time from scullion to cook, and had lasted out a dozen of her countrywomen of less adaptability also brought to the castle by Sir John. She wanted now the dignity of marriage, having indulged in any number of random couplings since the age of twelve. And, of course, she wanted a share of the treasure.

All of this was Una's story, as Wylkin understood it.

Dutifully, he had passed the same along to his employer, for although he would have liked to discover the treasure himself and keep it all, he realized that a treasure of that magnitude would have to be judiciously spent. For nothing was more likely to get a poor man hanged than a sudden and unaccountable display of wealth. And thus his absolute need for Stafford. Stafford already had wealth and power, and Wylkin could not imagine advancement, no matter how bountifully financed, save on the skirts of some great man.

Wylkin was content therefore to be a hireling. To work for a generous percentage of the gross, even though he knew that without the intelligence he had provided Stafford, the gentleman would have remained as ignorant as a babe of his neighbor's booty, which, if it was all Una claimed, would keep Wylkin in good wine and fine linen forever.

Now Wylkin's hard, calculating grin remained frozen as he watched the Irishwoman disappear among the trees. He put on his shirt and his jerkin and his hat and started walking to the place where he had left his horse. He was still grinning, despite the dark, for he had an overpowering feeling of being very close to what he sought.

Una made haste to return to the castle but was not so preoccupied with the fresh memory of her lover's embrace that she did not catch the movement at the corner of her eye, and, pausing briefly, saw the patch of cloth she recognized as the new housekeeper's. Reasoning that where the cloth was the gown was, and where the gown, the wearer thereof, she knew she was being spied upon. Her heart raced; she expected the Stock woman to rise from her place of concealment and denounce both her and Wylkin. For surely Joan Stock had *seen*. And *heard*?

That was another question. One with even more dangerous implications. To be caught playing the harlot under the castle walls was one thing; to be discovered as a betrayer of the house with the servant of Thorncombe's greatest enemy was quite another. But when Una heard no shrill denunciation of either sin, saw no motion, she quickly concluded that for some reason the new housekeeper did not wish *herself* to be seen.

Puzzled, Una resumed her way, trying to act as though she were as unaware of having been observed. She began to sing to give color to her deception, and she kept singing until she was clear of the woods and halfway to the kitchen porch.

She had agreed to meet Wylkin again. She resolved to ask him then what he supposed the Englishwoman's spying meant.

14

It was fully dark by the time Joan returned to the castle. With fear for her safety mitigated only by her eagerness to tell Matthew of her discoveries, she dashed across the cobbled courtyard and burst into the kitchen, where she found Matthew and Edward at the table and Una nowhere to be seen. Matthew thanked God that she had returned and was in the middle of questioning her as to where she had been and why, when Joan, eager not to be too direct before Edward, asked the hostler if he had a sturdy ax he might put to good use if she bade him.

"A door to be breached?" Edward asked good-humoredly when Joan had made her needs more explicit. "Does not Moll have the key?"

Joan explained that it was Moll herself who had suggested this method of entry.

Edward scratched his head and said he would do anything within his power to please and, as soon as his back was turned, Joan by sign and whisper made Matthew understand that she had much more to tell if he would be patient until they were alone, for in the meantime Una had returned and was busying herself as though nothing had happened that concerned her.

Then, when Edward returned with his ax, the three set out for the White Keep.

"There's a thing—someone—behind the door, but no mouse stirring nor another cat," she explained as they climbed the stairs.

When they reached the chamber, they found the door ajar. All stood there looking at it, wondering what that meant. Matthew stepped forward and nudged the door with his knee. He took Edward's lantern and held it forward to illuminate the interior.

Confused and mortified, Joan said behind him, "Oh, for heaven's sake."

"There's no one here now," Matthew said. A few furnishings—a small bed with canopy, very dusty even in the candlelight. A delight of spiders. A chest, which proved empty upon inspection, several battered chairs with curved backs, cold stone floors. Walls bare of adornment.

"There *was* someone here," Joan insisted. "I heard a stirring within. So did Una."

The thought of the Irishwoman brought back the recent discovery of her treachery and she twinged at the image, felt a flush of embarrassment. How the woman had made a fool of them both! She was eager to tell Matthew but could say nothing with Edward standing there, looking very useless and foolish himself, holding the great ax.

"And you're *sure* the room was locked before?" Matthew asked, turning to her.

"Upon the Holy Scriptures, I swear it," she said.

"I believe you without the oath," Matthew said reassuringly. "Yet there's no sign of occupancy—not in twenty years."

Nor would there be, Joan thought in dismay. At least *Matthew* believed her. That was something.

In their new quarters, deemed as suitable by Matthew as by Joan, she shut the door firmly behind her and said, "I have much to say, husband, but could not speak before."

"I have much to tell you, too, but forebore speaking for the same reason."

Joan quickly recounted her tour of the castle, her confrontation with Conroy, and her suspicion that he was up to no good. Not content to give over her opinion that *someone* had been concealed in the White Keep earlier that day, she ventured to say that it was Conroy. "A very sneaky sort," she said.

"But why should he have been lurking within?" Matthew asked.

"God knows," she said. "Pranks, perhaps. That would hardly be above him. He's full of resentment because I ordered him from the house to the stables. Perhaps he wanted to give two silly women a fright, although he seems to be friends with Una and she was as unnerved as I, if not more so."

"He may be trying to scare us off," Matthew suggested. "Making capital of the old stories about the Black Keep. Perhaps he's heard about Aileen Mogaill—perhaps he killed her himself. Perhaps she found him prowling and he took her head for the cause."

"Oh, a goodly cause for homicide," Joan said.

But Joan left behind the Irishman's behavior to proceed to greater news, not in the order in which the event occurred but in order of its importance in her mind. She told him what she had seen in the woods.

Matthew had no trouble identifying Una's hawk-faced lover as Stafford's manservant, Wylkin. "There can be no two faces so alike." But when he asked her what was said she could give him no satisfaction beyond the assurance it was English spoken rather than some other tongue. Of that she was sure.

"So Una understands English after all," Matthew said, shaking his head in wonderment. "That's a new fact to be reckoned with."

"She made fools of us," Joan said bitterly. "Moll, too, for surely the horrid woman knew all along. It was she who told us Una could not speak."

"What must we have uttered in her presence, then!" Matthew said, shaking his head, pinching his chin with thumb and forefinger.

But she had already considered that. She was positive they had not spoken of their secret mission except in privacy, as now. Perhaps the cook's deception had failed of its intent then. "At least we've been warned. Henceforth forearmed."

"Against Una and Moll," said Matthew. "But did Wylkin see you in the woods? There's the danger."

"I was very careful," Joan said, hurt a little at the suggestion she should be so maladroit a spy. "A naked savage stealing on his prey could not have been more circumspect. I crouched down low in the ferns and thorns. On my haunches. Wylkin saw nothing, and Una passed by unawares and singing upon her return to the house. I waited then until I was sure both were gone completely."

"Thank God," Matthew said. "Had Wylkin seen you crouched there, who knows what he would have done. Edward speaks very ill of him."

Then she told him about her visit to the lake. She had saved this for last, for she regarded both her glimmering and the chest that had provoked it the first of their clues to Sir John's drowning.

Matthew listened to her story without interrupting. When she had finished he put a sympathetic hand on her hand and said, "A terrible vision, indeed!"

Then he wanted to know all about the chest—its contents, size, and color; its quality and all the details of its construction that Joan had only half noticed. "What," she exclaimed in exasperation. "Am I a carpenter that I should observe these things? It was a chest, a plain wooden chest, such as might store clothing."

"Well, it might be a clue," Matthew conceded.

But she protested his weaseling *might be*. "Of course it's a clue. Anyone can see that! In the first place, it was no chest for casual discarding. Who but a fool would throw away a chest so fine? In the second, it was not hidden where I found it but half-submerged—an incompetent concealment if there ever was one. I'll wager it floated ashore and foundered like a vessel at low tide. Only it was deep in the sedge, very deep. Seeing it was a stroke of luck. But oh, Matthew, such a midnight melancholy seized me when I touched the thing—and a vision and waking dream of black water—like murky jelly all about me and loathsome creatures gaping and sucking."

She shuddered at the recollection, and seeing how distressed she was, Matthew put his arm around her shoulders and drew her forehead against his cheek. Her skin was cool; he could feel her trembling.

He asked her what she thought her vision meant and she shook her head, puzzled. She was almost afraid to speculate. But she said she was sure the chest meant *something*, was connected to the baronet's death, and perhaps with Aileen Mogaill's, too.

Her certainty seemed to settle the matter, and Matthew admitted the empty chest into his inventory of clues, as small an inventory as it was. He had too much respect for his wife's intuitions and visions to contest her interpretation. Partly to distract her from her gloomy memories, he told her about his visit to the wretched tenant farms, about his meeting with Stafford and Wylkin, repeating all that was on either side as best he could recall it. He told her about the child's cry he had heard while at the Bastian cottage. And about the fire that had been laid shortly before his arrival, but not by the old man, who, Matthew was convinced, would have been incapable of it.

Joan agreed it was very suspicious. "A child in the cottage, whose existence Edward denies. Could it have been a mewing cat you heard? Or a squealing pig?"

"The Bastians keep no pigs, and I saw no cat," he said, at the same time thinking that one often saw no cat, yet there might have been one. Yet he insisted he knew what he had heard: the wail of a human child—a singular, isolated note he could have discerned in the mighty cacophony of a tempest. He said again, "It was neither pig nor cat, but human child. Edward denied hearing it, but the lie was writ large upon his face."

"But whose child?" Joan wondered.

"His own, some other. But Edward *knows*."

She sighed heavily and felt regret, for she liked Edward. He seemed an honest, decent young man of stalwart parts. He had been their only ally in the castle. Now he, too, had come under suspicion.

Exhausted from her adventures, she gently released herself from his embrace and began to prepare for bed while the multiplying mysteries vexed her soul. "So," she said a little later, "our store of facts are these: that Conroy is lurking about the castle locking doors behind him, but we don't know why; that Edward has a child he keeps mum about, but we don't know whose; that an empty chest has something to do with Sir John's death, but we don't know what; and that a poor wretched girl was cruelly slaughtered under this roof and we can make no more sense of it than to say it happened, and that's that."

It gave Joan little comfort for Matthew to remind her that most of the facts she had recited were not facts at all, but mere supposes. She said, "At least we're on firmer ground with Una. The purpose of her deception is clear."

"To find our secret purposes out," he said.

"I detest a household spy," she said categorically, and then she remembered that she was one herself.

"Her amorous encounter with Wylkin makes the case stronger against her," Matthew said. "He's Stafford's eyes and ears at Thorncombe. It's impossible to think that one such as he could love without ulterior motive."

"She who lies down with dogs must rise with fleas," Joan said.

But Edward's duplicity bothered her most. He seemed such a pleasant young man, yet she knew the devil had power to assume a pleasing shape. Perhaps Edward was an ally of Una's, and therefore in league with Wylkin. Or a co-conspirator with Conroy?

The household of Thorncombe offered to her imagination the prospect of any number of entangled alliances.

He was already asleep when she woke him with her complaint—a draft from the casement, and would he be a good dear and see to it.

He murmured yes, crawled out of bed, and groped his way toward the window. He could see as his eyes adjusted to the dark how the curtains fluttered nervously. He pulled them back and saw the casement was ajar. He looked out on the view that Joan had seen for the first time earlier that day and it held him there for a moment.

The moon had risen over the distant hills and had transformed the lake into a breathtaking scene. The island at the lake's center seemed impaled upon a shaft of yellow light expanding from the base of the hills at the farther shore to the nearer.

He stood there long enough marveling for Joan to be aware of his delay. She called out sleepily, "Matthew?"

He replied, not wanting to leave the scene. "I'm here. At the window. Coming to bed soon, my love."

He continued to watch. The moonlight and the awesome stillness caused his heart to beat a little faster. His sleepiness fell from him.

She called again, "Come, Matthew, back to bed." There was impatience in her voice. He started to obey. Then he stopped, thought for a moment, and then returned quickly for a second look.

He had seen *something*. Something moving in all that stillness of light; something that had belatedly registered upon his consciousness and which now curiosity drove him back to the window to confirm.

"Matthew, will you come to bed, or do you think to stand there all night gawking? What *are* you looking at?"

"I thought I saw something moving, down by the lakeshore," he said. He pulled the curtain and stared hard through the glass. Down across the greensward to the water's edge he could see a solitary figure. Then it moved again. Toward the water. Within seconds he saw the human figure merge with an oblong shape. He knew what it was. Sir John's boat setting forth.

"Who is it?" came Joan's voice.

Her irritation at his delay had been replaced with concern. He was aware, without looking behind him, of how she would be propped up now, upon her elbows, staring into the darkness. Or into the moonlight rather as it filtered through the glass. He strained his eyes to see again. There was nothing; only the shimmering water.

"I'm going down there," he said. "I saw a man, and Sir John's missing boat."

"Surely, you're not thinking—"

"Yes. You stay where you are. I only want a closer look."

"But, Matthew!" she protested. "It must be eleven o'clock. The whole house is abed. The night is cold, and a young woman of the house has been cruelly murdered!"

"Someone has found the boat and set forth upon the water. I want to find out who."

"A lunatic—or worse."

"Lunatic or demon from hell, I'll find out who it is," Matthew said with determination.

"I'll come with you," she said, making an effort to free herself from the tangle of bedding.

"Absolutely not," Matthew said sharply. "I'll be back in no time. I only want a look."

"But it might be that rascal Wylkin," she said.

"Or Conroy," he said, planting a kiss upon her head. "Go to sleep. I said I'd be right back, and so I will."

"See that you *are*," she said in what was more plea than command, for with all his hardihood she had great fears for his safety.

A candle helped him down through the sleeping house. Outdoors, the effulgent moon sufficed. He crossed the greensward swiftly, making directly for the lake. Soon he was standing where he had stood earlier that day when Edward told him the history of the lake and pointed to the place where Sir John had drowned.

The water shimmered magically in its yellow light. Matthew, straining to see or hear, saw nothing but the placid water. Nor was there any other sign that what he had seen from his casement had material substance. But Matthew knew what he had seen, and he knew it had been no spirit.

His suspicion fell on Conroy Conroy was strong, an experienced soldier, a practiced braggart who exulted in his physical prowess. It was Conroy, too, who had had charge of his master's shallop.

Matthew conjectured that Conroy had hid the shallop, had come down in the dead of night to fetch it, and was now upon the lake in the same craft, rowing with his powerful arms.

But to what end? For exercise? To convey himself to the opposite shore, to which a reasonable man could as easily get by walking around?

Matthew was left with the island.

The assumption gave him a platform to build on. But having theorized as to the identity of the person and his activity, the next question was one of motive. Why should Conroy (or whoever else) want to journey to the island at midnight? Indeed, why go at all?

Matthew was starting to shiver a little. He realized that his vigil might go on all night. Joan would be beside herself with worry. He decided to go back. But first he resolved to establish more firmly one of his assumptions—to promote it from assumption to fact, if possible. He retraced his steps through the woods, then went to the stable, where he knew from Joan that Conroy had been exiled. He thought that if Conroy was in bed, then he was not rowing upon the lake, and although the opposite fact did not necessarily hold, it would strengthen mightily the assumption that it was Conroy whom Matthew had seen.

Warm odors of horse and hay assailed him as he opened the door, then he groped in the darkness of the stalls until he came to the little room that had been Edward's and was now, according to the hostler, Conroy's.

There was enough light from the moon to show him what was there and what wasn't. There was no Conroy, but the man's doublet and cloak were spread out on the pallet in the corner, and beneath were the sword and heavy soldier's boots Matthew had never seen the man without.

While Matthew was gone, Joan turned and tossed in a fit of worry. Then she collected herself and planned just what words and phrases she would use to chide him for his foolhardiness.

If he returned alive. Of which she was in grave and painful doubt.

"Thank God!" she exclaimed when she heard his knock and reassuring voice that it was he and no other. But she was also curious to learn what worthy fruit he'd plucked from his recklessness.

Matthew told her that he thought it was Conroy he had seen and that the lake isle was his destination. He told her all the evidence he had gathered to that effect, hard fact as well as tentative supposition. She agreed it was very likely Conroy was their man.

"Rowing to the island! At this hour! A mad practice unless well motivated," she observed.

"Mad indeed, and therefore I infer it to be well motivated. Surely he's not doing it for the exercise."

"But searching for what?"

"God knows, but I'll find that out, too," Matthew said.

"Well," she said. "Confront him tomorrow. Demand to know what he's up to. Tell him we know it was he who lurked behind the door in the White Keep to frighten silly women and rows by night to islands."

"That might be unwise," Matthew cautioned. "If he's murderer as well as prowler—"

"And boat thief as well," she inserted.

"It would be better to keep him ignorant of what we know. For now, at least."

Joan agreed in principle, remembering the dangerous looks Conroy had given her.

"Did you make fast the door?" she asked.

"Thrice over if it were possible," he said.

"Searching for what?" she wondered aloud.

It was another question badly wanting an answer. And soon.

Joan fell asleep and dreamed of the lake and the island and Conroy rowing across the dark water.

15

ALICE STAFFORD was a plain-looking, plain-speaking woman of about thirty. Short and plump like a partridge, she ruled her house and her husband with boisterous efficiency. She was the daughter of a well-to-do farmer in the shire, and her marriage to Thomas Stafford eight years earlier had been considered an excellent match on her part—a step up the rung of the social ladder. The only blemish upon the cheeks of her fortune was that there never was enough money in the household coffers to suit her purposes. Therefore she regarded her husband as a failure and reminded him of the fact at least twice a day. They quarreled endlessly about matters great and small, but the truth was they had a good deal in common. Both husband and wife were preoccupied with themselves, were arrogant and peevish; each was inclined to do things behind the other's back. Her domineering impulse was complemented by his uxoriousness.

Both Alice and her husband were relieved that she had never borne children, and both had an inordinate desire for money and were terribly frustrated at not having more of it. They were, therefore, of one mind with respect to Sir John

Challoner's Irish plunder. They agreed they deserved it more than the baronet's niece, and even more than Her Majesty the Queen, who, after all, was rich enough already and was very near unto death, if rumor spoke true. Alice Stafford's reasoning in that regard was that the Queen would hardly miss what she never knew she had, didn't need, couldn't use. Neither husband nor wife had qualms about securing the plunder by any means necessary. While neither would have stooped to rob a church; the church having been robbed, the plunder was up for grabs to whoever should grab first. And Sir John having neither need (since he was dead), nor right (since the plunder *was* plundered), neither did young Frances Challoner.

By the Stafford's logic, the ill-gotten gains were best distributed to those Sir John had wronged by his aristocratic arrogance in general and his egregious tampering with nature in particular. And thus it was that since the happy hour in which Jack Wylkin had proved his worth by bringing word of the hidden treasure of Thorncombe, a period of unusual domestic harmony had prevailed at Stafford Hall. Uniting in their larcenous enterprise, husband and wife smiled tenderly upon each other. Alice's carping about money ceased, and the couple spent many a pleasant hour contemplating what they would do when they were truly rich. The only difference in their attitudes toward the Irish booty was that while Thomas Stafford sometimes feared the story might be but a dream, Alice's faith never wavered. She coaxed her husband forward in the project, encouraged him to engage Wylkin in ever more desperate efforts of espionage, and insisted on being a party to every aspect of the conspiracy.

It was to that end that on the evening of Stafford's encounter with Thorncombe's new steward, the husband having divulged that merry tale to his wife, Alice and Thomas Stafford were waiting with great eagerness the arrival of Wylkin from his most recent rendezvous with Una. They were seated in comfortable chairs in the withdrawing room of Stafford Hall, which, although not as commodious as its counterpart at Thorncombe, was well heated, and secure from the pryings of their servants.

"What does Wylkin intend to have from the Irish wench?" Alice Stafford asked with a coarseness she affected when participating in her husband's scheming.

"Intelligence concerning the new steward and his wife," Stafford answered. Above the fireplace there was a mantelpiece upon which sat a stolid German clock. It ticked very loudly and then began striking the hour. Nine gongs. Wylkin was late.

"The pair could make trouble, couldn't they?"

Stafford turned from the clock and his irritation at Wylkin's tardiness to face his wife, for they were not seated opposite each other but very nearly side by side, both facing the fire. "Nothing I can't handle," Stafford said.

"You mean nothing Wylkin couldn't handle," she answered dryly. It was her turn to stare moodily into the fire.

Stafford winced at the remark. It was a casual slur, but it seemed to have graver implications. Although his wife had long professed her distaste for Wylkin, Stafford had noticed her looking at him more closely of late. And the looks she had given Wylkin seemed to Stafford to be quite bold, to say the least. Provocative, even!

He would have inquired of her whether there was not something passing between his wife and his servant but he was hesitant to start a quarrel. Yet the question stuck in his gut and he was beside himself to have it out.

Then Wylkin appeared, dressed in a sable doublet and hose that gave him an even more predatory appearance than usual. He bowed respectfully to his master, favored Alice with a deferential nod, and then presented his report.

"Una says the Irishman has been laying low since the new steward and housekeeper came. Sleeps in the stable now with his horse. The Stock woman made him do it. Una's convinced Conroy knows where the booty is hidden and is only waiting the right opportunity to snatch it."

"And how does she know that?" Alice asked, lifting her round face to address Wylkin.

"Pure instinct, madam," Wylkin said. "The way one dog sniffs out another though the chamber where they lie be as black as pitch. Conroy stays at Thorncombe for no apparent reason except for some ridiculous account of how he must wait upon his new mistress. Evidently, he also has some claim as a scholar of Sir John's papers, but Una has never seen the man read a sign properly, much less a book. It's all a gross imposture. Trust me, he's biding his time because he knows where the gold is, or doesn't know and is still looking."

"Well, tell the woman to keep a close eye on Conroy. I won't be cheated out of what's mine by a knavish Irishman," said Stafford, glancing toward his wife for support of this position.

"And what of the new steward and his wife?" Alice asked.

"Una says they're a nosy pair."

"How so?" asked Stafford, looking up suddenly.

"In act more than word; she distrusts them both, and more particularly the woman. The two of them spent the greater part of the day surveying the castle."

"But have they said anything about Irish treasure?" Stafford asked.

"Not according to Una. But then, if they did know about the treasure, they would not likely spread it about Thorncombe."

"What is the wife like?" Alice wanted to know.

"I've not yet seen her," said Wylkin. "But were she notable for brains and beauty, Una would have remarked upon it. The husband is a dull-brained fellow. Looks like a shopkeeper or corn factor. But I don't trust him more for that."

"It seems your Una isn't the only one then who works by instincts," Alice said coyly, cocking her head at her husband's servant.

Wylkin turned again to his mistress, and with a graceful inclination of the head an experienced courtier might have emulated, said, "I admit to my instincts, madam. They have kept me whole against more than one varlet bent upon cutting my throat for some real or imagined offense to his honor. I say the man Stock cannot be trusted. And since man and wife are one flesh according to Holy Writ, I conclude that Mistress Stock cannot be trusted either. To be what they *seem*, that is.''

''I'm in thorough agreement,'' Stafford said abruptly, displeased by the flirtatious exchange and thinking it was high time he interrupted it. ''Stock seems to be a good deal more than he appears. Wylkin is right to be careful. Will Una continue to watch Conroy?''

''She will, sir.''

''Very good. When do you meet again?''

''Tomorrow.''

''Good. Take care, Wylkin. Be wary of the Irishman. He goes armed.''

''Yes, sir.''

''And watch the Irishwoman as well,'' Alice teased. ''For the same reason.''

''I thought you couldn't abide Wylkin,'' Stafford remarked to his wife after his servant had gone.

''I can't,'' she said. ''He's so full of himself. A little Machiavel in his sable suit. I wonder he can afford it. What is it you pay him?''

He told her outright, while she regarded him with that skeptical expression she had—the right eye lifted in mock surprise, the round soft chin jutting forward.

''A princely sum for so princely a knave, but his doublet cost at least *that*. So whence comes the residue?''

He said, ''I don't know where he gets the 'residue,' as you call it, but you did seem overly familiar with him. Do you take me for a fool? Can I not read the look of lechery in your face?''

She eyed him coldly and turned her little body toward his. ''Overly familiar with Wylkin? Do you jest, husband? With Wylkin? My God, man, Wylkin is as ugly as a crow—as thin as a rail. He could wrap his body around a woman thrice before she knew who had her.''

"Do you speak from experience, dearest?" Stafford replied with reckless sarcasm.

The exchange had violated the little Eden their mutual greed had recently created. Each regarded the other across an abyss of silence. The German clock ticked; the faggots afire cracked and popped. Meanwhile Stafford withered under his wife's icy glare. He pulled at his beard and looked at her bleakly. Neither husband nor wife could believe what sudden anger had forced him to speak. But both understood the words could not be easily withdrawn. Like arrows shot skyward, they were now beyond the control of the archer.

"What did you say?" Alice said, as though there had been no stretch of silence and the accusation had just been minted.

He repeated the accusation—not because he meant it now but because she had asked him to and he wanted to withdraw it. But before he could find the words to make amends, Alice was upon him. She sprang from her chair and began beating his head and shoulders with her little fists, great tears of rage in her eyes and terrible curses and countercharges on her lips.

The conflict brought at least three of their servants from other regions of the house scrambling to see who was murdering whom.

"Get out, get out, you wretches! All of you, be gone!" Stafford bellowed, glaring at the intruders at the same time he was trying to fend off his wife's assault.

The startled servants shut the door again, suppressing their laughter. They had witnessed such scenes between their master and his wife many times and always found them more diverting than a bearbaiting or public execution.

Later that same evening, Thomas Stafford and his little wife declared a truce. Stafford apologized humbly for his slanderous accusation, and they both laughed at how silly it was for him to suppose that there could ever be anything between Alice and her husband's manservant. Alice in turn apologized for the bruises she had inflicted in defense of her honor. "The honor you assailed, who should have defended it to the death,'' she pointed out, thereby firing the last salvo in their war of words.

Stafford sighed heavily and leaned toward his wife. They sealed their truce with a good deal of wine and more talk of Challoner's treasure. The candles burned low and were replaced with fresh ones. A servant brought more wine, and departed the master's chamber marveling that such a tumultuous evening should have brought the master and his wife to this haven of marital concord.

''Will you come to bed, then, Alice my chuck?'' Stafford said in a wheedling voice he used when they were on good terms.

Alice Stafford considered her husband's proposition. She had kept up with her husband in his drinking and, like him, felt herself to be a quite different person—a cleverer, more attractive one. Ordinarily they slept in different rooms. He beseeched her a second time. She looked at her husband. His bedraggled, bleary eyed, hirsute appearance did not arouse her passion, but she supposed, even as light-headed as she was, that a simulated surrender would not be impolitic.

Stafford had the pleasure of watching his wife undress, which she did very slowly and with an undulating motion of her plump hips, as though she were dancing to the accompaniment of a lute. Pink and sensuous in the candlelight, she seemed a different woman. The candlelight flattered her bare, round shoulders and heavy breasts and thighs and quickened a response in his groin that had long slept. Naked as a babe but with a grin of triumph on her face, her golden hair unleashed from its restraints and her arms open as though to welcome his own, Alice Stafford moved with artful deliberation toward her husband's bed.

But she was not thinking of her husband in all these preparations. Rather, she thought of the princely villain Jack Wylkin and of what it must be like to feel that lanky, knotty body wound around her own. And even at the moment of her husband's most passionate fumblings, she had uppermost in her mind a stinging envy of the Irishwoman with whom Jack Wylkin rutted in his master's service.

16

MATTHEW went down to breakfast by himself next morning, leaving Joan to lie abed awhile and the Irish maids to commence their labors without a housekeeper's supervision, which they managed to do much more successfully than Moll had predicted. As he descended the stairs, he could hear voices and laughter coming from the kitchen. Among the voices, speaking in Irish, was Conroy's booming tenor.

Matthew entered and saw Conroy holding forth to Una and two grocers' boys who had brought provisions from the village and had lingered in the kitchen for a free breakfast of cheese and eggs. The boys, who spoke no Irish, were evidently by their expression enjoying Conroy's story as much as Una, but when they saw Matthew enter, the pleasantries ceased, the boys hurried on their way, and Una began automatically to prepare a breakfast for Matthew.

Conroy, dressed as was his custom with his sword at his side and in his canvas jerkin with the buttons, bid Matthew good day and asked about Joan's welfare as though he and she had never wrangled about his place in the castle.

"Oh, my wife does very well," Matthew replied, regarding Conroy carefully. The man did not seem the worse for wear from his previous night's activities. He asked Conroy how he liked his new accommodations.

"Oh, the stable, you mean," Conroy replied with a casual gesture of dismissal. "Well now, it's hardly a palace, but then it will do. I hold no grudges, Master Stock. And would be glad to have you and your good wife as friends."

Conroy offered to shake Matthew's hand, an amiable gesture Matthew did not decline. Warning himself not to be seduced by the Irishman's charm, Matthew said, "Consider us friends."

"Not that I spend much time there," Conroy said, picking up the thread of the conversation as it regarded his new quarters.

"You're gone much of nights, then?" Matthew asked, commencing to eat and trying to frame the question so that it did not sound accusatory.

But Conroy showed no reluctance to answer. He seemed instead delighted to reply in the affirmative. "A quick drink and an easy woman are a soldier's solace. I readily confess few nights will see me in bed before cockcrow."

"You must have a hardy constitution to maintain such a rigorous life," Matthew said.

"Oh, for a fact, sir," said Conroy. "Why, just last night I spent the better part of six hours drinking in the Black Duck. And a fine swollen noggin I have this morning for my effort."

"Is that so," replied Matthew, trying to sound sympathetic in the face of this obvious falsehood. Conroy looked anything but under the weather. "Well," he said. "That explains why you made no answer to my call when I was in the stable last night."

Conroy's expression changed at this. His eyes became serious and his lips formed a tight little smile. "You were in the stable *last* night? And what hour would that have been?"

"Oh, quite late. After the moon was up. Eleven or twelve of the clock at the very least."

"A very dangerous hour to be abroad," said Conroy nervously. "What did you want of me?"

"Oh, nothing but a good stout rope."

Conroy made a face to suggest he hadn't heard Matthew's answer.

"A rope," Matthew repeated, slipping into the falsehood with the ease of a practiced liar. "My good wife made me promise to fetch it for her earlier in the day and I forgot. She wanted it to hang clothes upon. But she remembered my promise, as women will. When I begged her love, she recalled it, asked me if I had complied. No, said I. So she sent me to do her bidding, maugre the hour and the darkness, telling me I should have no satisfaction from her body until she should have joy of my obedience. Down came I to the stable half-naked, with only the moon as a lamp, to do what I should have done earlier. But I found no rope. I called you out, thinking you might know where one was."

Conroy grinned broadly. The story seemed to put him at ease. "I was in town when you came to find me," he said. "With a good half-dozen stoups of the innkeeper's ale to my credit and an Irish song in my heart. A local wench, too, on my lap—the fairest skin and most amiable disposition this side of heaven. But if it's rope you want, well, there are ropes aplenty. In the saddlery."

Conroy explained where the saddlery was, while Matthew pretended that he didn't know. He had not liked lying about the rope—worse yet, the implication that he was ruled by his wife. But the Irishman seemed to accept the story and perhaps, too, think less of Matthew for having told it. Which was all to Matthew's purpose. As long as the Irishman believed Matthew to be a fool, Matthew might fool the Irishman at will.

Conroy said he had to go off about some errand. Matthew said good-bye and finished his breakfast. Afterward he went to the stable, arriving just in time to see Conroy riding off in the direction of town. He greeted Edward, who was busy filling the horse trough with water and explained what he sought.

"There's rope in the saddlery," Edward said, without asking its use.

Matthew went into the saddlery and found a length of rope that seemed about right. The story of the rope had been pure invention—a device for drawing Conroy out and learning how the Irishman would explain his absence the night before. Conroy's lie confirmed all of Matthew's suspicions about the young soldier's nocturnal voyage and its ulterior purpose.

Matthew had come to the stable to acquire the rope largely to make his story good. But while he had walked across the greensward he'd glanced down the sloping lawn to the lakeside and beyond to the island and a new idea came to his mind. It was a more practical use for the rope. And it had nothing whatsoever to do with hanging out clothes.

"At least we know he wasn't trying to drown himself," Joan said when later in the morning Matthew told her about his conversation with Conroy and the lie the Irishman had told. They were sitting in the parlor of the new house, whispering even though Matthew had taken the precaution of seeing that none of the maids or Una were listening at the door.

"No, his story about going into town last night proves I am right. It was he. Looking for something that he wants to keep to himself when he finds it."

Then Joan announced she had some news of her own. A letter had arrived from London while Matthew was in the stable. It was from Frances Challoner and announced her imminent arrival at Thorncombe. The wedding day had been advanced. There was no explanation why.

"What's on her mind?" Matthew asked.

"She's to be married in a week," Joan replied. "Here, read for yourself."

Joan held out the letter to Matthew, who took it and began to read. The small, cramped penmanship of the Challoner heiress was not easy to decipher, and Joan, who had had greater opportunity to peruse the letter, gave Matthew some help with the more difficult words.

"It says the husband's name is Master Thomas Cooke."

"A gentleman, doubtless," Joan said.

"I am sure of it."

"She says they plan to live at Thorncombe."

"Yes, strange, isn't it?" Joan said. "I can't think of a less savory place for a honeymoon. Especially in light of her uncle's murder. But perhaps her suspicions have waned since we left. Love may be all she thinks of these days."

Matthew thought of Frances Challoner—the willowy court beauty that someone had said resembled the Queen when young. Yes, Dan Cupid might have changed her desire for vengeance to desire of a more pleasant sort. Joan was right. Love was known for such miracles. The question was: Where did that leave their investigation of the murder? "Did she say anything about her uncle's death?"

"Read on. It's all there," Joan said.

Matthew read on. "She prays our inquiries have good success and says she hopes to hear from us soon."

"By the way," Joan said. "Have you written again to Sir Robert?"

Matthew shook his head. "I've decided to wait. I have nothing to report as of now—nothing of which we're sure. And yet I feel we may be on to something. This business of Conroy and the island."

Joan reminded him of the chest she'd found. That, too, seemed a part of the conundrum.

"I have a plan," he said.

She leaned forward, her eyes full of curiosity.

"It's not without it's risks."

Her curiosity changed to concern. "Well, speak, I pray you. Don't keep me hanging. What is this risky thing you plan?"

"I reason thus," Matthew said. "If Conroy had found what he wanted on the island, he would be gone, for I can hardly imagine why else he would remain. I think therefore he'll be rowing back to it. Probably tonight. The full moon will be his guide."

"And so what is it you intend, husband?"

He turned his eyes from her. He knew she would not be

pleased with what was in his mind, but the truth was he was getting desperate. Their month at Thorncombe was half spent. Now, Frances Challoner was on her way to Thorncombe. Their task would not become easier, and perhaps it would become impossible. It was not merely failure he feared, but disgrace: humiliation for him; grave embarrassment for Sir Robert, who had sung his praises before the Queen.

She repeated: "What *is* it you intend, Matthew? Tell me!"

Matthew strolled down toward the lake across the smooth grass with the ease of a man without a worry in the world. It was past dinner and he had fed himself well. But he had chosen this moment carefully. He knew Conroy was still in Buxton. Getting his drinking out of the way early to leave his night free for more athletic endeavors, or so Matthew hoped. Edward had gone home at noon to care for his father and would not be back to Thorncombe until three or four o'clock. Joan had the supervision of the entire female staff in cleaning and moving furniture into the previously unused sleeping chambers. And so Matthew could trust that his movements would be unobserved.

He slipped into the woods, and when he was safely enveloped there, he drew the length of rope from his pocket.

17

At dusk, Matthew looked out over the broad sheet of Challoner's lake. As a boy he had waded in his own Chelmer, a languorous winding stream, and the cool running water had given him pleasure. But deeper, more turbulent water made him uneasy. He had never learned to swim, and even his efforts to float only proved his capacity to sink like a stone. An involuntary plunge into the Thames a year or so earlier during an adventure in London had nearly been fatal. The experience still haunted him.

He had given thought to Joan's vision, too. But duty was a demanding mistress and curiosity even more tyrannical. There had only been one way to find out what Conroy was doing on the island, and that was to see for himself. Since Sir John's shallop was unavailable, a raft seemed Matthew's only means of transport.

Earlier he had found several good round limbs shorn from their trunks, and with the rope he had brought from the saddlery he bound them together. He dragged the raft over to the water's edge and then sat down and waited for night. He knew Joan would keep the women of the castle well occupied, despite her vociferous reservations regarding his purpose, once she had got it out of him. Between the time he completed the raft and dusk he had slept, for he was very weary from the night before and was uncertain as to the rigors before him.

Now the lake's surface was a mirror of dark, shifting hues. The island floated upon it like a demasted galleon. He tried to estimate how far off it was. About a hundred yards, he reckoned. About the space between his own shop in Chelmsford and that of his neighbor, Malachi Braden. An easy walk. But this was across water. The lake looked shallow, and so Edward had said it was. But perhaps the water was deeper than it looked. The hostler had also mentioned holes and old mines. Certainly, parts of it would be over his head.

He eyed his raft. It was the first he had ever made. How buoyant would it prove to be once he had left the safety of the shore and waded out through the sedge? He decided optimistically that if the raft sank or rolled, it would probably do so upon launching. The water would certainly be shallow near the shore and he might get a dunking for his pains but nothing worse. If things fell out that way, he would take the disaster as a sign from heaven that the whole enterprise was as dangerous as Joan had warned.

But still, while he thought these things, he could hear Joan saying, "Foolish, Matthew. Foolish, indeed." And he felt guilty about the worry his adventure would cause her.

The day had now been reduced to a sliver of light along the rim of the western hills. He reached down and removed his shoes, then stripped off all but hose and shirt. He hid his clothing under a bush, then waded into the sedge, pulling the raft in behind him.

The water was colder than he had expected, and the sensation of his bare feet sinking into the unseen muck at the lake bottom unnerved him. It was not drowning he feared so much as his vulnerability to what he could not see, and in such water, even in the broad light of day nothing could be seen. He recalled again now with special pertinence Joan's glimmering, and his imagination filled with the watery horrors depicted in books and broadsides—of slithering serpents, eels, poisonous toads. He took a deep breath and tried to clear his mind of these images. He said a prayer for safety of body and soul and finding courage again, he moved beyond the sedge to open water.

He was now up to his waist, his feet sinking into the ooze, bumping against submerged logs, stones. Like an old man with a bent back he pulled the raft after him, facing toward the island. When the water was lapping against his navel he brought the raft around before him and, taking it firmly in hand, he pulled himself up onto it.

For an anxious moment he thought the raft would roll over, or sink. Water surged around him; he clung desperately to the logs, a spasm of terror in his throat. He quickly adjusted his weight. The raft lifted out of the water and his legs dangled in watery space.

He maintained momentum now with a slow, methodical kick and steered toward the island, his face thrust forward. He tried to fix his mind exclusively on his goal, if only to avoid the terrors of his imagination. Above him the stars shone boldly, a multitude of witnesses. But cold and indifferent. Somewhere in their midst were God's eyes, or so Matthew devoutly prayed.

How far had he traveled? The island seemed no closer. Yet already he was weary of the exertion. For a while he stopped, floated, his legs dangling free in the water. How far to the bottom? He extended his legs into the depths as far as he could without jeopardizing his hold on the raft. Nothing. He looked up at the stars. And for a moment something of the awe he had felt the night before quickened his pulse. But his admiration for the beauty above him, cold and distant and mute, was mixed with apprehension. His legs loose and dangling, he felt more dependent than ever on the raft. What if the cordage should slacken or snap? What if the logs lost their buoyancy?

These fears made him so nervous he decided to resume treading, even though he was not fully rested. He turned toward the island. Was it merely hope, or did the island appear closer than before? Yes, it was closer. The darkness of the island had enlarged, had begun to take a shape. He could make out the tower and the vegetation around it. He was making progress, and his heart was beating with a steady anxious rhythm to match his tread.

Then his left foot struck something hard, then his right. Rocks. Beneath the water. He extended his legs and touched bottom, hard now, not soft and yielding as before.

He was not sure how long the water had been shallow enough for him to stand, but when he got to his feet he was surprised to see the water came only to his thighs. A few additional steps, the raft pushed in front of him, lowered it to midcalf. He could see the finer features of the island now. He could see a narrow beach of rocks and pebbles where he might land. But he decided to circle the island as a precaution.

He had waded only a few feet when suddenly he was head under, his feet extending into nothingness. Struggling for breath, he groped about in the oily darkness, realizing to his horror that he had stepped into some hole and the raft was floating beyond his grasp. He went down, down, and then touched a hard, invisible bottom. He pushed himself upward with the last of his strength. His head broke through into the night air and for a moment he saw the stars again, shining as before. It was his near-drowning in the Thames all over again. His body remembered what his mind could not; automatically he began to beat his arms, kick with his feet. A yard or so ahead he could see the raft. He extended his reach toward it, and his lower parts floated upward. He kept reaching and reaching, gulping down the water, catching what desperate breaths he could. Then he caught hold and with one final kick propelled himself far enough onto the raft that he could sustain himself without vigorous effort.

He floated for a while, not twenty feet from the island shore, afraid to try wading again for fear the water was too deep. Was it possible the island was surrounded by a trench? Or had he simply and unluckily stepped into an old mine? He floated until the wave of panic passed him and his breathing returned to normal. Then he maneuvered the raft toward the island and kept kicking until the water was too shallow to kick and he knew it was safe to stand.

The part of the island he had selected as a landing place was heavily overgrown with bushes. The bank was steeper and there was no natural harbor. But he did see a spot that seemed to afford cover for his raft. He secured the raft with the loose end of his rope and then, using the bushes as handholds, he scrambled up the bank.

Matthew was muddy and shivering and nearly exhausted but relieved to be on dry ground again. He had completed the first half of the perilous journey from the mainland, despite Joan's worst fears and his own. And in good time. Already the glow of the moon could be seen. Then, slowly, the great disk itself. Matthew waited, shivering. There was no purpose in his stumbling about, breaking his neck in the tangle of weeds and bushes. He thought Conroy would wait too.

Then the moon was up, coating the island in its pale, sickly light. He made his way through the dense growth and came to the crown of the island and the tower. From there he could look down on the narrow beach where he had been afraid to land and to the other side where he had hidden the raft. A path led up from the beach to the tower. The tower was a foot or so taller than he was. There were a wooden door and one window, higher than the door. Not more than a slit.

If there was time, he would enter the tower and look around later. First he circled the tower to have a look at the other end of the island. He found a scraggly bush about a dozen feet from the tower door that also gave a view of the beach below the tower, and he concealed himself in its foliage.

During the next hour—and it must have been the most of that—Matthew had cause to wonder whether the most foolish decision he had made that night was not his voyage to the island but the assumption that Conroy would make another one himself. What if Conroy didn't come? Should Matthew stay there all night waiting, or should he proceed to examine the tower while there was moonlight? But he was afraid that if he began to move about, Conroy would come.

And so he waited.

It was another half hour by his best reckoning when he heard the telltale sound of oars being dipped and lifted. It was so subtle at first that he thought it his imagination. But then the sound grew louder and the splashes more regular. He peered through the leaves to see down across the water. The moon had turned the water into thousands of glittering spangles. He could see nothing, but his heart had begun to beat rapidly with anticipation. He had not waited in vain. It was Conroy. He was sure of it.

Foolishly, Matthew now reflected, he had brought no weapon with him, not even a knife. And as he continued to search the waters for Conroy, he began to be afraid. Conroy was a brawny, younger man, inured to manslaughter and not likely to be happy to find a spy on his island.

Matthew hardly had time to worry more about the danger when he saw the shallop nosing toward shore. He could see it was Conroy at the oars.

Matthew held his breath and watched while Conroy pulled the shallop up on the rocks and then began to climb up the trail that led to the tower. The Irishman had dressed for vigorous work—he wore nothing but his shirt and his long hose, and the sleeves of the shirt were rolled to his elbows.

Conroy opened the door to the tower and disappeared inside.

For a while Matthew heard nothing. Then a glimmer of light appeared in the narrow slit that was the tower's only window and Matthew could hear the sound of digging.

Matthew waited.

The moon rose to midpoint of its course and then began its descent; still Conroy dug on. Meanwhile Matthew was suffering from his cramped position, which was something between a kneel and a squat. He was colder than ever, and he almost envied the physical exertion and freedom of movement of the man digging inside the tower.

Since Conroy had brought nothing along, Matthew now

believed his earlier supposition was correct: that Conroy's purpose was to find rather than conceal. But to find *what*? Something hidden, obviously, but by whom and why?

He was pondering these questions still when the digging ceased and the light inside the tower was put out. Conroy emerged. Without chest, box, or sack. He went the way he had come, down the trail and then to the shallop. Matthew waited until he could hear the rise and fall of the oars again before he left his place of concealment and even after until he was confident Conroy was to shore again.

Standing was both a relief and an agony. His joints ached; he flapped his arms and jogged where he stood to warm his blood. The exercise rejuvenated him and made him curious. He went over to the tower and looked inside.

There was still enough of a moon to show the interior—an empty chamber of about a dozen feet squared with an earthen floor and the dank smell of a tomb. In the corner Matthew could see Conroy's tools—a spade and pick. There was also an oil lamp. He could see, too, that Conroy's excavations had been thorough. The entire floor had been plowed and smoothed again. Whatever Conroy had hoped to find buried here, he had not found. Yet Matthew felt strongly that Conroy had not finished his search. He would be back—perhaps not stopping until he had dug up the entire island.

Matthew went down to where he had hidden his raft, uncovered it, boarded it, and pushed off, having accustomed himself on his outward voyage to its handling. His return was uneventful and, mercifully, it seemed quicker. He was nearly to shore when he remembered he had not covered his footprints in the tower. Surely when Conroy returned he would see the evidence that his nocturnal mischief had not gone unobserved.

It was half-dark when Wylkin finally saw Una hurrying toward him through the trees. He was vexed by her delay and made no effort to conceal it. He was not in an amorous mood for once and felt therefore no compulsion to be courtly.

"God's bodkins, woman! In good time, you've come. Did we not agree to meet at six o'clock?"

"Faith, Jack, I could not come sooner," Una said breathlessly. Her hands, swollen and red, lay upon her breast, as though to still her racing heart. She looked around nervously. "The housekeeper has had the lot of us at work since dinner. She would not take her eyes from us, I swear it. It's only now that I was allowed to go—to make supper. I can't stay long."

"Damn her then," Wylkin said.

"But that isn't the worst," Una said, looking up at him sheepishly.

"What is the worst?" he asked.

"She *saw* us."

"Who?"

"Mistress Stock, the housekeeper."

"When?"

"Yesterday. She saw where we met, where we lay. Where we talked afterward."

He seized her by the shoulders and shook her, as though she were responsible for their betrayal. And he believed her to be so. "What, did she accuse you? Where was she hidden? Tell me, woman, and be quick about it."

"She was hiding, hiding over yonder, amid the ferns," Una said, trembling at her lover's outburst. She pointed to the place. "She didn't think I saw her. But I did. I saw her gown."

"Then why in Christ's name didn't you say something, but let the two of us talk with her within earshot?"

"I didn't see her until after we had parted. I thought she would rise up and denounce the two of us, but she never did. Nor did she say anything later."

"She said nothing?" he said.

"Nothing. She treated me the same as before, by nodding and pointing as though I had no wit."

Wylkin released her. He stood there thinking, thinking hard what it meant, the housekeeper's spying and her even stranger failure to denounce the wantonness in a servant.

What housekeeper tolerated such behavior under her own nose? It was most unnatural, the Stock woman's silence.

But then perhaps not so unnatural after all—if the woman was more than a housekeeper. If the women was a spy by commission rather than a mere eavesdropper by nature. Wylkin regarded Una with contempt.

"You fool," he said. "Of course Mistress Stock kept you working the long afternoon. Of course she treats you the same. Where was the husband all this time? Not by his wife's side, I'll warrant."

She shook her head, slow to follow his reasoning.

"That's because he was away, looking for the treasure. She kept you and the maids busy for that reason. Don't you see what she was up to?"

He was so angry he could have throttled her.

"There's other news," Una said fearfully. "The new mistress is coming to Thorncombe. Coming any day, so says Mistress Stock. She's to be married."

Wylkin cursed roundly. "Are we to be visited by a host!" he declared, slapping the side of his forehead. His brain began to work rapidly, assimilating this new information. First Conroy had been his major obstacle at the castle. Now it was the Stocks. Should the new mistress arrive with the inevitable train of servants and houseguests, Wylkin's chance of locating and stealing the Challoner treasure would vaporize like mist. He realized that time was of the essence. Angrily, he asked Una when Mistress Frances Challoner was to arrive. Una said she didn't know. No one knew for sure. But it would be soon.

Her ignorance infuriated him. She stood before him dumb and quaking. She had never seen him in such a temper. A dread swept over her. She wanted to return to the castle but she was afraid. He had turned his back to her and she touched his shoulder in a conciliatory gesture but he turned on her abruptly and struck her across the face with the back of his hand.

It hit her hard, but the stinging blow was not so painful as it was humiliating.

"Stupid bitch, stupid old woman!" he shouted. Then he angrily turned and strode off into the darkness.

Great scalding tears blinded her. She realized now how little he cared for her and she felt dirtied by his embraces and deeply regretful that she had ever told him about Sir John's hidden treasure.

She stood there a long time in the darkness. Finally, she roused herself and wiped the tears from her cheeks. Feeling abandoned and disconsolate, she walked back through the gloom, anger growing within her. It was as though she had been impregnated by Wylkin's slap and what was growing at a vastly accelerated pace was not a human child but a devil of vengeance to which she would presently give birth to the undoing of him who had betrayed her so remorselessly.

Bone-weary and frustrated from a long night of futile effort, Conroy passed through the dark stable cursing to himself, thinking how he might have better spent the night in Buxton with his boon companions and the fair-haired wench with the long legs than in digging up half of Challoner's island seeking a treasure that might not exist at all. As he kicked open the door to his quarters his nostrils were immediately assailed by a foul odor he knew only too well from his experiences on the battlefield: putrefying flesh. It was unmistakable, for there was no other smell like it, on earth or in hell.

Alert to danger and vulnerable without a weapon in his hand, he assumed a protective stance, his muscles tense, his eyes straining to pierce the darkness.

Slowly his vision improved and he could see his pallet, his clothes there as he had left them, but not the sword, which at the moment was his chief concern. In its place was a burlap bag.

A practical joke? After a few minutes, when he was sure there was no other person in the chamber, he walked over to the table where the nub of a candle was, struck a flint, and lighted the wick. A little flame appeared and he looked around.

He decided that if it was a dead animal inside the bag, as he suspected it was—considering at the same time which of his companions at the Black Duck possessed such a mad humor as to plague him so—the prankster would be very sorry indeed when Michael Conroy laid his hands on him. And if the same prankster had also stolen Conroy's sword, then the fellow would be sorrier still.

He hefted the bag, judged its weight to be about that of a cat or small dog, and turned its contents upside down upon the floor.

Even by candlelight it took Conroy a few moments to recognize what fell, went bump, and then rolled toward the pallet. He felt his gorge rise and heavy beads of sweat break out upon his face.

He had seen the heads of hundreds of men fixed upon pikes as warnings to other traitors or malefactors—in Ireland and England both. But he had never seen a woman so treated—and especially a woman he had known, in senses both common and biblical—for he recognized, despite decomposition that made mock of the once winning countenance, the hair, face, and dull staring eyes of Aileen Mogaill.

He thought she had run off, like so many before her. He was too stunned by his discovery, too disgusted and perplexed at how Aileen's head had come to be where it was to hear what under less stressful circumstances would have at once sent every nerve and sinew of his powerful body to their stations. When he did become aware of the soft tread behind him, it was already too late. Alarmed, he swiveled to face the unseen threat and saw nothing before his eyes but a headlong rush of something cloaked and muffled, wielding a thing with a crescent blade like a sickle, now sweeping through the air in a wide arc.

The blow nearly knocked him off his feet. Blinded by pain as intense as he had ever experienced, he lifted one hand to staunch the warm river running down his chest and instinctively raised the other to ward off a second assault.

But it was an ineffectual defense, and Conroy's life was draining from him faster than he could feel it go.

In the next moment he was as dead as Aileen Mogaill.

18

MISTRESS Frances Challoner's excitement at the thought of her impending marriage to Master Thomas Cooke of the Middle Temple had done much to alleviate her melancholy preoccupation with her uncle's death—especially since the date of the wedding had been advanced upon the Queen's urging. Mistress Frances wondered now, in absence of proof to the contrary, if her uncle had not simply drowned by accident after all. A clever girl, she suspected that the Queen's suggestion that she marry sooner rather than later was intended by the Queen to be a distraction—a way of diverting the young woman's attention from the inadequacy of her champion, Matthew Stock, and perhaps, too, the hopelessness of her cause. "Vengeance is a most tiresome passion," the Queen had observed.

Her Majesty had also quoted Saint Paul on the legitimacy of marriage: that it was better to marry than burn.

Frances thought these wise words indeed, and as for the little Chelmsford clothier-constable and his wife, she supposed, there having been no report from Thorncombe, that Stock and his wife had failed in their mission.

The Challoner heiress was hardly surprised, for although she had a heart as kind as her countenance was gentle, she never doubted the implicit merit of being of old Saxon blood, or the moral deficiencies of being of ordinary stock. Thus, while she granted the unprepossessing country constable might be honest and earnest, these qualities, admirable though they were, hardly compensated for a lack of heroic mettle.

Young Thomas Cooke was another matter. He was nineteen, a year her senior, the younger son of a Sussex knight of good reputation and modest income. Thomas' older brother and their father's heir was a soldier who had distinguished himself in Flanders, while Thomas' younger brother was a student at Cambridge—preparing for the Church. Thomas had spent two years at Cambridge and then gone to the Middle Temple, where he hoped for a career in the law. Tall and lean, he had become a great frequenter of plays and a young man of fashion. He had a little blond mustache and a spade-shaped beard that was a bit thin now but gave promise of growing fuller with time. His manner was very polished, very courtly—he was witty and eloquent and he could recite verses of all the fashionable poets from memory. These accomplishments impressed Mistress Frances greatly, even though the Cookes were relative newcomers to the gentry, their grandfather having been a London scrivener.

And so, if she had had someone like her intended husband to make the proper inquiries at Thorncombe, her confidence would have been much stronger.

Her first view of this paragon had been in the form of his portrait, which showed Thomas Cooke to be very handsome indeed. But when he manifested himself in person several days thereafter, she found him even more wonderful in reality than in art.

Although Thomas' ardor was somewhat restrained, he seemed fully in accord with the match. They had met at court, fallen in love without the sponsorship of parents (she had none to sponsor; his did not object to the engagement), and had come to agreement as to terms. That their marriage was to be solemnized in the ancient seat of the Challoners had been established early in their engagement and was for Mistress Frances as set in stone as the marriage itself.

But while all these arrangements were as she wished, one great concern remained. It was a concern not unusual in young virgins anticipating the termination of that state. She was reluctant to throw herself so completely on the mercy of her new husband, to lose her identity in his, to trade noble Challoner for gentrified Cooke. And this concern, as preoccupying to her now as her uncle's unexplained death before, caused her to doubt the motives of her intended husband. She was not so inexperienced in the world's ways as to be ignorant of the plight of younger sons whose patrimony was of necessity curtailed by the rights of the firstborn. That Thomas Cooke was a young man of promise was true. The question was: How substantial was his income? About such practical matters Thomas, his knighted father, and the Queen herself had been vague. And that made Mistress Frances suspicious too, for she knew the Queen to be much too clever in money matters as to ignore the question of the bridegroom's financial resources. Her silence on the point suggested that Thomas had more promise than present means, but, of course, he *would* be much better off after his marriage to her.

"He's a young man who's expressed a most gratifying interest in becoming your husband, child. The family is well-enough off, and you shall not want for a new gown once a quarter," the Queen had said, by way of laying the matter of Thomas' money to rest.

And so now she was sitting in her bedchamber in the palace waiting to depart London for Derbyshire. The couple had decided after the wedding to reside at Thorncombe. Frances was weary of the court but would have been content to live in London. It was Thomas who wanted to be a country squire. His head was full of plans for restoring the productivity of the land, for raising the tenants' rent. Frances was not sure how he could stand to be deprived of his beloved theater, his elegant, witty friends, and his career in law. What prospects for advancement were there in dull Derbyshire?

But without a husband—and the right husband, too—Frances had no future in London.

About her uncle's death she had been discreet in her conversation with Thomas. The drowning was, after all, a thing of the past. A year gone might as well be a lifetime, especially to one like her who had seen only eighteen winters. The Queen had encouraged her reticence. "No use filling the young man's head full of horrors, especially when his thoughts should be on his bride." This the Queen had said in an unwonted fit of enthusiasm for matrimony. "Let Matthew Stock resolve things in Derbyshire—*if* there's anything to resolve." She, too, had become more accepting of the coroner's verdict.

"And if he cannot?" Frances had asked, worrying not so much about the defeat of justice as how a murderer at large might put a damper on her honeymoon.

"Should it fall out so," said the Queen, "it would be well to leave it all in God's hands." Her Majesty had mumbled something in addition to this pious thought. Something about a wager. And she seemed very pleased about something.

But Frances supposed none of that pertained to her. She thanked the Queen for her goodness and sought permission to leave the royal presence and service.

The Queen granted permission for both and kissed Frances on the forehead with cool, dry lips. "Pray come see me once more before you depart for the north."

Frances promised she would. She curtsied with as much genuine affection as requisite obsequiousness, backed away from the royal presence, and then stood and turned, threading her way through the ranks of hangers-on and courtiers, servingmen and ladies. She went to her bedchamber. Earlier, she had directed Susan Harwood, her own maid, to pack her belongings for the journey. Susan, a round-hipped, raven-haired girl of Frances' own age, had at least begun the task. The chests were open in the center of the chamber. One seemed fully loaded; from the other, various items of clothing dangled, as though tossed there from a distance. Susan, at the moment of Frances' entrance, was primping before the looking glass, striking seductive poses and pinching her cheeks to make them ruddier. All this, Frances suspected, designed for the brood of lecherous cooks and scullions with whom Susan kept riotous company.

Frances continued to watch these antics with amusement, then adopted a more serious mien and cleared her throat to herald her return. Susan quickly gave over her posturing and twisted around to face her mistress. She assumed an abashed expression of one caught in the act. Frances decided to let the scolding Susan deserved pass and settled for a cold, censorious regard with sarcastic query: "Not *yet* finished. When you are, perhaps you will be at leisure to pack my clothing. And properly."

"I was only resting, ma'am."

"Well, you have rested enough," Frances said curtly. "Just thank God you are not maid to Mary Throgbottom, whose wardrobe is fivefold mine and her patience less."

Mary Throgbottom was another Maid of Honor. She shared the chamber with Frances and had a reputation among the lower servants of being a tyrant.

Susan resumed packing while Frances watched. Frances envied her servant's buxomness, her smooth skin, short stature, and untrammeled lust. When Susan was finished, Frances inspected all that her servant had done and then told her to go find Jasper Prince and tell him she was ready to have her chests taken below.

When Susan had gone, Frances began to think more seriously about the practical matter of her journey. She would not be traveling alone. She would be attended by Susan, by Jasper Prince (Thomas Cooke's personal servant), and William Wallace, whose services had been procured by Thomas Cooke as footman and bodyguard. Then, since no young woman of good breeding and fortune could travel unaccompanied by a social equal or relative, that charge had been given to Priscilla Holmes.

Priscilla was Frances' best friend. A pleasant woman of about twenty-five, Priscilla was of middle height, had a round, cheerful face, and winsome gray eyes. She had been widowed two years before and had recently remarried a man twenty-five years her senior. Her status as a married woman with a reputable husband thus qualified her as a suitable chaperone. The party was to leave early the next morning, hence Frances' concern that the packing be done expeditiously.

Priscilla, a newlywed herself, was delighted by the opportunity to give advice to Frances about her impending marriage. The two women found a quiet corner of the royal garden where Frances received the benefit of Priscilla Holmes' experience. Indeed, Priscilla spoke so explicitly of the pains and pleasures of the marriage bed that Frances felt herself flush along the throat and up to the very roots of her flaxen hair, while her heart burned in anticipation of the handsome young man with whom she would share these delights.

"Young men are very eager," Priscilla observed candidly. "They do not always allow for a virgin's bashfulness by mitigating their first thrusts."

Frances had reflected a moment on her friend's comment. Then she had said, "I am sure Thomas will be gentle with me—as gentle as a dove."

In making her comment she was also thinking of Priscilla's present husband, whom Frances had met. An old man—fifty if he was a day. Was he gentle with his young wife? Worse, was he fully capable of being otherwise? She had heard it was often so with men of later years. Especially those who had taken young wives, whose demands intimidated their husbands into impotence. What did it mean to be old? Surely, at best, it meant wrinkled skin and flatulence, a drooling mouth, missing teeth, waning virility. Frances could not understand how her friend could be happy with a graybeard for a mate and accept her lot with such equanimity.

Priscilla seemed to read Frances' thoughts. "Henry is a very gentle, patient man. My first husband was hot-blooded and amorous. He pleased me well—I won't be hypocritical and deny it. But he swore violently and drank overmuch and—"

Priscilla paused. Frances leaned forward with intensified interest in this catalog of vices.

"And," Priscilla continued, "he was unfaithful to me."

It was the worst of Frances' own fears. Her heart sank. If her winsome companion and friend could not hold her husband to fidelity, what chance did Frances have—especially with a husband so attractive to women as Thomas Cooke?"

"Henry gives me what my first husband did not—constancy," Priscilla said.

The two women fell silent, too good friends for such silence to be a breach of good manners. This talk of marital fidelity had further undermined Frances' confidence. The fear of betrayal enforced her low opinion of her own attractiveness. Was Thomas only marrying her for her money?

She could hardly imagine in her present state of mind another motive, and to her shame she began to weep.

Frances' tears alarmed her friend. "Beshrew me for all this talk of pain and faithlessness," Priscilla said. "What a fool I am to speak to you thusly, especially when you have so much to fret of—our long journey as well."

Frances assured Priscilla that she would be all right soon. It was only a passing mood, these tears. Such tear-storms brides-to-be sometimes fell afoul of as they contemplated the demands of their wedding day.

To cheer her, Priscilla told a joke about a certain bishop, whose scandalous behavior was at the time the theme of every court gossip, Frances dissolved into laughter so completely that for a while she forgot about her fears of Thomas' motives, just as she had put behind her her preoccupation with her uncle's death.

But the night she was to travel to Derbyshire to take possession of her inheritance, she had a disturbing dream. She had never been to Thorncombe, but her mother had told her of it, and she had enough of an image in her mind to furnish forth a dream of the place. She was walking near her uncle's lake, which was in her dream hardly more than a pond with pale, clear water and surrounded with shrubs and flowers like the work of Her Majesty's careful gardeners at Whitehall. Above her, great billowy clouds floated like housewives' sheets blowing in a March wind and white birds skimmed across the water, laving their wingtips by sudden dips. Watching these things, she felt very free and happy, unburdened from worries and fears and proud that she was the mistress of such a place. She turned to include the castle in her view. The castle occupied a whole hilltop. It was very ancient and very grand in appearance—a domicile an earl might have boasted of. As she continued to marvel at the noble edifice, it seemed to grow larger, its wings, towers, and stories multiplying until she thought that Sir Robert Cecil's magnificent mansion at Theobalds was a mere gatekeeper's lodge by comparison.

But then a sudden frisson of fear passed over her. The birds that had been singing a moment before suddenly disappeared. The sky darkened and the billowy clouds that had seemed like housewives' sheets turned into great black thunderheads. The clear water of the lake now appeared to be dismal and thick. Looking around her for the cause of this transformation, she suddenly felt something grip her ankle.

Startled, she looked down and saw that she was standing near the edge of the water and what had shot up therefrom with such suddenness to fasten an iron grip upon her was the mottled and maggoty arm and hand of a rotting corpse.

She woke herself with her own scream ringing in her ears. The vision of horror was replaced by the face of a very angry Mary Throgbottom, bent over like a snarling gargoyle and saying, "You stupid girl. Quiet! You were having a dream, nothing more. Go back asleep. Another outburst and we shall have the guard streaming in to gawk at us in our nightclothes. You'll wake the entire palace."

Mary Throgbottom returned to her own side of the bed, her back to Frances. Frances lay with her hand tight over her mouth to stifle her sobbing. Ashamed of her tears and her scream, Frances knew she deserved Mary's censure. But what else could she have done? *Never* had she had such a dream! And the worst was what the dream might portend, for she held it sound doctrine that a nocturnal vision of such vividness and strangeness could not be without meaning.

She lay quaking until dawn, listening to Mary's soft breathing and thinking terrible thoughts about putrefying corpses. When dawn broke at last, she was much too grateful for the light to be sorry that she had slept so little and now would be tired during the long first day of her journey to Thorncombe.

She was dressing when she noticed the pale flesh of her delicate ankle bore an ugly bruise. As though what she had dreamed had been no dream at all.

19

AFTER breakfast, Moll sent her husband down to the lakeside to look for a variety of edible mushrooms that grew in the moist earth along the shore. When he did not return right away, she was neither vexed nor surprised. The truth was that she did not care a fig for mushrooms. She only wanted to get Cuth out of the way for a while. Accustomed as she had been to the run of the castle, her present confines in the run-down lodge made a difficult problem of adjustment. She also missed the command she had enjoyed as chief servant in the castle. Now she had to content herself with ruling her husband, and he hardly began to gratify her passion for control and manipulation. Slow and deliberate, he seemed always in her way. He irritated her with his mumbling and complaining, his doddering and long heavy sighs and tedious reminiscences of life at Thorncombe in the days when the master spent ten of the twelve months in Ireland. Moll often made up errands for Cuth to attend to, just to get him out from underfoot.

The mushroom expedition was such a one. And yet, when Cuth was gone, Moll found the cottage lonely. Especially since the death of the worthy Nebuchadnezzar, whom she continued to mourn as she might have mourned the loss of a beloved child.

She had not given up her desire for revenge on Joan Stock, who she was sure was to blame for the death. Yet she had yet to determine a punishment worthy of the crime. She would not have been satisfied with direct action. What was needed was something devious, something spectacularly clever and monumental. She wanted, in short, not only the punishment of the wrongdoer but a personal triumph of which she might boast to her husband and others for the rest of her life.

Since Joan's arrival, Moll had been observing the interloper from afar. Joan's illness her first week at the castle had been profoundly gratifying to the old woman but had fallen short of complete satisfaction in not having been terminal. More recently she had been disappointed in finding Joan a competent housekeeper, for Moll had intended to ask for restoration of rank on the grounds of Joan's failure to control the Irish bitches, as Moll was wont to term ungraciously the castle's maids. But no failure was evident, nor could it be easily falsified. The house and castle were efficiently and properly being made ready as ordered. The Irish girls seemed to work more willingly for the Stock woman than for Moll. In sum, there simply were no chinks in the armor of Joan Stock's adequacy.

Obviously another course of action had to be taken. And Moll was in the middle of contemplating what that course might be when she heard her husband's voice outside the lodge, bawling out her name.

Moll hardly had time to rise from her stool to see what the matter was before Cuth burst in the door all pale and breathless. He looked at her strangely and said, "By God, Moll, you killed the Irish bastard after all!"

She was too bewildered by this proclamation to be angry. "Why, what is it you say, husband? An Irish bastard? What! Is one of the maids with child, say you?"

Cuth was clutching his chest, trying to get his breath. He started to speak again and then fell helpless in a fit of coughing and gagging so that Moll had to press a cup of water on him to clear his throat.

"Conroy, the Irishman." He sat down on a bench in front of her and put his elbows on his knees and stuck out his face. He looked at Moll with eyes full of wonder, as though he had never truly understood this woman to whom he had been married for over forty years. "Cold, stone dead. Like Aileen Mogaill! His throat was cut. From ear to ear. Old girl, you know how to wield a kitchen knife, you do, you *really* do."

"Fool!" Moll said. "What makes you think *I* killed him?"

The question took Cuth aback. He had no immediate response. Then he said, "I thought you hated him for his insolence."

"And so I did," she said. "And so I might have brained him with my cudgel at hand, or taken a kitchen knife to his privates, if it had struck my fancy. Marry, he would have richly deserved neutering. But the bald fact of the matter is that *I* didn't do it."

She wanted to know where her husband had discovered the body.

"I went even as you said, down by the lake where the willow arches over the bank. I saw something afloat there and wondered what it was. Thought it was a huge fish, I did. No, it wasn't a fish. I thought then it might be a log or a dead sheep."

"Out with it, man!" Moll cried impatiently in an effort to stanch the flow of useless words.

"He was floating face down."

With mordant relish, Cuth gave another gruesome description of the dead man's wounds. She stopped him in midsentence.

"He was *plainly* murdered then, and like Aileen?"

"Nothing but murder makes such wounds," Cuth said, nodding as though his knowledge of these bloody matters were extensive.

"No chance of it being self-slaughter?"

Her husband laughed grimly and shook his head. "Self-slaughter! Him? Why, he was too mean. He would never have given the world so much pleasure."

She had to admit he was right on that score.

"Well then," he demanded, looking at her curiously. "If it wasn't *you* that did it, who did?"

It was the very thing she was wondering herself. And the first person she thought of was Joan Stock. Not because she reasoned that whoever would murder feline innocence would not stint at murdering an obnoxious Irishman, but because she knew full well that whoever would murder a harmless cat deserved *to be blamed* for killing an Irishman, guilty or not.

"The Stock woman murdered him, *that's* who," she said decisively. "Murdered him in cold blood. With ill intent and motive malicious. It was because of some quarrel the two of them had."

"Did she?" gasped Cuth. His jaw fell slack. For a moment he was speechless. As an alternative to his wife, the hostler had struck him as a likely candidate. He had not even thought of Joan Stock—or her husband either.

Moll warmed to her theme. "Did you not hear the quarrel the two of them had—what threats were exchanged and bloody oaths uttered? What weapons were brandished on both sides!"

"No, I didn't. You told me—"

"Foolish old man," Moll interrupted, glaring at him threateningly. "You *did* hear such a quarrel and were a privy witness to the threats she made to him and he to her."

"But I don't remember—"

"You *do* remember," Moll repeated.

And then Cuth understood what he was to say if he was asked. He envisioned the quarrel she spoke of—and to which he was supposed to have been an eavesdropper—with startling clarity and conviction. He nodded in agreement. He approved of his wife's plan. Besides, he was eager to see her have her revenge. It would put the matter of the dead cat to rest, once and for all.

"Where's Conroy's body now?" she asked.

"Where I left it. Beached, fly-blown, and rotting in the sun."

"Go hide it so no one tampers with the remains. At least until our constable's had an eyeful. Then go find Edward. Tell him there's been another murder done and the Stock woman did it. Tell him there's a world of proof. Say her husband was her accomplice. It will be the salt to a narrative already well seasoned with plausibility. If he inquires as to the cause, say it was because the Irishman spoke uncivilly to them and would not willingly forsake the house."

Cuth rushed back to where he had found Conroy's body. He was greatly relieved, now that he thought of it, that his wife had not murdered the man. For one thing, he would have been tolerably sorry to see his wife hanged. For another, her murder of Conroy would have set a worrisome precedent. For certainly she would murder him next if she ever found out it was he that had dispatched Nebuchadnezzar. Cuth trusted the hostler would keep his little secret as he had promised, since Cuth had promised in turn to keep mum about Edward's Irish whore. Tit for tat it was to be between the two men.

But when he came to where he had left the corpse he found it gone. He looked about him in a panic. There was the same willow. The same overhanging branches, the same clump of sedge. The same slimy bank.

And Conroy was gone!

For a moment a supernatural dread seized him. Into his confused imagination came a parade of horrors—bloated corpses that walked, skeletons that danced. Or perhaps Conroy had not been dead after all. But then he remembered the half-severed head. No, not even the Irishman could have survived such a wound.

He backed away from the spot, afraid to take his eyes from the water. His old heart beat so violently against his chest he couldn't catch his breath. When he had walked backward a good dozen paces and had come near breaking his neck stumbling over stones and roots, he turned and broke into a frenzied dash for the lodge again, bellowing out his wife's name as though he were a child come running home to Mother with a skinned knee.

"Now don't piss yourself, but tell me what it is," she said.

"He's gone."

"Who?"

"Conroy."

"You said he was dead."

"I swear he was dead. Bloody enough for a dozen Irishmen."

"Then he only seemed to be dead," she said. Moll's heart sank as her plot began to crumble before her mind's eye.

"Nay, he *was* dead. If not by his wounds, then by the water."

"Well, then, Master Know-It-All," Moll asked scornfully, "pray tell me where he has gone. To find a grave digger?"

Her husband had no answer.

Moll snorted with disgust and stood elbows akimbo as she often did when she was thinking. Here indeed was a puzzling turn of events. A disappearing body! She believed her husband's description of the wounds. She knew her husband was an ass, but surely too poor a liar to fabricate a story in such a wealth of detail. Yet she held it as a matter of principle that no man with his throat cut walks away. So someone must have discovered the body and borne it off. She knew they must act quickly now or all might be lost.

"Go to Edward. Tell him what you saw and what we suspect. Then let him go to the house and confront the housekeeper and the steward. If she claims ignorance of any bodies or murders, then we'll accuse her of murder all the same and say she did away with the body herself so as not to be caught red-handed; just as she and her husband did with Aileen Mogaill—and contrary to our better judgment, too, for we urged them to fetch the constable when the wretched girl was found, but they would rely on their own wisdoms."

"Why, that's true, Moll," Cuth said enthusiastically. "If

she murdered Conroy, she might with equal logic conceal his corpse. And 'twas her husband and Edward that buried Aileen huggermugger and without a priest to bless her bones."

"Let her deny it, let her deny it!" Moll cried. "I'll say I saw Conroy floating in his gore—that we went down to the shore together and dropped the mushrooms we'd collected in sheer terror of the body. We'll match stories. That's two 'gainst one."

"But what if her husband stands by her?" Cuth said. "There's two against two."

"And so it is, husband. An even match. Yet we'll come out on top because Conroy won't be around and where else could he be but dead? Besides, we're natives to the place, the Stocks strangers. If it's to be *them* against *us*, then we'll prevail."

Cuth felt bolstered by his wife's confidence. Pleased to have such a clever wife, he hurried toward the stable to find the hostler, rehearsing, as he ran, everything his wife had instructed him to say.

Edward was in the paddock, grooming one of the horses. Cuth rushed up and told his story, but the hostler seemed unimpressed. "Floating in his gore?" he replied incredulously. "Nonsense, surely. The man was hale and hearty this morning when he left the castle."

"Left?" Cuth exclaimed in amazement, thinking of the bloated corpse he had seen.

"He and his horse and his gear. He didn't say where he went or when he'd be back, but he took everything with him and I judge thereby he's gone for good."

"But the Stocks murdered him, slit his throat and gutted him too, because he would not quit the house," Cuth protested, his panic rising again.

"But the man *has* quit the house—and probably the country as well. By all signs, he's gone back to Ireland. The Stocks would have no cause to murder, and I saw the man alive just this morning."

* * *

Cuth walked out of the paddock in total and devastating confusion. He was sure what he had seen—or at least he thought he was sure. But the worst was that he now had to return to tell Moll, who would hardly be pleased to learn that her stratagem of revenge had foundered.

He walked back to the lodge in fear and trembling, and with a vague, distant expression on his face. As soon as he crossed the threshold, he told his wife what the hostler had said.

"Left this morning—quit the country?"

She sat there looking at him, trying to piece things together herself. Then in her eyes came the gleam of recognition. "Why, you dolt! Left this morning! You fell asleep by the lake instead of bringing me my mushrooms and then made up a story of a corpse to cover your own sloth! Napping, were you? And dreaming too, I warrant. Bloody corpses! I'll make you a bloody corpse, I will."

Moll seized her broom and gave Cuth a few good whacks before he managed to dodge out of her way. She drove him out-of-doors, where he remained the rest of the day, while in her solitude the enraged old woman studied other means to avenge the worthy Nebuchadnezzar.

The two men walked quickly toward the stable, each in a hurry for a different reason and their common interest yet to establish itself. Stafford's hostler went to bring out his master's favorite mount; Stafford remained at the paling to think about his wife and his future riches. When Wylkin returned, Stafford made mention of the Challoner treasure. He said he wanted a report of Wylkin's progress, a report of his espionage at the castle.

Stafford's request gave Wylkin a chance to announce offhandedly that he had discovered where the same treasure was hidden.

The effect of this nonchalance was a thing of beauty, according to Wylkin's view of things. For a moment Stafford just stood there by his horse, his mouth agape, his face wrinkled up in puzzlement as though he had lost his hearing—or kept it and Wylkin had lost his mind.

"What did you say, Jack?"

"I said, sir, I've found out where old Challoner hid the booty."

"Why, speak, man; my God, if this be true, it's wonderful news."

Hardly surprised by his master's joyful response, Wylkin told of his most recent meeting with Una, of Joan Stock's spying, of his own increased suspicions of Matthew Stock. He told how he searched the castle grounds looking for the new steward and how he found instead Conroy (although the Irishman did not see him), drawing a boat from its hiding place in a thicket and rowing out onto the lake with only a bold-faced moon for a lantern. Wylkin had watched from shore until his suspicions were confirmed. Conroy's destination was clearly the island.

"The island!" Stafford exclaimed. "Why, I should have thought of it before this. Beshrew me, I should have known—and yes, you, too, Jack. What better hiding place? Tricky devil, that Challoner. God knows when he started planning this. Why, he must have built that cursed lake to protect the treasure, which even then he must have been hoarding."

Stafford was beside himself with happiness. He said he would not go riding after all. He wanted to go back to the house to inform his wife. The news would be as welcome to her as it was to him, he said. But then Stafford looked very seriously at Wylkin and said, "My God, you don't think Conroy found the treasure and then made off with it, do you?"

"Believe me, the booty is still on the island," Wylkin said. "I feel it in my bones. I waited for his return to shore, a lonely vigil, but he brought nothing home that he had not taken abroad on the lake."

"But why hasn't Conroy found it?" Stafford said.

"He hasn't found it *yet*, sir."

"By which you mean we must find it first."

"Exactly."

"But I can't swim—shall we walk on water?"

"We shall go dry-shod," said Wylkin, supremely confident.

"Dry-shod?"

"Mark my words."

Wylkin had saved the best for last—a plan to obtain the treasure and destroy the Challoner pride in one fell stroke.

20

MATTHEW and Joan lay long abed the next morning, both drifting in and out between sleep and wakefulness, while the timid November sunlight filtered through the curtains and in the lower regions of the house footsteps and distant voices could be heard, signaling that the Irish maids were already at their appointed tasks.

Joan's first words when she was fully awake and saw that Matthew was likewise was a request that he tell her again of his night's adventure. She said she had been too over-whelmed with weariness when he returned to hear him all out, and what she remembered she could not now be sure was fact or dream.

Matthew told it again, while a strange torpor seized him.

"Digging by lamplight. A sinister work indeed," she observed when he told her that part.

"And not burying," he said.

"Nor finding?" she inquired.

"No. I saw him leave the tower. He had nothing but what he had brought with him."

She said, "We could put it to him that you *saw* him. That we know."

"Poor bait for the larger truth," Matthew said. "He'd deny everything, or concoct some fantastical fiction."

Joan thought of the lake, so dismal and treacherous with its submerged stumps, its murky water, and God knew what creatures in its depths. She shuddered and looked at her husband, wondering at his hardihood—indeed, at his incredible bullheadedness, for she had reminded him before he left of her glimmering. Had it not betokened grave peril?

But now that she looked at his face, she realized he did not look well at all. Against the pillow his face was drawn and flushed, his eyes lusterless.

He sneezed violently.

"Well, now," she said. "See, you have caught your death."

A second sneeze, more violent than the first, prevented his reply. He groaned and shut his eyes. "I don't feel well. Not since waking."

She ordered him to remain in his bed. He protested and tried to rise, but fell back down again. He felt a fever coursing through his blood. His muscles ached, especially those in the calves and thighs, which had borne the brunt of his labors.

"Conroy must be watched," he said weakly. "If his digging hasn't something to do with these strange murders, then I'm no Englishman."

"You are as true an Englishman as ever walked the earth," she said, very sorry to see him so unstrung. She felt his forehead and listened to his chest. He was burning up. She heard a definite wheezing about his heart and lungs. She smelled his breath. It was sour. And in addition to all these untoward symptoms she could detect about his body the rank odor of the lake. Alarmed, she said, "I'll be your nurse, as you were mine. You have made your last voyage to the island."

She was very definite about that.

She dressed, went downstairs, and prepared a concoction

of herbs and spices she had learned from her mother for the curing of colds and other distempers. It was a remedy of proven virtue, and yet Joan knew the best remedy was rest. Then she went back upstairs, gave him several spoonfuls, and sat by the bedside until he fell asleep again.

She watched him for some time, and while she watched she thought of Conroy and Una and Edward, of Jack Wylkin and his master, of poor Aileen Mogaill, and of the chest she had found by the lake and about Matthew's excursion to the island. All swirled in her head with their competing claims for significance.

Matthew seemed better. She felt his forehead. It was cooler, his breathing more regular. She decided the investigation must continue.

She thought that despite what Matthew had said about the unlikelihood of Conroy confessing anything, it would be of some value to see what the Irishman was up to. She went downstairs and then out to the stable.

As she entered she saw Edward at his workbench and asked him if he'd seen Conroy.

The hostler paused in his work. He was in the midst of repairing a saddle and had a sharply pointed tool in his hand. He looked at her and said, "He's gone."

"Where?"

"Where he willed," Edward answered, returning his attention to the saddle. "He's cleared out. Go have a look for yourself."

She decided that under the circumstances the invitation was well worth accepting. Joan slipped around Edward and into the stable where Matthew had told her Conroy slept.

Despite the hostler's assurance that Conroy had cleared out, she expected to see the chaotic mess that had characterized Conroy's quarters in the castle. Instead, the little room was well ordered and clean. The straw pallet had been covered with a piece of new canvas. There was no sign of the Irishman's gear.

She was turning to leave when she noticed a large dark stain on the planks. She knelt down to have a closer look.

Whatever had spilled had been in ample supply, and someone had made a serious effort to clean it up, for there were abrasive marks all around the edge of the stain, as though the floor had been scrubbed hard with a thick-bristled brush.

"I noticed a stain on the floor. Something spilled," she commented to Edward as she was on her way out.

"The floor is filthy with stains," the hostler said without looking up. "Most of it blood. Animal blood. My father tells me the cabin was once used to slaughter chickens and pigs."

"Oh, was it?" Joan responded casually, as if the hostler's explanation was of no importance to her.

A slaughterhouse for chickens and pigs? she thought as she walked back to the house. Who would believe that a stable room with a solid wood floor would be used to butcher beasts—a filthy work all the world did out-of-doors? And, moreover, who could believe, knowing the natural slovenliness of Michael Conroy, that he would spend a minute of his time cleaning quarters he had never sought and was on the edge of abandoning forever?

The only conclusion to be drawn was that Edward was lying. But if Conroy really had cleared out for good, why didn't Edward simply tell the truth?

And then she wondered if perhaps he hadn't—at least in part. Perhaps the stain was blood. But no animal's.

She shuddered.

She reasoned that if Edward was lying, then it was his second lie, for she recalled Matthew's account of the hidden child. She wondered if Conroy might be dead and if Edward had killed him and had then cleaned up after the murder. The silly story about the slaughterhouse might have been invented on the spur of the moment. Perhaps he thought no one would see the stain, or attach any significance to it. If so, Edward had woefully underestimated her housewife's eye for detail.

She went upstairs again to see how Matthew was doing. Finding him still asleep, she applied cold compresses to his forehead while she tried to decide what to do next. When Matthew awoke she told him what Edward had said.

"Gone! I can't believe it. He wouldn't go save he found what he was looking for, I'm convinced of it."

She had to agree. She told him she thought Conroy might be dead. Murdered. Perhaps by Edward.

"But why would Edward kill the Irishman?" he asked. "I must get up."

"No, you don't. Keep to your bed. You're not well, and while I think you are mending, if you do too much you'll make it worse again. I'll be back in a little while."

"Where are you going?"

"Out to see Edward's father—and perhaps Edward's child."

"No, wait until I'm well enough to accompany you."

"We can't wait. Things are happening too fast, Matthew."

He protested futilely. In the next moment she was gone.

She recognized the cottage from Matthew's description, which had been very exact. As she approached, she saw an old man seated in the doorway sunning himself. At his feet sprawled a large dog. Indoors, a woman's voice was singing. The dog, catching her scent, stood and began to bark. The singing stopped. Joan advanced quickly, maneuvering around the man and the dog, who she could see was tied to a stake and was at the end of his tether and beyond reaching her. Joan's foot was on the doorstep when the woman appeared, a startled expression on her face.

She was in her early twenties, Joan supposed. With fair skin and dark hair, full on her shoulders. She was holding her hand over her mouth in a gesture of surprise. Joan greeted the woman, identified herself, and stepped into the cottage, as though the younger woman's astonishment at Joan's sudden appearance had been a clear invitation to enter.

Not certain as to how long she could take advantage of her hostess's confusion, Joan took in as much as there was to see. She noticed the interior was simply furnished, and, as Matthew had said, clean. She saw the baby at once. Joan judged it to be about a year of age, perhaps more. It was lying on its stomach on one of the two pallets, its round pale face protruding from a coarse-spun blanket. The child was asleep.

Joan turned from the child to look at its mother. The woman had come into the center of the room and wore an expression of confusion and dismay. Joan noticed, now that she could study the woman's features, that they were delicate and winsome, the eyes wide-set and the mouth small and well-shaped.

The woman still seemed too astonished by Joan's invasion of the cottage to speak. Taking advantage of her confusion, Joan turned to have a closer look at the child.

The child's coloring favored the mother. There was a thick growth of ruddy hair on the smooth scalp and the child's flesh was pale, almost translucent. But there was a deformity in the mouth that marred the little face. It was a harelip, a lamentable defect.

Somehow sensing his mother's alarm, the child awoke and stared up at Joan and began to wail.

The baby's distress brought the mother hurrying to the bed. She snatched the child up in her arms, putting the blanket over the lower part of the child's face to hide the deformity.

Joan decided to be direct. "Who are you? And who, pray, is this child?"

"The child is mine," the woman said in a heavy Irish accent. "He's my son. My name is Brigid."

"You are Edward's wife, then?" Joan said.

Brigid paused before answering; then she said, "No, not his wife."

"But that is *his* child," Joan said.

In the comforting embrace of its mother, the child had ceased crying and was watching Joan out of large blue eyes. But before Brigid could respond to Joan's question about the child's paternity, Joan's attention was drawn to the yard, where the dog had resumed barking. This time, however, the quality of the bark had changed from fierce aggression to excited welcome. Joan heard a familiar voice. "Stand, Dagger. Peace, cur!"

The next moment Edward appeared, stern-visaged and breathing hard, as if he had run in pursuit of her.

"What's your business here, Mistress Stock?" he inquired coldly.

She was tempted to answer in kind—to say that she had every right to be where she was and to demand what right the woman and child had to be under a roof that was property of Thorncombe without the owner's permission. But then, remembering that a soft answer turned away wrath, she said, "I came to visit your father. And this young woman. And her child."

This response seemed to take Edward by surprise. He appeared less angry now and came deeper into the room to stand next to Brigid.

"You came to visit my father?" he asked suspiciously.

"You told me he was old. And infirm. I thought it within the scope of my duties—if not an obligation of a Christian."

"My father needs nothing that I cannot provide," Edward said defensively. He looked down at the baby in Brigid's arms as though to see if it was all right and then back at Joan. His face was full of resolve. "This woman and I are betrothed. If our union has not yet been blessed by the Church, yet it has been blessed by this child, who is truly ours."

"It's a fine, healthy child," Joan agreed, not sure how to respond to this speech and its note of defiance. "But I don't understand, Edward, why you have been so secretive—about Brigid, I mean, and your son. Certainly there is no cause of shame here. You did say you were betrothed."

Joan decided that she would not reproach him with the lie he had told Matthew. But she was still not unconvinced that the hostler's handsome countenance was not a murderer's, for there was still the matter of the bloodstain on the stable floor.

"Well," Edward said, "some might not approve of our living as husband and wife before our union has been blessed. I'm of no mind to have my son called a bastard."

Joan thought that was a good enough reason. If the pair weren't married by law, then it followed that the child was a bastard by the same law, despite the dubious "bed-rights" often claimed by betrothed couples and sanctioned by their families. Yet the word "bastard" had a sting to it, and she could see another reason for Edward's secrecy. Since it was common thinking that bastards wore the outward sign of their illegitimacy on their bodies, it was sure that the child's hare-lip would be construed as a curse and stigma.

"*Bastard* is a hard name, a cruel name," she said. "I'm sure your little son is as innocent as any other child. As for your unmarried but housed condition, I will be no hypocrite and say that I completely approve. Yet I will be no judge of you."

Edward's hard manner seemed to soften at these words. "Thank you, Mistress Stock. We didn't know how you and your husband might think. The old steward and his wife cast Brigid off when she was great with child. We keep to ourselves here, as you can see. Dagger isn't used to company."

"I could see that well enough," Joan said good-naturedly. "Yet a dog that does not bark is hardly worth what it takes to feed him."

Brigid smiled and put her baby back down on the bed. Edward said, "We'd be obliged if you didn't say anything about the baby at the castle."

"As you please," she answered. "It's your business—yours and Brigid's. The matter is closed as far as I and my husband are concerned."

Then Joan said it was time she must be going. She explained that her husband was taken ill. Both Brigid and Edward expressed their sympathy. They said they hoped he would be himself again soon. They waved to her as she left.

The old man was still in the yard. Unmoved since her arrival, he now lifted up pale, watery eyes in her direction as she passed, and the dog, having accepted her status as an invited guest, was too busy scratching its fleas to take note of her departure.

She was disappointed that the mystery of the crying child

was so easily explained—and more disappointed that the explanation cast no greater light on what the child might have to do with the castle murders.

Matthew had been awake since his wife left, thinking he really should get up, imagining that while he languished recuperating, events of great moment were taking place of which he was woefully ignorant. And so get up he did, although not without a few protests from his ailing body, despite Joan's remedies and compresses. Still in ill sorts, he knew he had paid the price for his foolhardincss. He could see that now—and Joan had seen it too and therefore had spared him the scolding his foolhardiness warranted.

He felt not only physically weak, but morally chastened.

But what lay heaviest upon his mind and heart was a sense of failure. In London the Queen and Sir Robert would be waiting his return. But when he did, what could he report—a second mysterious murder and perhaps a third to add to the first he had been charged with solving?

The Queen would hardly be pleased. She would forget his great service at Bartholomew Fair, perhaps even demand the return of the silk purse and its contents on the grounds that it had been earnest money for greater service promised and yet unperformed. Matthew knew the Queen to be a canny businesswoman. Yes, would she not have the purse back?

And there was Sir Robert, who had praised Matthew so generously. Matthew's failure would be Cecil's too. And with that thought, Matthew slid even further into a slough of despondency.

He went over to the casement and looked out. How long had Joan been gone? To the cottage of Edward's father. That had been her destination. He wondered what she would find. Perhaps the concealed child. And the reason for the concealment?

He turned at the sound of her voice.

"The child is one of the maids," she said without prologue. "She lives with Edward. They're betrothed."

"Not Una?" Matthew asked, imagining for the moment the triangular complexities of Una, Wylkin, and Edward.

"The girl's name is Brigid. She was once a servant here but was sent away when found with child. By the Fludds, or so says Edward."

"Cast the maid off because she was undone by another servant!" Matthew exclaimed, disapprovingly, climbing back into bed folding his hands beneath his head. "Why,.if that were made a rule, half the houses in England would be untenanted by servants. Besides, they are betrothed. Some say that gives bed-rights. Whence comes this moral severity on the old couple's part? Neither strikes me as a Puritan."

Joan took off her cap and cloak and sat down on the bed beside Matthew. She asked him how he did and he said he felt better, much better.

"Liar. Stay in bed," she said.

She addressed his question.

"With people as bad-tempered as the Fludds, there's no great mystery. I imagine Brigid got on the wrong side of Moll. The girl is quite beautiful really. Her features are unusually fine for a country girl's."

"Jealousy, then?"

"Envy, spite, the cankered nature of the awful old woman," Joan said. "When Brigid's folly began to betray itself in the swelling of her belly, they asked her to leave, and Edward took her in. Took her to his father's cottage, where she looks after the child and his father. He didn't want you to know she was there because he was afraid you'd send her packing, just as the Fludds did. But they trust us now to keep their secret."

"And so we shall," Matthew said.

Joan told her husband too about the child's deformity, the little red fissure dividing the upper lip and marring the otherwise flawless countenance.

"Our grave divines and moralists would make much of *that*," Matthew said, shaking his head sadly, for he loved children and felt a natural sympathy with other parents who were protective of their little ones.

"There remains one cause of suspicion about Edward," Joan reminded him. "The bloodstained floor."

"Well," Matthew said. "However that is explained, I'll believe Conroy dead when I see his body for myself. But if he *is* dead we may never know what he was looking for on the island, or why he killed his master to get it, if Conroy's our man."

"Perhaps it was in the chest," Joan suggested. "The empty chest I found."

"Perhaps," he agreed.

For a moment each thought his or her own thoughts. Then Matthew said, "Conroy may have misunderstood Sir John's intention—about the island, I mean. Maybe he thought that because Sir John was in his boat he was setting out for there. But maybe the island wasn't in the man's thought at all."

"What do you mean, husband, not in his thought?"

"I mean, maybe he wanted to row out to the center of the lake and give whatever it was he had with him a toss into the water and let it sink to the bottom."

"Something that he may have carried with him in the chest I found?"

"It is possible," said Matthew.

Joan considered this, for her husband's new speculation had its appeal. It made sense of the chest, their only hard evidence. But what would the baronet have been so eager to throw away on the night of his homecoming? The larger, more compelling question remained unanswered.

"Well," she said with a heavy sigh, "much good whatever he cast off will do us or Conroy now. Unless the lake goes dry."

"Would we could drain the pestilent thing."

"*Could* the lake be drained?" she asked, thinking suddenly that what man had made could be unmade.

"Mistress Frances would hardly approve," he said. "All of what we've said is guesswork. How could we justify it to her? Could we say: *Madam, your honorable uncle concealed some unknown thing beneath the lake waters—something for which we suppose the good man might have been murdered, although we have not a jot of proof of the same. We humbly request your permission to—"*

She conceded the point, indicating with a bob of her head and a wry smile that he need not proceed further with his fanciful conversation. They could not ask *that* of Thorncombe's new mistress. The implication that some disgraceful revelation would follow upon the discovery of whatever had been cast away and since hunted for so covertly by Conroy was too grossly palpable. They had been commissioned to find a murder, not expose a family scandal.

"No, the Challoners are a proud race," Matthew said. "Only if Mistress Frances' curiosity is greater than her sense of family honor would she consent to such an undertaking."

"Or her passion for truth, should curiosity fail," Joan said.

But both Joan and Matthew knew that neither truth nor curiosity nor the two in consort would prevail over family honor.

They seemed to have arrived at another impasse.

21

THAT night Jack Wylkin made three trips from Stafford Hall to the dam, bearing on each trip two twenty-pound kegs of black powder hoisted on his shoulders like a peddler's pack. He had secured the powder at no little expense and trouble from an unscrupulous captain who would sell anything for money; but it was good-quality powder, purloined from Her Majesty's own navy vessels and guaranteed by these virtues to blow the dam to hell.

He made the difficult journey on foot, for there was no horse trail, only the streambed with its puny trickle, sharp rocks, dead branches, and pits—all navigated with great difficulty because of a teasing moon that would appear and then disappear behind swollen clouds.

But Wylkin performed his labor cheerfully and would not have complained even if he had had a companion to complain to. For already in his mind's eye he could envision the catastrophe his labors would produce—an explosion of fire and smoke and a deafening noise that would release the contents of Challoner's vile lake down their true and natural course, making accessible at the same time Challoner's treasure isle.

Wylkin contemplated this outcome with great pleasure. His motive was more than greed. He was an arsonist at heart.

With the care of one long experienced in such work, he placed the kegs at intervals at the base of the dam to maximize the effect of the blasts. The last two of the kegs he decided to hold in reserve, concealing them in a shallow cave just above the dam.

The dam had been well constructed but was in need of repair. Time had violated its integrity, and all along its foundations an ominous seepage could be detected. All of this was to the good, Wylkin thought. He took a length of fuse and linked the kegs, giving special attention to the fuse's end, which he splayed into a downy tassel to improve its ignition capabilities. Then, as a precaution to premature discovery, he hid the kegs beneath loose rock and uprooted bushes.

The plot, to his mind, had the simplicity of a child's game; for he was preparing for a special moment to come. He would set fire to the powder on the wedding night of the Challoner bride, when bride, bridegroom, and guests, besotted with wine and merriment, would be asleep, or, if by some miracle awake, think the blasts the roll of distant thunder.

Thereafter, if Wylkin did his work aright, Challoner's lake would drain like a pierced carbuncle. Come daylight, Wylkin, his master, and other stout fellows secured for the service, would walk to the island and appropriate with impunity whatever treasure was concealed there, fair field and no favor.

That arson was a capital crime meant nothing to Wylkin; he would have received as severe a sentence for stealing a loaf of bread or a good round of cheese.

An important element in his plan was Una, whom he required as accomplice in his demolitions, for through her he might learn at what moment it was safe to proceed. And for that reason he regretted now that he had lost his temper with her at their last interview. Reconciliation would be difficult, given his harsh words. He would have to resume the guise of the jolly wooer, swallow his hateful language as a bitter pill to a desirable end. Could it be done? His growing excitement at the prospect of laying his hands on Challoner booty had given sexual conquest a lower priority than it normally enjoyed in his mind. That morning, before leaving Stafford Hall, he had found Alice Stafford's subtle hints and flirting tiresome. Had she offered herself to him stark-naked in her husband's bed, with the air perfumed like a rose garden and the lascivious plunkings of a lute to accompany their coupling, still he would have leapt over her body to deliver the powder to its destination.

He slept for a few hours on the hillside, with only his heavy cloak and cap for warmth, but he slept dreamlessly and without thought for the hard earth or the fearsome loneliness of the hills. When dawn came, he proceeded to the castle.

He knew at this time of the morning Una would be in the kitchen. He lurked around the wellhouse until she came out on the kitchen porch and stood there in the crisp morning air shielding her eyes. Did she know he was there somehow? He didn't wonder long. He whistled a string of notes they had agreed on as a signal. At once she lifted her head. He knew she had heard. She began to walk toward his hiding place.

He showed himself briefly and then moved quickly back into the trees, trusting that she would follow. He walked for a dozen or more paces before looking behind him. When he turned he was not surprised to see her following, like a sheep following the bellwether.

At their usual trysting place he stopped and watched her come through the trees toward him. He could see that her face was slightly altered in its expression. She seemed neither angry nor expectant, and this puzzled him. Suddenly he realized how much he despised her for her docility, and in so doing he remembered what he had called her—fool, stupid bitch, *old* woman—words that would have instilled undying hatred and loathing in a soul of any pluck, hateful words deserving no forgiveness in this world or the next.

He greeted her uncertainly, watching her face. She returned the greeting and kept on coming until she threw her arms around his waist and kissed his cheek as though there had never been strong words between them.

He was amazed. Dumbfounded. And had he not been so convinced that her pliancy was a testimony to the defect in female nature, he would have been more suspicious than he was.

But he suspected nothing and immediately began to press on her his need for a trustworthy friend in a daring enterprise. He told her that their hour of opportunity had come, that soon the both of them would be rich and, yes, free to marry. She listened without expression or comment, staring at him as she might have stared at a perfect stranger. Sensing her sudden unresponsiveness and more than ever aware of how greatly he was in need of an ally at the castle, Wylkin stooped to beg her pardon for his ill-considered words during their last meeting.

"Take it as Jack Wylkin's anger, and not as Jack Wylkin himself. I was possessed of a terrible demon of choler. Forgive me for it."

Her lips curled into a thin smile; she did not speak.

"Still angry, are you? I tell you, I need you in this," he declared with unfeigned urgency. "Your master's treasure stands within our reach. But we must act in concert."

"What will you have me do?" she asked.

Taking her answer as a sign that greed was an adequate route to regaining her goodwill and cooperation, Wylkin now placed his plan before her in its fullness. "Of risk there is but little," he said. "Only signal to me when the castle is asleep so that I may work my mischief in the greatest privacy and half my gain shall be yours. The best is that your part will never be known."

"But is the plan not dangerous?" she said, still seeming reluctant. But the expression in her eyes had changed; he had noticed that, and in the change he felt she was yielding. Hopeful, he cast his repentent manner aside and played the wooer again. "Come," he said. "Say you will do it and we will seal the bargain with our lips."

"And then," she said, looking up at him with mild eyes, "seal it with our bodies too?"

The smile came again. It was a smile he had not seen before. She seemed somehow a different woman and the novelty fired his lust. He reached out to grab the fullness of her body and was delighted when she yielded to him without further protest or reprimand. He kissed her neck and shoulders. She laughed a little as he took her, and this he interpreted as a sign of her pleasure in his lovemaking, for he could not imagine that she would have anything to mock.

Una did not find her lovemaking with Jack Wylkin unpleasant, even though she had resolved to betray him. In her mind, he had now already received the reward for his treachery, and somehow they were even again, quite without his knowing it. Her love for the man had been displaced first by a desire for cruel revenge, and now by a kind of pity for one who stumbles forward in blind ignorance of a pit everyone can plainly see.

When their rendezvous had concluded and he had given her instruction, he kissed her good-bye and said, "When we meet again we will quarrel only as to which of us is the richer by this deed."

He told her to take care. "You are an engineer now, a soldier of the wars. Go into battle with a high heart."

She assured him that her heart had never been so high. She told him, too, savoring the irony of the double meaning, that she had him to thank for the joy she felt.

He grinned with self-satisfaction at her words, and by his expression and general manner she knew he suspected nothing. What fools men are, she thought. How easily deceivers are themselves deceived.

When he was out of her sight she went directly to the house and told the steward and housekeeper everything—about Stafford, about the treasure, and about Wylkin's plan to discover and snatch the same while all were asleep. She asked forgiveness for her deception—her feigned ignorance of their language—and her complicity with the man who now had earned her hatred.

"A bold plot," Joan exclaimed, astonished at the audacity of Stafford's servant.

Matthew echoed his wife's sentiment. "Many thanks to you for revealing this. But tell me, for what reason would you betray your lover?"

Una's eyes filled with tears. "He did not love me. He said he did, but he loved only the treasure I was to bring him."

"I believe you," Joan said, taking the Irishwoman's hands. "And forgive you also."

Una went her way, beginning for the first time to regret a little what she had done. Yet she knew recanting was too late now. She scorned herself for her lack of resolve, but then she remembered what Wylkin had called her in his choleric fit and she realized his eager embraces and honeyed words had no more substance than breath upon cold glass.

As soon as Una had departed, Matthew and Joan commenced an earnest discussion of this new information and what use they might make of it.

"So it is *treasure* then for which Conroy searched."

"Robbed from churches and Catholic households—a dishonorable kind of soldiery, if you ask me," Matthew said.

"So much for Sir John's reputation—a thing of naught."

"The worst will be his failure to give the Queen her due," Matthew added. "Which makes him traitor as well as brigand. Had this been known, he would have been tried and convicted for his crimes. He would have died upon the gibbet rather than drowned in the lake."

"Our immediate purpose should be to prevent Wylkin's stratagem," Joan said with resolve.

"I've been giving that some thought," Matthew said. "Especially in light of our discussion yesterday. Why prevent him at all?"

"What! Allow the man to drain the lake and find the treasure?'' Joan wondered if Matthew's illness had not also affected his good judgment.

''Let Wylkin do his work,'' he repeated.

''Husband, you confound me!''

Matthew laughed, ''*Think*, Joan. Did we not lament that the lake could not be drained?''

''So we did.''

''Consider this, then. Wylkin shall have his signal as he supposes, fire his powder, unleash the flood, but it is we who shall have the element of surprise.''

''And Mistress Frances' permission will not be sought.''

''Nor needed,'' he answered.

22

IT was a warm day for so late in the year and the windows of the Privy Gallery at Whitehall stood open to let in the mild air. The Queen, dressed in a white taffeta gown lined with scarlet and ornamented with pearls and rubies, was seated in private conference with Master Secretary Cecil. In her lap was a little volume of Seneca, whose Stoic doctrines gave her much satisfaction in her days of pain and suffering. Her attendants, her Maids of Honor, stood at a respectful distance, for few at court enjoyed the intimacy with the Queen that Cecil did.

During a long morning they had talked of weighty matters of state. *She* had talked, rather, for it was Cecil's special wisdom to be ever the listener, to advance his own ideas with proper caution. This strategy the Queen well understood. And encouraged. For at her advanced age and in her weakened condition she was impatient with debate.

In due course, their conversation came around to the Challoner drowning, as Cecil was sure it would sometime before his dismissal.

"The girl is gone from the court, you know," the Queen

said. "Off to be married to Thomas Cooke. Why, she must be in Derbyshire by now. And no word as yet from Constable Stock?"

"None, Majesty," Cecil said regretfully. He took the liberty of reminding the royal mistress of the terms of their wager. Stock had a month to discover the murderer and return. "We lack a good week or more of that," he said.

In fact, he had hoped she had forgotten the wager. But that was a foolish hope. Although she was old, her ability to recall minute details of earlier conversations was uncanny. And he knew that she was much too fond of gambling to overlook the forty crowns hanging in the balance.

"A few days," she said dismissively. "Fie upon *them*! What can be done in so little time that has not been done in a fortnight? You've lost, Robin. You and your constable of Chelmsford. Now pay up!"

She stretched out an open palm as though she expected him to have the money ready. And for a moment he really believed by the severity of her expression that he must surrender it.

"But, Your Majesty," he protested good-humoredly, "surely you won't violate the terms of the wager. We agreed to a month, and though nothing was put in writing, yet it was spoken by the Queen's lips. I *do* trust Your Majesty will keep your royal word, for a Queen's word is a sacred thing."

She laughed at this adroit response and slowly withdrew her hand. By which gesture he knew his money was safe. At least until the end of the month's time. But she continued to press him about the matter. Why had Stock not written? What *was* going on in Derbyshire?

"The Chelmsford constable's long silence betokens failure—or worse," she said. She waited for an answer.

It was not soon in coming. Cecil was loath to admit failure—on his own part or on the part of his servants or agents. It was not the forty crowns. That was a mere pittance to one as rich as he. He knew that the Queen had been skeptical of Matthew Stock's abilities from the time she gazed upon his plain, simple countenance. Her skepticism had egged Cecil on, made him bold in wagering. His pride was at stake—and perhaps more. The Queen's confidence was mixed up in it, too.

He looked at his royal mistress and noticed how frail she seemed. Her cheeks, heavily rouged to disguise the pallor of her recent indisposition, seemed as thin as parchment. Her eyes were tired, as though she had strained them by reading in poor light. Her jeweled hand shook with a palsy. Surely old age was no jest. It came to fell both King and clown and would be at his side soon enough.

He had to agree that Matthew Stock's silence did not bode well. And yes, perhaps he had erred in judgment.

He deftly changed the subject, reminding her that she had promised an audience within the hour to the French ambassador.

"Ah yes," she said without enthusiasm. "The Frenchman again."

With a subtle motion of her hand she made him understand their interview was at an end. Yet she had one final word on the Challoner business.

"Don't worry yourself, Robin, about the Chelmsford constable and his wife. Sir John may have not been murdered after all. I do believe that's Mistress Frances' opinion now. Or perhaps thoughts of wedded bliss have given a large draught of the river Lethe to her gloomier meditations."

Cecil expressed no opinion himself of this interpretation. He did acknowledge, with an elegant, congratulatory bow of the head, that Frances Challoner had made a very good match for herself. He did not know Thomas Cooke, but he knew the father and he knew that no apple falls far from the trunk.

"I made the match," the Queen said with a toss of her head. "Frances is full of pluck, bright and winsome. Indeed, in her I see my own youth, for I was very like her in countenance and, yes, an orphan too."

"But not husbanded," Cecil remarked teasingly.

She put the Seneca she had cradled in her lap aside and rose, taking Cecil's hand for support. He gave her his arm and the Queen and her Principal Secretary walked to the end of the gallery. "Never husbanded," she said, but whether with regret or satisfaction, Cecil could not tell. "To have been husbanded would have been to be mastered. I have allowed one master of my soul, Jesus Christ my Redeemer. But I would have none for my body. Frances will have a master for her body and I wish her joy of him. He seems a stalwart, promising youth. Although he's a second son, there's grit in him. He'll advance and be advanced."

"With royal approval I am sure he will advance," Cecil said.

"I only pray he's gentle with her. For she's a sweet child and I would fain see her free from suffering."

"Are you not worried about her going to Thorncombe?" he asked.

They had come to the end of the gallery. Her attendants began to advance toward her but she warned them off with a stern regard. She was not yet finished with Cecil.

"I am worried a little," she admitted. "Not that I fear for her life from a murderer, but because I fear for her. *You* will think, Robin, that what I've just said makes no sense whatsoever. That I am an addled old woman."

He started to protest, but she put her hand to his lips to silence him.

"I have an uneasy feeling about Frances. I blessed her marriage. I encouraged her to advance the date, thinking it would rid her of her morbid preoccupations. If anything happens to the child, I will not forgive myself."

"What would Your Majesty have me do?"

"Send someone after her. Someone you can trust. Let him be no mere servant but a person of authority and intellect. Someone with a strong arm."

"A soldier? One of the captains?"

"Not necessarily," she said. "Just so he is no ordinary constable."

"Very well, Your Majesty," Cecil said, bowing low but feeling the sting of her implied rebuke.

"And, Robin."

"Yes, Majesty?"

"I will gladly risk the loss of twenty crowns we wagered but not the loss of Frances Challoner. If he whom you send has the least inkling of murder having been committed at Thorncombe, I will have Frances fetched home straightway to London. As I said, if anything happens to that girl because of arrangements I have made on her behalf I will never forgive myself—nor you, either, for it was you who recommended Matthew Stock to this post, wherein he has so plainly failed."

"Yes, Majesty."

"Have him whom you send inform Stock he has not pleased me in this."

"I will so instruct him."

The Queen's attendants now were summoned to her side and Cecil watched while they led her away. He could hear the Queen's voice chiding the women for something, but the substance was lost in the midst of the other voices. It did not matter. He had been given his dismissal—and his instructions.

Later, riding through the crowded London streets in his coach, Cecil mulled over both. Feeling the burden of Matthew Stock's failure himself, he tried to think whom he might send to Derbyshire. The Queen was right, of course. No use sending some hanger-on, overjoyed to travel at the Queen's expense. A dependable sort was what was needed, someone keen of mind and discerning of falsehood, should it be presented in the guise of truth. Someone like Matthew Stock.

There was his own personal secretary. No, *he* wouldn't do. There was too much work for him in London. Besides, the man detested travel. There was Sir John Harington, the Queen's own godson. A witty fellow, with experience in Ireland, but perhaps too witty for his own good. He had, too, barely escaped disgrace in Essex's rebellion. No, Harington wouldn't do, either.

By the time his coach had stopped at his own residence on the Strand, Cecil had considered and dismissed from consideration twenty candidates for the assignment. Some were clearly deficient in some requisite, others merely unavailable for service. By the time he was being made comfortable in his own apartment by his servant, he had concluded there was but one person to send. Cecil needed a change from the smoky, unhealthy London air. The Queen had given him leave to send whomever he chose. Could he presume that included himself?

When, within the next hour, Matthew Stock's letter arrived (unexplicably delayed), recounting the horrible murder of a female servant of the castle, Cecil was fully resolved.

Frances Challoner had indeed been gone from London for three days, but she had not yet reached Thorncombe. Her journey had been troubled by minor accidents and consequent delays: a broken axle near Coventry; a misdirection farther on that took them thirty miles out of their way, to the great embarrassment of their guide, who was beside himself with anxiety that his master would flog him for distressing the ladies; and by Priscilla's severe stomach cramps, so severe that she thought she would die from them.

"It must have been something I ate," she complained when she had recovered sufficiently and they could continue their journey.

Nor were the roads a help. For the rains of late autumn had set in, and the earth was soggy and the skies so dreary that both young women felt an oppression of spirit that made them poor traveling companions.

And the worst, for Frances, was the night before their arrival. They had stopped in Buxton, it being too dark to continue to the castle that day. Their inn was small but clean and comfortable. But there she experienced another disturbing dream. She dreamed she was in what must have been the master's chamber in the castle. She could tell because of its size, its fine furnishings, its massive hearth with the Challoner arms carved in the stone. She was sitting in bed, wearing a loose-fitting nightgown of silk. Her body was sweetly scented with rosemary and lavender and other perfumes; her flaxen hair was loose about her alabaster shoulders. It was her wedding night, and he for whom she waited was her bridegroom.

In her dream she was very excited but apprehensive, too. Her hands trembled on the bedcovers.

Thomas did seem to dawdle. Whatever *was* he doing? she wondered impatiently. She could hear voices in distant rooms—whisperings, footfalls, knockings, giggles. These she ignored, never wondering at the incongruity of such an apparent company of folk in her castle.

Finally, when she was as close to despair as sleep from waiting, a soft knocking came at the door, and she heard a voice say her name. "Frances?"

"Come," she said, alert and quaking.

Her chamber was very dark, the fire having burned low on the hearth, and she could not clearly distinguish her bridegroom's face. But she knew it was Thomas. Her heart raced and she almost swooned with happiness as he knelt down by the bed. She shut her eyes and leaned her head back on the bolster, sensing him arching over her. She felt his lips touch hers, his hand upon her cheek, a gentle, slow caress of admiration and devotion.

But no! The lips were hard lips and the touch was cold and the breath upon her face was foul like the odor of wet ashes when the rain had run down the chimney.

After the revulsion, the disgust, she felt offense—offense at his inexplicable delay, offense at his failure to sweeten so foul a breath with cloves or mint. She opened her eyes to rebuke him for his discourtesy. Did he think because God and law had made her his, that he could treat her as chattel?

It was then she saw her visitor was not Thomas.

The thing was in burial weeds, misshapen and ghastly to look upon. And the face was the very image of Death, a grinning skull.

She awoke in a sweat as cold as the bony hand that had caressed her cheek, struggling for air and with a heavy weight upon her chest, as though the creature of her nightmare, invisible to the waking eye, lay there still, sprawled upon her like an incubus of old legend, satisfying its lust upon her white, vulnerable body.

The next day, the day of their arrival at Thorncombe, Frances did not tell her dream to Priscilla. Two dreams of a death's-head within the week? She would not have to pay tuppence to a cunning woman in Cow Lane to tell her what *that* portended.

"I hope your thoughts are pleasant ones," Priscilla said, noticing Frances' silence.

"I am thinking," Frances lied, "of how sadly beautiful the country is."

Priscilla said she had traveled this road before. "Soon there will be but few habitations and only hill, wood, and open sky."

"You have seen Thorncombe before, then?" Frances asked, turning sideways to her companion.

"Never, but I suppose it to be a fitting place for your marriage. You need but a poet to celebrate your solemnities with an epithalamium or two."

"Pray God it be fit," Frances said, shuddering.

Priscilla seemed to notice Frances' reaction. "Why shouldn't it be?"

Priscilla then jokingly accused Frances of having cold feet about her marriage, but Frances paid only half attention to her friend. The road was rougher now; the coach labored over the ruts and bumps of a steep incline, and the coachman's whip was in constant use to urge the team of horses to greater effort. Then suddenly the coach came to a stop and, above the angry shouts of the driver telling someone to make way, Frances heard the anguished screams of an injured animal. She lifted the window flap to see what had caused the stop.

A little way ahead, a cart lay overturned in the middle of the road. A man she took to be a farmer by his ragged coat and cap stood looking helplessly at the beast that had pulled the load and now struggled on the ground, kicking its hind legs against the overturned cart. Another man, perhaps the first's son, stood by also watching the scene. The coach jolted forward, pulled over to the side of the cart, and Frances had a full view of the accident.

The horse had apparently broken its forelegs in the fall. Its remaining vitality was now being expended in its hindquarters in a futile effort to stand. The horse's eyes were wide and bright with fear, and its screams were terrible. Frances leaned out the window and told the coachman to give what aid he could, but the farmer, overhearing, turned to her and said, with a brutal insolence that shocked her, that no help was needed, as though he and his son and his fallen horse were above her charity.

The footman climbed down off the top of the coach mumbling to himself, and with pistol in hand he went up to the farmer. Frances watched as the two men came to some agreement and then the footman went over to the injured animal and put the muzzle of the pistol to the horse's head.

She jumped at the loud report and turned away quickly—but not before she glimpsed the great splash of blood and the mortal shudder of the horse.

The footman fired again, but Frances did not see. She had buried her face in her hands. She heard the footman climbing back atop the coach and only in her mind's eye saw the white, accusing faces of the farmer and his son.

"You shouldn't have looked," Priscilla said prudently.

Frances heard the driver command the team, heard a sharp crack of his whip; the coach lurched forward and resumed speed.

23

THE coach carrying Mistress Frances Challoner and her companion came into view, and Matthew and Joan, standing somewhat apart from the other servants in the castle courtyard, continued to debate what Matthew should say to the new mistress of the house now that the necessity of a report was beyond question.

"She must be told of Aileen Mogaill," Joan advised in a whisper. "Not to tell her would itself be criminal."

"Perhaps she does know already," Matthew whispered back. "I wrote of it in my letter to Sir Robert."

"Which letter pray God he received," Joan responded doubtfully. The silence from London since their arrival had been ominous, even though Cecil had warned them not to expect official letters. She forced a smile for the occasion's sake now that the coach was coming to a halt just a dozen feet away, but she felt no joy in her heart for the young woman whom Joan could only deem unfortunate to have come into such a bloody inheritance.

"All evidence points to Conroy. That I'll say to her," Matthew said resolutely.

The rub, Joan reflected in these final moments before Mistress Frances' face appeared in the coach window, was that evidence of Conroy's guilt was small. A brute, prowler, and treasure hunter—Conroy was undoubtedly all that; but that he was a murderer, too, did not necessarily follow. Besides, Joan retained the strong impression that the Irishman was dead—as dead as Aileen Mogaill or Sir John. And, for all she knew, dead by the same hand that had killed them!

Mistress Frances waved in greeting and Joan and Matthew waved back. Matthew murmured, hopefully, "The wedding will put her in a better mood, I warrant."

But Joan's returning glance—there was no more time for words—was not intended to affirm her husband's optimism. Joan had grave doubts in her heart and a multitude of unanswered questions in her head. No pessimist herself, yet she was of no mind to temporize the facts, much less prevaricate. Blood had been shed at Thorncombe, blood shed by an inhabitant or neighbor of the house and not by some passing stranger, as Matthew had told her Edward Bastian had suggested, or by ghostly agency, as the Fludds supposed. Surely more blood would flow. The facts were horrifying and threatening, mind-numbing to contemplate, so that she wondered that she had had the hardihood to stay in the castle so long. No, Joan was convinced Mistress Frances must be told—and told the unvarnished truth.

As for the wedding—it was scheduled for that very week—Joan thought the timing most ill advised. It was not that she doubted the bridegroom's qualifications, or that she revered the proverbial wisdom that those who married in haste might repent at leisure. And certainly Mistress Frances was old enough to consider and consent. It was, rather, that the circumstances of doubt and violence in the castle could only poison the feast, and that, to Joan's mind, was the *least* harm that might befall it. After all, when she had married Matthew, her mind, properly, had been fixed on marriage, not murder; she had delighted in the newfound paradise of their common bed, not agonized with visions of decapitated corpses, ghostly legends, and ancient family curses. Yet the letter she had received from Mistress Frances a week earlier had made the headstrong young woman's determination perfectly clear. The wedding date had been announced to family and friends, the precise day had been named, the minister's services had been secured, and all requisite documents and deeds had been engrossed. Most importantly, the advancement of the wedding had received the Queen's special blessing and commendation.

Joan's only consolation among these worries was that the coming event and attendant festivities had put a better face on the grim old castle. The new house had been cleaned from top to bottom. The banqueting hall, before as uninviting as an abandoned barn and as filthy, now had been redeemed by a veritable forest of boughs, mixed in with brave martial banners untrunked for the nonce and draped where before only spiders spun their silken habitations.

Then all pondering stopped, and, with a graceful curtsy, Joan welcomed the new mistress of Thorncombe to her domain.

"Let me see if I understand you aright," Mistress Frances said when later in the day Matthew and Joan had opportunity to speak to her privily. "This Irish captain and manservant to my late uncle drowned him for his treasure, or knowledge of where it was hid. Then, shortly before your arrival, the same man murdered a young servingwoman of the castle, who you think may have been his confederate."

"There may have been a falling-out," Matthew conjectured. "Or Conroy, having discovered the treasure's whereabouts, or so he believed, then killed her for her share."

"Which treasure was concealed on the island in the lake?"

"So Conroy believed."

Matthew provided a shortened version of his own voyage to the island. He told her of observing Conroy's digging and assured her that the Irishman had found nothing.

"So there may have been no treasure at all."

"That's possible," Joan said, thinking at the same time

that there remained some mystery about the island, even though it might not be a treasure.

"The treasure consisted of Irish plate, jewels—all pillaged from Irish Catholics in the wars," Matthew explained. "Or so rumor alleges."

The allegation did not seem to faze the accused man's niece. Preoccupied, she sat erectly in a chair by the window overlooking the courtyard while the slanting afternoon sun streamed into her lap. There was a short silence, then she sighed heavily and said, as though she were coming back to the subject of her uncle's crimes from some other, more personal, concerns: "Whatever my uncle may have done, he has doubtlessly paid for his sins with his most treacherous murder. You are in a better position than I, Master Stock, to assess the strength of your contention that this Michael Conroy drowned my uncle for his treasure and cruelly murdered his former helpmate. All seems within the scope of belief, and so I fear his menace. He has disappeared, you say, but there's no proof he's left the neighborhood?"

Matthew hesitated before answering, then spoke the blunt truth Joan had advised: "Conroy has disappeared. I have no evidence he has left the neighborhood."

"Why, then he's still at large and dangerous to me and mine!" she exclaimed, a sudden wild look in her eyes.

Matthew assured her she should have every protection. "It's a mad murderer indeed who would invade a house full of guests," he observed.

"But after the wedding, when the guests have gone home? Am I to fear for my life and the lives of my servants until this dreadful person is arrested?"

To this Matthew and Joan could give no answer, and the young woman stared dolefully from the window as though the solution to her quandary were etched upon the glass.

Mistress Frances had arrived on a Tuesday, the wedding was scheduled for Friday, and in the hectic interim, Joan, still functioning as housekeeper, had precious little time for contemplating mysteries, for there was still much to do to make the castle ready for the guests, many of whom would be lodged there for the better part of a week. These included the bridegroom's immediate family; fifteen to twenty other persons allied to the Cookes by blood or business; and a half-dozen friends of the groom—young bachelors from the Middle Temple. The sheer number of servants alone was not inconsiderable.

Along with the gentlefolk were a large number of guests not to be housed at the castle because they lived within a day's journey or because they lacked the requisite social standing. The latter category included Buxton burghers and their wives, officials of the town and their wives, several local clergymen, none of whom was married, the local justice of the peace, his secretary, and several other dignitaries and lesser dignitaries. All these, too, were accompanied by servants, who would be feasted in the courtyard and on the greensward along with most of the local villagers, who would regard a share of the feast as their traditional right.

The Staffords, to no one's surprise, had not been invited.

To help serve this great company of guests, the Fludds had been recalled to duty, and many of the Challoner tenants and their wives had been impressed as doormen, waiters, drawers, and maids. Una, half hysterical for worry as to how she would prepare food for such a multitude, had been given the assistance of three cooks and four bakers—all very experienced, according to Moll, who had been put in charge of recruitment because of her superior knowledge of the local work force—and a dozen scullions of such villainous countenance that Joan swore they had been snatched that very day from the Buxton almshouse.

Meanwhile, Matthew was no less occupied. To his lot had fallen the provisioning of the castle, the supervision of the carts that daily brought foodstuffs from the village and from Buxton, the slaughtering of cattle and sheep, the securing of fish and fowl, and the procurement of the great quantities of wine and ale that on no account could fall short of what was needed for fear that bad luck should haunt the wedded couple ever after.

In all this bustle, however, Joan thought in her periodic interviews with the mistress of Thorncombe that the shadow of apprehension had not passed—indeed it seemed to have lengthened and deepened as the hour of the wedding approached, if Joan was any judge. Since, to Mistress Frances' way of thinking, the alleged perpetrator of the Challoner murders remained at large, Joan could understand this apprehension even though Joan herself continued to be dubious about Conroy's guilt. Indeed, she and Matthew had had several heated discussions upon this very point.

Matthew, of course, had informed Thomas Cooke of Conroy's history, but the pleasant young man had hardly seemed to believe it. "What," he had declared with a broad smile rich in incredulity, "my sweet Frances' uncle drowned by a manservant! A tale hardly to be credited. This talk of treasure likewise, Master Stock, as though Sir John had been a crusty old pirate instead of a soldier of distinction and valor. Yet if there's danger, my brothers and I will see to it quickly enough. An Irishman, you say, named Conroy? We'll give him a taste of good English steel if he sets a foot within the park pale, mark my words!"

Joan overheard this declaration and dismissed Master Cooke's crowing as a young man's right. His breadth of shoulder and length of shank gave some reason, however, to believe it more. Later, she told Matthew how worried she was about the bride. She seemed so wan, as though tormented by more than the thought of a murderer at large.

But Matthew said he believed all would be well. He speculated that Conroy had fled to Ireland. "Next week, the nuptials done, we'll take horse for London. There'll be ample time to arrive within the month's limit and satisfy the Queen's conditions. Surely she will be pleased with our discovery of Sir John's murderer, even though I cannot present her with the guilty man himself."

"I pray Her Majesty will not be overly demanding of evidence," Joan replied pointedly, and then moved away, for she and Matthew had covered this matter time and time again and as yet had reached no mutual agreement. In her heart she felt there were cracks in Matthew's theory. Cracks? She thought them, rather, great trenches! Instinctively, she felt Mistress Frances shared her doubt.

Just after dawn on the wedding day, Cecil arrived quite unexpectedly at Thorncombe, bedraggled but in good humor despite having ridden half the night, and boasting of his mount that had brought him so many miles in good order. He explained his presence by saying he had some state business in the neighborhood, which no one questioned. Indeed, the prospective bride and groom were so honored by the great man's presence that he was immediately invited to stay for the ceremony and however longer he should wish. With Cecil had come his manservant Sears and two gentlemen named Moppitt and Hargrove, whose houses he had lodged in along the way and who had agreed to keep him company for fellowship's sake.

Joan and Matthew were as greatly surprised as anyone in the castle at Cecil's arrival, for they had not expected to see him again until they returned to London. But they were very pleased, too.

They conversed privately in the second-largest bedchamber of the new house, a room previously occupied by Thomas Cooke's parents but gladly relinquished by the same for the honor of having so distinguished a guest as Master Secretary Cecil.

"It does my heart good to see you well," Cecil declared, when the door was shut behind them and Sears had been sent on some quickly contrived errand belowstairs. "Your letter, Matthew, I received belatedly the day I left London. I came posthaste, both at Her Majesty's command and out of my own concern. What is this lurid business you wrote of—headless serving girls?"

Matthew gave a more complete account of Aileen Mogaill than he had presented in his letter. He also told Cecil about Conroy, how he believed him to have been the murderer of Aileen and Sir John, the island treasure being the link.

"The man is in custody, I hope," said Cecil.

"At large, sir."

"Or dead," Joan couldn't help adding. The remark, which Cecil invited her to explain, gave her occasion to tell of her discovery of the bloodstains on the stable floor.

Cecil listened attentively while she told her story, but he neither affirmed nor denied her conclusion that Conroy might be dead. Cecil seemed far more interested in the argument for his guilt, for which he turned again to Matthew.

Matthew summarized his own experiences, his journey to the island, his conflict with Stafford and Wylkin. He told him about Wylkin's plot to destroy the dam and drain the lake, and about his own plan to let Wylkin do it. Cecil approved.

"I agree in letting this varlet do his worst at the dam and thereby damn himself. Then we'll see what turns up on the lake bottom or on this island you speak of. Treasure confiscated from the enemies of the Queen is the Queen's property and must be secured at all costs. I'm sorry to hear an officer of Her Majesty abused his office so abominably. As for these conflicting opinions regarding Conroy's guilt, I can say only that while there is not as much evidence as one would wish, there is sufficient circumstance to warrant his arrest—if we can find him." Then Cecil said to Joan, "You may be right, too, about him being dead. But until we know for sure, possess the *corpus delicti*, as our learned lawyers say, we must assume otherwise and guard ourselves against further harm to members of the household."

Remembering that Cecil had said he had come upon the Queen's behest as well as his own inclination, Joan asked him to explain. Cecil's expression darkened; he stood and walked to the long lancet window. Looking out, he said, "The truth is that the Queen is most worried about Mistress Frances' welfare. She seems to have an unusual affinity for the girl."

"You related the contents of my letter to her, then?" Matthew asked, well understanding how the Queen might be disturbed if she knew what had transpired at the castle since their arrival.

"In truth, I did not communicate it," Cecil admitted.

"There was no time. Her Majesty's not pleased, Matthew. You must know that the Queen, for all her sterling virtues, is not the most patient of women. When two weeks passed without report, she assumed the worst. She doesn't understand that fruit such as you sought is not plucked from the wayside."

"The Queen *is* angry, then?" Joan said, fearing this was what Cecil was saying by indirection and feeling suddenly at fault for having been ill abed that week—a week lost to profitable investigation.

Cecil admitted it was true, but then he said more brightly, "But look how pleased she will be now—now that the murderer is known and the fullness of his perfidy. Why, she will have no cause to complain—or to fear for Mistress Frances."

"As long as we can provide ample defenses against Conroy," Matthew said.

A knocking came at the door. It was Sears, looking very anxious. Cecil, seeing the expression, asked at once what the matter was.

"It's a body, sir, nothing more nor less than a man with his head nearly severed. Some of the young gentlemen and friends of Master Cooke were swimming in the lake on a dare and found it."

Cecil said, "We'll have a look then at once! Come, Master Stock, you're still steward. Surely this discovery merits your attention as much as it does mine."

News of the body's discovery had quickly spread, and about a dozen of the wedding guests and a few servants had gathered at the shore to see it, although the female contingent stood a little farther off for decency's sake.

A way was made for Cecil through the onlookers, and Matthew and Joan followed. The body was sprawled face upward, with the arms extended at right angles to the trunk, and the head, nearly severed from the body, as Sears had reported, lolling against the right shoulder, so that the impression given was of a man crucified on an invisible cross.

The two boys who had found the body stood shirtless and shivering in the brisk air.

Joan glanced at the corpse and then joined the other women. A glance had been enough: the dead man was definitely Conroy. Neither his having been several days in the water nor wounded so viciously could obscure his identity—the brawny physique, the flaming red hair. Like Aileen Mogaill, whom Matthew was convinced Conroy had killed, Conroy had been overcome by a strength greater than his own. Only the thick musculature of the neck had preserved him from total dismemberment.

While Joan watched, and a greater crowd gathered, Cecil and Matthew talked to the boys who had found the body, speaking loudly enough so that she could hear. They were relatives of Thomas Cooke, distant cousins. The one had dared the other to swim in the lake and the dare had been accepted. One of them had tripped over the body while he was returning to shore and had reached down into the water to investigate the impediment. Having brought forth more than he had bargained for, he now swore he would never go near water again, not if he should hang for it.

Cecil gave orders that the local constable be summoned, although he wasn't to make inquiries until the next day. "The dead man will wait," Cecil said. Edward and several other servants were directed to find something to cover the corpse and in a few minutes they were returning with an old horse blanket of which they made a makeshift shroud. They picked up the body and carried it to the stable.

While this was being done, Matthew and Cecil walked over to where Joan was, and Matthew conceded it was Conroy who was dead. "Dead for several days, maybe a week."

"As I feared and hoped both," Joan said in response, keeping her voice low so that the other women couldn't hear. "It's well this lot has not heard of the Challoner ghost. The castle would be cleared in an hour, despite Mistress Frances' wedding."

"As it is, a blight will be put upon the feast, I warrant.

The corpse cannot be hushed up, as was Aileen's,'' Matthew said.

''You're both sure it's the Irishman?'' Cecil asked.

''Or his perfect twin,'' Matthew said, and Joan agreed.

''Mistress Frances will be relieved then, for her fear of the man was great,'' Cecil said.

Joan looked at her husband; it was clear he too saw the incongruity—the reason there was no occasion for rejoicing. She said, ''Conroy was murdered in the exact manner of Aileen Mogaill, which fact I take to mean a third party, as yet undetected, murdered them both. I've said it all along—we've been trailing a rabbit, not a fox.''

''The whole fabric is rent,'' Matthew lamented when he and Joan were alone again in their room.

''Perhaps only in part,'' Joan said, feeling as much vindication at having been proved right about Conroy as sympathy for Matthew's confusion and disappointment.

''What do you mean, 'in part'?''

''Well, *Edward*,'' she said, regretfully, for she remained fond of him and yet she could not stifle her suspicions. She was sure Conroy had been murdered upon his return from the island, sure that the blood on the stable floor had been his, sure that Edward had dissembled or been, at best, too casual in regard to the plain evidence to the eye. Then the murderer had dumped the body into the lake, hoping that it would never rise from its watery tomb. A nasty piece of work. What she could not conceive and therefore what hampered her enthusiasm for accusing Edward was why *he* should do such a thing—lie about the stains—perhaps even lie about the murder. *Could* it have been he?

She remembered his face when he looked into the wardrobe. A face as appalled by what he saw as surprised. She was convinced Edward was not the murderer.

''Mistress Frances must be told about his death too,'' Matthew said. ''If she's not already heard.''

''But what about Edward?''

"There's no time to talk to him now. Within an hour the wedding party will leave for the church."

"I'll tell Mistress Frances about Conroy," Joan said. "She's being dressed. No man will be allowed to come near her."

"As you wish," Matthew said, looking pleased to be relieved of the duty.

Joan was right about the difficulty in getting access to the bride. She was also right in supposing the word of the dead man had penetrated the group of women helping to fit Mistress Frances out. No one spoke of it but the bride and her attendants were visibly shaken. A pall had settled on them all: the murder, revolting in itself, had also been construed as the worst of omens.

Joan waited until the dressing was completed and she could speak to Mistress Frances alone. Then she told her the dead man was Conroy.

The revelation did nothing to reassure the young woman, who quickly inferred that Conroy had been the victim of some other malicious person. There was an expression of despair on her face.

"This doesn't mean there is any personal danger to *you*," Joan said in an effort to mitigate the effect of her announcement.

"I wish I could believe that," Mistress Frances said.

"Is it so beyond belief?" Joan asked.

Then Mistress Frances confessed that she had had disturbing dreams—three in all, each more horrible than that which went before. Joan urged her to tell them, assuring her that she would find in Joan a sympathetic listener.

The young woman looked away and stared into the middle distance; her brow furrowed as though she were experiencing some physical pain. "Each dream was a vision of assault upon my person, each set in this very place—either by the lake or within the castle walls. In the first I was seized by a dead man's hand, springing suddenly, to my surprise and horror, from the dismal waters themselves as I walked nearby. The second, more distressing than the first, showed me myself, ravished upon my wedding night by a creature from the grave. The last and most recent found me in a castle chamber, searching for something, I know not what. I saw a large chest which when opened revealed costly garments, all unfamiliar to me save one, my shift of Italian cloth that I did intend to please my bridegroom with upon my wedding night. I unfolded it carefully and found the bodice most bloody and shredded."

"These were terrible visions indeed," Joan murmured sympathetically. "I don't wonder that you are distressed."

Mistress Frances turned to look at Joan again. She said, "Pray speak the truth for love of me, Mistress Stock. Are these nocturnal visions a young bride's fears writ large upon the sleeping mind, to which I should give no credit? Or are they supernatural warnings I ignore at my peril? My heart tells me the latter is the case. What say you?"

Joan was too firm a believer in the power of dreams to reject them out of hand, and the visions that Mistress Frances had just related had that consistency of theme and tone that argued their validity as warnings.

"I believe," Joan said after a few moments of consideration, "that these dreams of yours are true cautions, given of heaven for soul and body's sake and not to be ignored. But of what *may* be, perhaps, not necessarily what *must*, and to ensure it is not otherwise than I have said, I and my husband, Sir Robert, and every brave man within these walls will protect you from what dangers these dreadful dreams betoken."

"Oh, you mustn't tell *them*," Mistress Frances said, a new alarm in her face. "I won't have my wedding day ruined or delayed. If death is my fate, then let it come. I will go down to the grave a married woman at least."

Joan chided her for such despair, telling her it was neither in accord with common sense nor with true religion. "It need not be as you fear. No guest will know, nor your bridegroom, if that's your wish. I repeat, the dreams you have experienced may bespeak possibilities rather than fate. Why, they may be sent from heaven for the very purpose of preserving your life! But you must do what reason bids. Protect yourself against the envisioned threat."

Mistress Frances was slow to reply to this counsel, but in the young woman's gaze Joan thought she saw more determination than fear. Mistress Frances was clearly a woman of courage, not because she was unafraid, but because despite her fear she would do her own will, danger notwithstanding, and her will was to marry Thomas Cooke.

"You may tell Sir Robert, and the others," Mistress Frances said at length, "but not Thomas. I pray you will not tell him of the dreams."

Joan gave her promise. Priscilla Holmes entered to inform the bride that her coach was ready, and Joan went to find Matthew, more concerned now than ever for Mistress Frances' safety, for she feared the dreams the young woman had had.

24

HALF past eleven of the castle clock, the weather fair and wholesome for November, the bridal party left for the village church, since the humble house of God had been the site of every Challoner marriage within living memory, and because the larger and finer edifice in Buxton was thought too far for the guests to travel. A gaily decorated coach led the procession, carrying the bride, her female attendants, and Priscilla Holmes as matron of honor. It was followed by another conveying the bridegroom and his parents. Thereafter, on horse, came Sir Robert, who had consented to give the bride away, and his gentleman friends Moppitt and Hargrove, and the other guests. Matthew and Joan, as befitted their station as servants, remained at Thorncombe to supervise the preparation of the wedding feast that would occupy the long afternoon and extend far into the night.

But before the wedding party set out, Joan had told both Matthew and Sir Robert about her conversation with Mistress Frances. Matthew had believed Joan's intuition about the dreams at once, but Cecil had been more skeptical, making light of dreams in general—and especially those of skitterish brides—but conceding that it was unwise to ignore any warning, no matter its source. He said he doubted there would be any grave danger on the wedding day, given the multitude in attendance. "Who would attempt a murder in so great a confluence of visitors, especially by one who had previously worked only by stealth?"

But with all due respect Joan reminded the Queen's Principal Secretary of the recent case of the assault upon the Queen at Bartholomew Fair, when the assailant had attacked in the face of an armed retinue and a press of thousands—all after a series of gross and secret murders!

Cecil granted her point, and in the few minutes before Cecil was to ride to the church they discussed plans for protecting Mistress Frances.

Within two hours' time, Joan could see from a window in the long gallery the wedding party returning—heard them before going to the window to confirm it, for the solemn procession that had left, depressed in spirit by the discovery of Conroy's corpse, now returned in a mood of raucous merrymaking as though nothing untoward had happened that morning. Behind the coaches and mounted party of distinguished guests came a disorderly rout of villagers dressed in plain homespun garb. They sang and chanted, and gave ample evidence of their readiness to celebrate, whatever the occasion might have been.

The bridal party came indoors and filed into the banqueting hall, where long trencher tables were already groaning under a rich assortment of meat, dainties, and drink. Outside on the greensward the tenants, their families, and the villagers were to be entertained under three brightly colored pavilions. The castle grounds were rapidly taking on the appearance of a rural fair.

The bride and groom, looking very merry, were seated at the head table with Sir Robert as the most illustrious guest on one side and the parents of the groom on the other. Joan observed that during the feast that followed Cecil never left the bride's side, except when she danced with her new husband, and that Masters Moppitt and Hargrove, Cecil's friends, hovered nearby, for Cecil had apprised them to some limited extent of his concern for the bride's safety. Matthew was constantly around, too, acting as chief butler and majordomo, and introducing the series of musicians, jugglers, and dancers that constituted the official entertainment. Their performances on the dias at the end of the hall were generally ignored, even though the applause following each act seemed thunderous no matter its quality.

During all these proceedings, Joan circulated between the hall and the kitchen to ensure the uninterrupted provisioning of the tables. But she never ceased to think of Mistress Frances' dreams, for coupled with her own vision and inklings, her reasonings and speculations, they made a powerful cause for concern.

Matthew, she had decided, had been right when he complained that Conroy's death had rent the fabric. The problem, she felt, was that Matthew's solution had been too easy. It had, like a poor job of weaving, merely intertwined a plenty of loose threads that gave way at the first proof of its strength. Now she saw her duty: to unravel the cloth and weave it right—and to do it before the murderer could strike again.

By early evening there was a lull in the eating but not in the drinking, and several of the servants who had surreptitiously sampled the abundant supply of wine having demonstrated their uselessness (and one sick unto death in the pantry!), Matthew had sent Cuth to find Edward and bring him indoors to assist with the serving. Matthew told Joan what he had done when she protested that Una was nearly exhausted and it was simply essential that she receive more help in the kitchen. She said, "Cannot Cuth Fludd give some help? I trust kitchen work is not beneath his dignity."

"I've sent him to find Edward for the same cause," Matthew said. "The service at table is slow, the guests continually call for more wine, and until the cellar is bare, they must be served."

Joan wondered if anyone had seen Edward since that

morning, and indeed, she had quite forgotten him herself, so occupied she had been with worry about Mistress Frances. She realized that the hostler remained their chief suspect, now that Conroy was dead.

"Surely the man knew he would be wanted," Matthew remarked with a mixture of disappointment and disapproval. "Where could he have gone?"

"Perhaps he's at the cottage looking after his father," Joan ventured to suggest. "Or perhaps he's fled, fearing that Conroy's death will be blamed on him. You know he was either dissembling or woefully simple about the bloody spot in the stable. Conroy's death confirms it."

"There may be another explanation," Matthew said, "which we can discover when we discover him."

Joan went into the kitchen to see what relief she could provide for Una. She was surprised to see Brigid there, clutching her baby to her and looking very distressed.

Brigid came up to Joan and said, "I can't find Edward. He's not come home. His father's gone, too. I fear something dreadful has happened."

Joan explained that no one had seen Edward since early that morning and that Cuth Fludd had been sent to find him only a few minutes before.

"He always comes home by this hour," Brigid said anxiously. "And while his father sometimes walks around the yard by himself, he rarely goes beyond call."

Joan explained apologetically that although she understood Brigid's worry, she could not leave her present duties to conduct a search for the young hostler or his father. "It's likely the two of them are together," Joan said. "Even now they may have returned to the cottage while you are here. Go home, Brigid. See if it isn't as I have said."

Joan watched worriedly as Brigid did as she had been advised, realizing the great sacrifice the young woman had made in coming to the castle—and with her child. Joan had a definite sense that Edward's disappearance betokened something dreadful, and she did not know what to think about the elder Bastian's behavior, for she had supposed him too infirm to ramble on his own.

Within the hour Cuth had returned to report that he had searched the stable and the grounds and could find Edward nowhere, nor had any of the servants celebrating on the greensward seen him. It was all a great mystery, Cuth said, and Moll, who had come into the kitchen to help Una, agreed, although she professed to have never trusted the holster from the day he was born, nor his father.

It was nearly midnight when the bride and groom rose to go, accompanied by howls of mock protest from the guests, who pleaded with them to stay and made many bawdy remarks that caused the bride to blush furiously. The groom, more than a little drunk, dug deep in his purse, drew forth a fistful of coins, and threw them across the table as a gratuity for the servants, upon which the servants breached decorum and began scrambling for the coins, to the great merriment of the guests.

By this time the feast was long past its prime, yet the celebration went on, the society resembling more now that of a tavern than a company of guests in a great house. Men and women who would not have willingly given each other the time of day now talked intimately, danced, and sang. As the bridal couple began to thread their way toward the door, they were followed by a file of the groom's friends and relations, several of the women of the company, and, of course, Moppitt and Hargrove, who continued to take their roles as bodyguards with grim seriousness, although both seemed as besotted as the groom and had lost their place of proximity to her whom they had been assigned to protect. Some of the guests, not content that the newlyweds should take their leave without a proper sending off, had secured pots and pans from the kitchen and now hurried in with the same instruments and in a riotous manner were treating them like drums and tabors, howling and shouting and making such a deafening racket that Joan thought she was in Bedlam with a troop of lunatics. Joan had attended many a country wedding—and her own to

Matthew twenty years before had not been without its predictable harassment of bride and groom—but she had never seen anything like this. It seemed incredible to her that a day that had begun on such a macabre note should end with such hysterical festivity. But then she remembered the bizarre stories of the plague years and how people then, despairing of survival, had eaten, drunk, and been merry on the very porches of the charnel house, their merriment fueled by unspeakable fear.

Joan's fear now was more a dull ache; she had no heart for merriment; it would cease soon—the bride and groom gone to bed, the guests, exhausted from their revelry, would follow. The castle would be quiet.

And the bridal couple would be alone.

It was strange, she thought at that moment, that she had not considered the dire implications of that fact earlier. Mistress Frances' protectors—Cecil, his friends, the great company of guests—would soon go their ways. Quickly. Her uneasiness grew into panic. If Mistress Frances' dreams had substance, did they not predict not only her murder but its very hour?

She elbowed her way through the crowded tables to find Matthew. She saw him among the groom's friends, who had formed themselves into a serpentine chain, each person's hands on the shoulder of him who came before. She realized now that while the banqueting hall had rung with celebration, the new house must have been virtually abandoned! Why, anyone might have entered unseen or unnoticed, stolen upstairs, and hidden himself, waiting for the revelry to cease and young Master Cooke and wife to come to bed.

But she saw that ahead of her the great dancing snake of guests following Mistress Frances had made its way through the kitchen and was into the new house. She followed quickly. Thomas Cooke and Mistress Frances had reached the top of the stairs and were looking down into a crowded, noisy throng, prevailing with them to be still. The young bridegroom's speech was slurred, his handsome face ablaze with a satisfied grin, but Mistress Frances, who clutched adoringly to his arm, looked yet more radiant, as though her past dreams had dissolved harmlessly in the bright moment of her present happiness.

Thomas Cooke's pleadings and threats having taken no effect, the groom's Templar friends, his tormentors and chiders before, now took it upon themselves to defend the stairs against further encroachments by other wedding guests. The bridal pair disappeared from sight and the little company of defenders of the couple's right to privacy challenged those below them to dare to cross the line. This offer was met with mockery from those who wanted to pursue the newlyweds to the very door of the nuptial chamber—if not to the marriage bed itself—which, their own upper chambers aswill with wine, they would certainly have done otherwise. They contented themselves, instead, to congregate in the hall, banging upon their pots and pans and making such a deafening din that Joan could hardly hear herself think.

She struggled to get to where Matthew stood smiling at the scene of misrule and shouted in his ear. Thrice she had to repeat herself, but Matthew was not slow to grasp her meaning. He told her he would go at once to find Cecil, that only the great knight's authority could penetrate the self-appointed guardians of the stairs, and even then he was not sure the "good tosspots united there" would let him pass.

But as she waited anxiously for Matthew to find Cecil, she saw Edward. He had come through the door and was staring around the packed, noisy hall as though looking for someone. She made her way toward him and asked where he had been the long day. His explanation was partially lost in the din of banging and shouting, but she was able to discern the words "father" and "lost" and she could read upon the handsome young man's face an expression of great concern. Yelling at the top of her voice, she expressed hers about the bride.

Edward glanced at the crowded stairhead and then back at her. He seemed to grasp her intent. "There's no time to wait for Sir Robert," he shouted. "There's another way to the chambers above."

Then, without further word, the hostler dashed out the door into the night.

Mistress Frances hardly noticed the uproar from downstairs, which might have served to represent a rout of black-faced hellions in an old moral play. They were her guests, deep in their cups. A good time was being had by all, and she herself was more than a little tempest-tossed. Her new husband had excused himself of a sudden to run to the adjoining chamber, where she could hear him throwing up in the chamber pot, and she began to giggle at the thought, for he had bragged all during the feast how he could hold his liquor, but she, who had matched him cup for cup by her last count, remained as sober as a judge. Suddenly a wave of dizziness overwhelmed her. She stumbled toward bed. Laid out, bless Priscilla's heart, was her fine nightgown, the bolster perfectly propped, flowers strewn upon the coverlet. She sat down on the bed, intoxicated as much by happiness as by wine.

She began to undress, fumbling and humming and anxious for Thomas to come, for surely she supposed he had recovered by now. Slipping into the nightgown, she went over to the cheval glass and admired her reflection; by candlelight her white skin showed to best advantage. She had never been so happy, not in all her years.

She brushed her hair, counting the strokes, waiting for Thomas to come.

But still he did not come; she called out his name. Below, the din continued. She was prompted to go find him, but then she remembered it was his place to come to her. She could not violate tradition.

She climbed into the bed, shuddering a little as her bare feet explored the lower regions of the cold sheets, and closed the velvet bed curtains around her. She splayed her flaxen hair out over the scented bolster, imagining how she should appear when he came, remembering, too, what Priscilla had said about the ways of men with their virgin brides. Her excitement grew. But also her drowsiness, stealing upon her before she was aware. Words she had spoken at the marriage service ran through her mind, mingling with fragmented visions—of her dead mother's smile, of the palace garden. And then not a vision but a sensation, of being touched upon the cheek by a dry, cold hand.

She awoke with a start, conscious that she was no longer alone, knowing that someone or something was beyond the bed curtain.

She heard a ripping noise, then another. She saw the curtain being parted by a sharp curved blade.

She tried to scream but no sound could she make. At the third strike, she rolled to the opposite side of the bed and dropped to the floor, entangled in bedding while she heard heavy footfalls moving toward her and raspy breathing. Scrambling to her feet to meet her attacker, she saw a cloaked figure with muffled mouth and glaring eyes. In his hand was the means by which he had shredded the bed curtains—a reaper's sickle.

She found her voice and screamed for Thomas.

Then there was a blaze of light and at the open door stood the hostler, holding a torch.

"*Put down the sickle!*" he commanded to the cloaked figure menacing her. "She's done no harm to you or me. Leave her alone or answer to heaven."

Her assailant had turned aside at this interruption. It was all she needed. She moved backward slowly, at the same time hearing new voices in the corridor, voices she recognized as those of Sir Robert Cecil and Matthew Stock.

Her would-be murderer bolted for the door, shoving the hostler aside. Mistress Frances screamed again, again, and again, as she watched her young protector recover himself, snatch the torch from the rushes before it could set them afire, and disappear through the door.

When Joan came in with Cecil and Matthew, she saw Mistress Frances standing by her bed, so sickly pale and quaking she seemed a very ghost. She was holding the shredded bed curtains as though the damage done them was the cause of her distress.

Joan went directly to ask how she was, and after some hesitation the trembling young woman said she was well enough now, but not so before. She gave a confused account of what had happened, from which Joan gathered that she had been attacked by a cloaked, sickle-wielding creature; that, had it not been for Edward the hostler's timely intervention, she would have been murdered; and that she feared *that* awful fate had befallen her new husband, else he would have rescued her himself.

Cecil assured Mistress Frances that she was safe enough now, and he sent Matthew next door to see to the bridegroom, while Joan offered what comfort she could. Then Matthew returned to say that Thomas Cooke *was* in the next room but asleep rather than dead, and that, if fouled linen and stench about his person were any clue, the young man had fallen victim to more dry sack and burgundy than he could hold, and he would be well enough off in the morning.

Moppitt and Hargrove now appeared, along with about a dozen of the groom's friends. They had just come from a search of the other bedchambers and had found no strangers. Cecil was in the process of organizing a more extensive search when Sears rushed in to say that the hostler had the assailant cornered in the attic and they should all come, for the man would not surrender and was threatening to cut his own throat.

Everyone, even Mistress Frances, went to see.

Like a fox at bay, the person whom Mistress Frances had described was standing in an alcove, his back to an open window. He was swinging the sickle in front of him as though he were reaping an invisible harvest and in consequence keeping Edward at a distance. Although Edward was begging for the man to put the sickle down, he refused and continued the threatening motions.

Joan and the others had crowded into the small room and were standing behind Edward, but the appearance of the men had its effect on the cornered man, who proclaimed in a hoarse, unearthly voice that they should all stand back if they desired to live.

Cecil commanded the man to put down the sickle in the Queen's name, but the man only laughed a mad, hysterical laugh, and then, before anyone could prevent it, he turned suddenly and dived head-forward through the window.

Joan heard a piercing scream. Then an awful stillness.

Mistress Frances' assailant—the Challoner murderer, as Joan now supposed—had fallen on his head and had been killed instantly, for those who had been standing in the courtyard and watched his plunge swore he never moved once he hit the cobbles. There was a great pool of blood beneath the body, and blood on the cloak, too.

It was Matthew who ran forward to identify the murderer and told Joan who it was. Then Joan looked around for Edward and realized the hostler must have stayed upstairs. It was just as well, she thought.

The dead man was Edward's father.

25

It was past midnight, a fact that only moments before had been solemnly pronounced by twelve strokes of the clock, and the wedding guests, chastened by the fatal climax of the feast, had retreated to their beds to dream whatever dreams God or the devil should send to each. In the withdrawing room a fire had been laid for the comfort of those few souls still awake—Cecil, Joan and Matthew, and Edward Bastian, who within the hour had seen his father dashed to pieces on the cobbles and was of so stony a visage and lusterless eye that he seemed almost a dead man himself.

To the right of the fire sat Cecil, his small body encased in a high-backed chair taller than himself, his legs crossed casually but hardly touching the floor, and a shadow across his eyes giving him an inscrutable expression of a wizard or prophet. To the left of the fire, Matthew and Joan occupied a long bench and were silent as in church, for each understood that Cecil's coming had usurped their own little authority and that any questions put to the accused would be framed by Cecil alone.

Between the Stocks and Cecil then was Edward, like a

prisoner at the bar—an apt comparison, since whether the hostler was to be hailed as defender of his mistress or condemned as an accomplice in her attempted murder was the issue to be resolved.

"You came to the castle this evening in search of your father," Cecil began, with an edge to the question, as though he anticipated that Edward would deny it. "Whereby I think it plain as day you knew his malice toward the Challoners, were privy as well to his other dreadful murders—I mean those of Sir John Challoner, the Irish maidservant whose name escapes me, and Sir John's own manservant, Michael Conroy. Speak, churl, and remember how God hates a lie and him that utters it."

There was a deep silence after this solemn admonition that seemed to Joan to stretch for minutes. Finally the accused answered in a barely audible voice, forced from his throat as though the hangman's noose were already about his neck and these were the last words he was to speak in mortality.

"As God is my judge, I did not know it was my father who murdered Aileen Mogaill, or the Irishman. Much less Sir John."

Joan heard Cecil laugh skeptically. She could not see his eyes.

"Inhabit the same cottage with a madman; eat, drink, and sleep with the same day in and day out and have no inkling of his depravity? How can a son be so ignorant of his father's mind?"

Edward said, his voice a little more audible now and, Joan thought, defensive. "He *was* my father, and for that very reason I was ignorant—perhaps as much by choice as by neglect. I admit that after Conroy was killed I suspected. Yet I had no proof. I could not accuse him to his face. I could not fathom a reason for the act. My father ever loved me, more than fathers are wont to love their sons, and to him I was equally devoted."

Cecil said, "Devoted were you? God save us from such devotion when it abets murder. You maintain you knew nothing about his violent urges?"

"I believed him incapable, for so the infirmities of age and his condition argued. Long days he sat brooding, without a word. Some days he could not move about or stand. His vision was poor, or so it seemed. Other days he would be lost somewhere in his addled brain and become like a child—look at me as though I were a stranger or ask who Brigid was or who the child she nursed. We thought him harmless in such grave ineptitude, his old hatred of Sir John notwithstanding. And as for this most strange and unpredictable assault upon Mistress Frances, why, Sir Robert, I know not how to explain it other than a mindless vengeance for that she was her uncle's niece and heir."

"What grievance did your father have against Sir John?" Cecil asked.

"Why, no particular thing, sir, or if it was, he never said, other than Sir John dismissed him from his service upon some infraction."

"You say you did not know your father's intent, and yet you did this very night rush to the castle in search of him and scramble across the rooftop most desperately, after Mistress Stock informed you of her fears. Do you mean to say you didn't know it was your father you pursued?"

Edward answered, "I sought to prevent the worst I could imagine, not what I was certain of. Father had been gone most of the day, Brigid had said, and she could not find him. I searched the fields myself, thinking he may have stumbled there and not been able to rise again. All day I searched. I came at last to a shed near the cottage where tools are kept. I noticed one removed—a sickle that it is my habit to keep razor-sharp, the better to mow with. Then I thought of the bodies—Aileen Mogaill's and Conroy's, whose body I had twice seen: when I found it first on the stable floor, and this morning when fate brought it forth from the lake. It came to me then what I had before dared not think, that no passing stranger had perpetrated these enormities but my own flesh and blood. When I went to the castle, Mistress Joan told me of her own fears. I acted at once, wishing no more harm to come, and least to Mistress Frances."

"And acted well," Cecil said after a few minutes of reflection while Joan grew very nervous as to how the great knight would accept the hostler's word. "But what of Conroy? Surely when you found him dead in the stable, you had cause to suspect that more than a passing stranger had murdered him."

"True, I did," Edward said. "I found Conroy weltering in his blood, killed as Aileen Mogaill before him, and feared the blame of both murders would be laid at my door. I am skilled in tools of every sort and it is my custom to keep them serviceable, honing the blades until they can sever a horse's hair with little effort. Conroy frequented the stable while he was alive, and it is no secret that he and I were not always of the same mind about things. I dragged the body to the lake and had no sooner pushed him in than I heard approaching steps. The old steward it was, Cuth Fludd, mumbling to himself. I left Conroy's body on the bank and hid myself, watched while the old man started at the ghastly thing, then bellowed to wake the dead man. He ran off; I suppose to report his find to his wife.

"I pulled the body farther into the lake, pushed it under and secured it to the bottom with rocks and sodden logs, thinking it would rot there. That it would surface soon was not within my reckoning. I swear, I never killed him, no; nor Aileen Mogaill, either. Nor had cause, just or otherwise."

"I can't believe in all this you would not have suspected your father," Cecil said.

"There may have crossed my mind the fear the way a cloud obscures the sun, then passes on. My worry, I confess, was all upon myself. For this reason, when Mistress Stock came to ask me where Conroy was, I told her he had packed his gear and left. In truth, I took his horse and gear and turned both loose in an orchard ten miles distant where, if found, it would be thought the horse a runaway."

Cecil sat for a long time considering Edward's version of events while Joan pondered her own feelings. Before them stood either a very clever confederate of a murderous father or a blameless son who deservedly could be called a hero. But which?

Finally, Cecil said to Matthew, "What say you to what this young man has told us?"

Joan waited for her husband's response, and while she waited a tightening in her chest prophesied that her own verdict might be required next.

She considered how she might respond if asked. To her memory came Edward's earlier denial that anything amiss had happened in the stable, his ready assertion that the Irishman had packed and taken horse for parts unknown. All had been presented to her with the frank, open countenance of one to whom a lie is as alien to the tongue as is mercy to the devil. She remembered, too, what Matthew had reported upon return from the Bastian cottage—how Edward had assured him that no child was there, had denied all, knowing in his heart the contrary.

Edward was a man, then, to whom deception, when deemed politic, came readily. And that realization Joan could not ignore in her deliberations.

On the other hand, she had watched with fear and trembling as Edward had climbed the ivied walls and scrambled across the roof to circumvent the blockade of the stairs and snatch Mistress Frances from his mad father's clutches. Had they waited for Cecil to come and exercise his authority over the rowdy guests, the bride might have died there—and perhaps Thomas Cooke, too. She had heard from Mistress Frances' own lips how Edward's sharp reproof had stayed the murderer's hand, how he had given chase. All this she realized as well, and to this she added her own intuitive sense that although Edward had lied before, what he had now confessed before them was more truth than not.

Finally, Matthew's own answer came:

"In faith, Sir Robert, I warrant Edward Bastian acted most bravely in defense of his mistress. He need not have come to the castle or risked his life upon the slippery shingles to save her—and surely would not have been so bold as to corner his father and subject himself to harm, for we both saw how Hugh Bastian slashed the air before him, and we examined the sickle to prove that one touch would have been his present death. As for Conroy, had Edward been his murderer, he would have found a better place to kill him than his own stable, where evidence of blood could not be easily removed. For these and other good reasons, I believe Edward speaks the truth."

"And what say you, Joan?" Cecil's voice said out of the shadowy recesses of the chair.

The verdict was hers, as she had feared. And before she was fully ready to render it in her own heart, much less speak it aloud as testimony to others.

And yet speak she must, for so Cecil commanded.

"What Edward says may well be true, Sir Robert," Joan said. "Of his courage in saving Mistress Frances' life I am a ready witness. Concerning these other matters—the murders of Aileen Mogaill and Sir John, I must confess some things remain unsettled in my mind."

"Are these matters of such a nature as you would condemn the man?"

"They are not," Joan said.

"Nor shall I then," said Cecil, rising.

"God bless you, Sir Robert," said Edward, his voice breaking.

"God bless us all," said Cecil, "that we may be kept from such evil as your father intended and executed. Let us also pray that murderous impulses are not inherited."

Joan whispered a silent prayer to add to Cecil's, and then Cecil reminded them that there was still a mystery to be solved. "If our Irish cook has done her work, even now she is conveying to Jack Wylkin the welcome news that the castle is asleep and, given last night's revelry, not likely to wake until noon."

"We should hear the explosion at any time now," said Matthew.

They all went out into the courtyard. The night was very still, and above their heads the stars shone clearly. Cecil told Edward what they all were waiting for, the distant thunder that should not be thunder at all but the beginning of the end for the lake. Cecil said, "We can use your courage, Edward Bastian, in apprehending Wylkin and Stafford when they come to seek what Sir John disposed of in the lake or hid upon the island."

"Gladly will I lend a hand," replied Edward. "For I have little cause to love either man, and would cheerfully see they get what they deserve."

No sooner had Edward spoken these words but a dull boom was heard, and immediately thereafter another. Even in the darkness Joan could see a smile spread across Cecil's face, and she thought, how much he loves the chase.

"The arsonist has done his work, it would appear," Cecil said. "Now let's to bed. Before dawn we must be up and on the lake. My brave companions of the road, Moppitt and Hargrove, will help us too, if we can rouse them from their slumber. And so shall we give these strange events at Castle Thorncombe their long-delayed period."

It had taken so long for Una to come that Wylkin began to think she had failed him, and he was heaping on the whole female race a hundred ingenious curses and was about to strike the fuse without her word when he heard footsteps and looked up to see her advancing from the trees.

"Are they asleep?" he asked in place of greeting. "In good time, for I thought you'd never come."

"Asleep as the dead," she answered.

"Let them sleep until the Resurrection so they sleep until noon," Wylkin said. He kissed her quickly on her cold cheek for her pains and without another word set off about his work, his mind totally fixed upon the task at hand.

Beneath the dam he struck the match and held it to the fuse he had so carefully concealed from prying eyes. It hissed as it burned, to him a very pleasing sound. He watched it for a moment and then scrambled up the hillside out of harm's way. Breathless, he looked down at the long ridge of earth and rock, watching the little glow that recorded the steady consumption of the fuse, until there was nothing but a little pocket of darkness where the light had been before.

Then the explosion came, explosions rather, for they came in such close succession, it seemed one but triggered the next.

Wylkin was first half-blinded by the flash and the clouds of dust and debris raining down around him. When it had passed and he could see the stars again, he strained to hear the sound of rushing water that would signal his success.

He cursed when he heard no sound.

He climbed down the hillside until he could get close enough to the dam to inspect his work. He could see now that a small breach had been made at the top of the dam and from this a little stream of water ran down the rocky slope into the old dry streambed, like blood pouring from a wound. But it was not enough. He cursed aloud the dam and him who made it, the Challoner tribe, and his ill luck.

He remembered the powder he had held in reserve for such an exigency and went to retrieve it from its hiding place. Within the next few minutes he worked quickly and skillfully to place it, groping around the earthen structure until he had detected every point of vulnerability. He had only a short fuse left of his store and that troubled him, but he knew he had to take the chance. He could not stop now. He reckoned there remained a good five hours before dawn, and that, if he was going to walk dry-shod to the island, he would need at least that time for the lake to drain. Like a pierced carbuncle, he thought, relishing the smile.

He lighted the fuse and ran for cover.

In the split second following the final explosion Wylkin knew he had seriously misjudged both the length of the fuse and the time it would take to return to his position of vantage above the dam. Debris from the previous explosions had created new obstacles in his path and he stumbled twice before he was halfway to where he was before when the first and second blasts detonated.

He was hoisted in the air and flung against the hillside with such force that he heard his bones snap when he hit the ground. At the same instant a sharp, agonizing pain in his left leg and in his ribs confirmed the seriousness of his injuries and the hopelessness of his escaping harm's way.

A hail of debris fell about his head, he heard a mighty roar like a cavalry charge, and then the black flood, more powerful than he could have dreamed, engulfed him.

26

IN the gray dawn Matthew could see that Wylkin's demolition had done its intended work. The lake was gone, and in its place was a brackish swamp.

With Cecil in the lead and Moppitt and Hargrove behind, Matthew trudged through the muck toward the island, thankful that he had worn his boots. A charged pistol in hand gave him an extra measure of confidence.

At Matthew's heels came Edward as a rear guard, armed with a stave and watching the shore for signs of Stafford and his crew. It had been Cecil's plan, announced before their setting out and while the new day was a mere promise in the east, to occupy the island, search it and its environs, and hold it against Stafford and any other trespasser, with deadly force, if necessary.

It was very clear to Matthew that Cecil was enjoying immensely his new role as general. Deprived by his diminutive stature from the ordinary joys of soldiery, he was at last getting a chance to indulge, if only on a limited scale.

The lake bed was treacherous in the immediate vicinity of the island, proving that it was not merely its watery covering that had made it inhospitable to the casual visitor. Deep pools, like the one in which Matthew had nearly drowned, remained, and waterlogged relics of the woods that had once flourished there made rapid advance difficult and unsafe. The island, too, was much altered. Now a round-topped hill, it appeared higher than before, and it reminded Matthew of one of the barrows Edward had shown him, which indeed it might have been for all he knew.

It was Edward's sharp eye that first detected the cavity in the rocky side, like a low, broad mouth with upper lip fringed with a thick growth of vines. "Look, good sirs, a cave!"

The men approached and Matthew could see that there was indeed a small opening in the hillside, the entrance to which was now apparent only because of the retreating water.

Advancing with growing excitement, Matthew bent down to peer. Despite the lack of lamp or torch, he could see that the small opening led upward to an interior vault of generous proportions.

But the cavity was neither natural nor the work of ancients. The opening had been hewn from the rock with modern tools, and Matthew agreed with Cecil's surmise that it had been constructed as a grotto, perhaps by the same French engineer who built the dam.

The larger chamber into which the men now entered was a natural cavern, perhaps discovered by accident by the grotto's maker. In the gloom Matthew was able to discern arches, grotesque erections of stone, and drooping icicles—a hoary congregation of petrified forms, as though the old ones who may have worshipped there before the Romans and the Saxons had for their unspeakable blasphemies been metamorphosed into stone.

But Matthew had not time to meditate on these antiquities. The question was not when Wylkin would come, but why he had not come already, and, as Cecil now pointed out, if there was searching to be done, it ought to be done quickly.

The men worked their way up the incline until they stood among the growths of rock. Matthew looked up to the cave's ceiling and then in the backparts of the cave. The cave was not deep, as it turned out. They could see all there was.

Cecil commented on the cave's expanse; his voice echoed strangely. Then Matthew saw that against one of the walls was a natural dais, a shelf of rock. He pointed it out to Cecil and the two men went over to investigate, Cecil voicing his regret that they had not brought torches.

Matthew realized with sudden amazement that the shelf was not an alter but a bier.

The corpse upon the stone seemed to have been laid out in state, for the hands were crossed upon the chest, as they were in marble effigies of the dead he had seen in churches. Rotting garments, once of good quality, clothed the skeleton, and upon the bony ribs lay a medallion bearing the Challoner crest.

Cecil noticed the gash in the skull. "Another murder. And a Challoner, unless the medallion he wears was stolen."

Edward said, "That's Arthur Challoner, Sir Robert. It could be no other."

"Arthur Challoner?"

"Sir John's brother," Edward said reverently. "He we all thought was lost in Ireland almost twenty years ago. My father often spoke of him as a most worthy gentleman, not like the others of his blood."

Cecil said, "Well, he did indeed die violently. The blow came from behind, cracking the skull, and since he is garbed for peace, not war, and he is buried obscurely here without the honors that were his due, it takes no great imagination to conceive him murdered. Doubtless by him who had most to benefit by his death, the second son, Sir John Challoner."

The five men now began to search for treasure, poking into every nook and cranny, feeling, when they needed for want of light, and assuring themselves at last that all within was as solid as it seemed, with no hidden passages or crypts. If there was booty at all, Cecil said at length, it was elsewhere on the island. "We came to find a treasure trove and instead have found a sepulcher. Marry, it's not the first time pregnant rumor has birthed an airy nothing. The devil must be given his due, for indeed, because John Challoner was a murderer, as it now appears, does not mean he was an extortionist to boot, although a man may swing for one crime as well as t'other."

Now voices were heard outside the cave. Matthew recognized Stafford's voice and warned Cecil and the others. They concealed themselves, Matthew where he could see the cave entrance without himself being seen.

He saw Stafford peering into the cave. With him were two other men, servants by their dress, one armed with pick and the other a shovel. There was no sign of Wylkin.

"You've come late for your treasure, Master Stafford," Cecil said, emerging from his hiding place as Stafford entered. "We're here before you and have made our claim on whatever of value is here."

Stafford squinted, his eyes adjusting to the dim light. Cecil moved closer, but Stafford showed no sign of recognizing him. "And who, sir, might you be to speak so? I have drained the lake and exposed this cave. Its contents are therefore mine by law."

"A very strange law would justify such a ridiculous claim." Cecil laughed. Behind him Moppitt, Hargrove, and Edward now emerged. Matthew also stepped out into the open.

Matthew said, "What, Master Stafford! Have you turned brigand, you, and these with you, that with impunity you invade a neighbor's property? Have you no shame?"

"Ha, our little Stock, the steward," said Stafford. "Brave words from a servant. But pray tell me, who's this minuscule hunchback that leads you? He looks as though he has escaped from an actor's troupe where he daily delights the multitude of unwashed and unlearned too stupid to appreciate better. Stand aside, the lot of you."

The two servants behind Stafford raised the tools they carried threateningly. In an instant, Cecil and his companions had drawn swords.

"If you would know my name, sir," Cecil said coldly. "I

am Cecil, Robert Cecil, and she whom I serve is England's Queen. Perhaps you've heard her spoken of?''

Stafford's jaw fell open and the effect of this announcement was even greater on his companions, who immediately dropped their tools to the ground.

Cecil said, "I arrest you, Thomas Stafford, for arson, assault upon a Queen's officer, and trespass—and for such other crimes as times and fact shall prove. You and these varlets with you."

One of Stafford's servants dropped to his knees, the other bolted and began running across the lake. Stafford himself seemed too terrified to speak.

Cecil motioned to Moppitt to move forward and take Stafford into his charge, while Edward went after Stafford's escaping servant. Cecil said,

"Before we take you back with us, Master Stafford, I'll be pleased to show you what a treasure our foreknowledge of your mischief has deprived you of."

Matthew reminded Cecil that Wylkin was yet to appear.

"He shall not appear," Stafford mumbled. "He's gone to hell in the flood. We found his body before we came."

"Then there's justice in the world after all," said Cecil.

While later that morning Matthew and Cecil questioned Stafford further about his strategems against the Challoners, it fell to Joan to bear the news of their discovery in the island cave to the person it concerned most, Mistress Frances. Of course immediately upon his return, Matthew had told Joan the whole story, and she was therefore adequately equipped to convey the same to the new bride.

It was well past noon before Mistress Frances came down, looking no better than should have been expected, given her night's ordeal. The two women spoke in the withdrawing room.

In the telling, Joan tried to be gentle, but she had no gift for mincing, and upon reflection later she feared she had been much too direct. But Matthew had presented to her all the facts, and Joan agreed they allowed but one conclusion. Certainly no other explanation came to mind to offer a palliative: Sir John had murdered his brother—and Mistress Frances' father—years before, doubtlessly for his title and his land, and concealed his body in the island crypt. The only good news was that the morning's expedition had not confirmed Sir John's extortion, since no Irish treasure had been found. As for the drained lake, Mistress Frances said, when Joan mentioned it, that she cared not a fig for the lake, which she regarded as her wicked uncle's toy.

Indeed, Mistress Frances took these revelations more calmly than Joan would have supposed. The young woman did not decry her father's profane burial without appropriate honors, exequies, or other tributes, nor did she roundly condemn his murderer, his treacherous brother. Compared to the horrors of Hugh Bastian's attempt on her life and the prophetic dreams that preceded it, she could cast a cold eye on these ancient wrongs.

Joan also explained—for there had been no opportunity the night before—what Edward Bastian had revealed when questioned by Cecil.

"But Edward was not his father's confederate?" Mistress Frances was concerned to know.

Joan answered in the negative. She herself was sure of that point, however many other doubts she might have, for no confederate would have acted with such bravery as the hostler did, or make himself the instrument of his own undoing when he might have kept silent and let his father's vicious plan take its course.

Joan's reasoning seemed to satisfy Mistress Frances, who said she was heartily glad to have Edward exonerated from any blame, for she owed him a great debt of gratitude for saving her life. Thomas Cooke, who presently joined them, agreed wholeheartedly with his wife's estimation. Shamefaced, he admitted his own negligence the night before. "I should have protected my wife. I did not. God curse me if I ever drink to excess again."

Thomas also said he would not hold the father's malice to the son's charge. "He shall be my personal servant henceforth, and in the matter of compensation he shall not find me ungenerous."

Mistress Frances said she, too, would like to reward Edward, and that she was sure the Queen would do likewise upon their return.

"Return?" asked Joan. "You intend to return to London then? I thought you planned to make Thorncombe your home."

Mistress Frances and Thomas exchanged glances, then she said, "Our plans have changed. This house, cursed with ghosts before, will now have more to haunt it. I could never be happy here, or feel safe. Thomas agrees. We will return to London and live for the time being in my father-in-law's house near the Strand. It would please us both if you and your good husband would accompany us on our way and be our guests in London until such time as you can see the Queen and make your report. I trust it will prove as satisfying to you as it is to us, now that these hidden facts are known at long last."

Joan received these thanks gratefully and said that she and Matthew would indeed keep the young couple company on their journey to London, which was to be accomplished as soon as possible; for Mistress Frances was of no mind to spend another night in the castle, which she said might burn to the ground, for all she cared, and its ancient curses with it.

But as to the mystery of Thorncombe and its recent deaths, Joan was not as satisfied as was Mistress Frances. Even as she had concluded her report, she had felt some material fact eluding them all, and she would not rest easy until she had put a name to it.

27

WITH the horrors of the previous few days behind them, the journey south was a pleasant one, and the weather, typically unpredictable for so late in the year, was on its best behavior, with dry days and clear skies of the most marvelous azure that no artist could have reproduced the like.

Matthew and Joan, who accompanied the Cookes in their spacious coach, were in very good humor, and Matthew most of all, for, as he said several times in the course of the journey, what was past was past, and having commenced a marriage, it was unwise for either the young husband or wife to look behind them.

Mistress Frances and Master Thomas accepted this counsel with good grace. And the second day of their journey, the bloom of Mistress Frances' complexion had been restored; her eyes were bright, and her wit had returned as well, for she entertained them all with court gossip and in her banter with her friend Priscilla Holmes, who traveled with them—as did Edward Bastian, who had left Brigid and her child behind at Thorncombe until they could be more conveniently removed to London and who had his seat by the coachman and relieved the same of his duties from time to time, showing how great his skill with horses really was.

But although Matthew was content to think his duty done, Joan's doubts increased. She could not rid her mind of the notion that even murder must have a method in it, which in Hugh Bastian's case had been cruel dismemberment of the victim by that dreadful sickle. But what was she to make of his first alleged venture into homicide—the drowning of Sir John—subtly done and covert and perpetrated against one who might reasonably have been supposed capable of defending himself against it? While she therefore was content to believe that Hugh Bastian had killed Aileen Mogaill and Michael Conroy, revived from his senility for the nonce to disable his victims by surprise and terror, and that he would have given Mistress Frances her quietus by the same instrument, her feelings about Sir John's death were more complex. In sum, she believed the mad old man not guilty of that charge against him.

There was also the matter of Joan's vision by the lake, prompted by her finding of the chest. That this was a vision pregnant with significance for the case at hand she had no doubt at all. Yet she still could not determine its place in the pattern of events, as Matthew now construed that pattern. For Joan, all that had been revealed to date was chaff; she had yet to come to the kernel.

When they arrived in London, Cecil left them to go at once to court. He returned the same afternoon to the Cookes' house to report the Queen was indisposed and under the advice of her physicians was granting no audiences but to certain members of the Privy Counsel and her astrologer, the renowned Dr. Dee.

"Your report must wait," Cecil told Matthew. "Which saddens me greatly, for I relish the thought of your presenting it within the Queen's allotted time."

That, Cecil did not have to remind them, was within three days, it being now twenty-seven days since the commission to investigate Sir John's death was first issued.

While they waited for the Queen's indisposition to pass, Matthew and Joan saw the sights of London, many of which they had seen on earlier visits but which remained a source of inexhaustible fascination—and especially those connected with the Stocks' earlier forays in the world of crime and treason: stinking Smithfield, site of Bartholomew Fair; the Tower of London, once a royal palace, now a prison; the Globe Theater, where the notorious Sir Henry Saltmarsh had been apprehended while watching one of Master Shakespeare's plays; and the most unpleasant recollection of all, Newgate Prison, where both Joan and Matthew had been briefly but perilously incarcerated during the most life-threatening of their adventures.

Then, just as their month was about to expire, word came that the Queen had recovered. An audience had been arranged, and Cecil was delighted. As was Matthew. But Joan continued to nurse her doubts, and with such constant care they grew so as to displace any little confidence she had earlier had that the matter of Sir John Challoner's murder had been resolved.

She had spent most of the day before in the company of Mistress Frances, since Priscilla Holmes had returned to her own house and husband, and Thomas, having been elected one of the controllers of the Middle Temple Revelers, had gone off to that worthy institution, dragging Matthew with him, to supervise rehearsals for a Christmas entertainment not to be surpassed, or so Thomas boasted. The men gone, both women felt somewhat abandoned and licensed thereby to go abroad and shop, which they presently did with full purses and wills to bring them home empty.

It was in a certain shop that Joan, seeing a locket of excellent workmanship, admired it, whereupon Mistress Frances said it was nothing compared to one she had among her own jewels. Mistress Frances promised to show Joan the locket as soon as they reached home again.

Later, Mistress Frances fetched the locket as she had promised and handed it to Joan. "Here, good Mistress Stock. You shall wear it on the morrow for your audience with the

Queen. Keep it—it's yours, for friendship's sake and in part reward for your service to me."

Joan protested that the gift was of too great a value, but Mistress Frances insisted. She said it was part of her inheritance from her uncle, and had no personal worth that she should keep it.

Joan held the locket in her hand admiringly. It was indeed exquisitely made, of finely wrought gold and equipped with a chain of delicate workmanship—obviously of much greater value than the one she had admired at the jeweler's. Noticing, upon closer inspection, that it was fitted with a clasp, she flicked it open.

Inside was a miniature portrait of a young man with broad, smooth forehead, deep-set intelligent eyes, and firm, beardless chin. She asked whose picture it was, and Mistress Frances, surprised at its being there, said it was her father, for there was a portrait much like it that her mother had had.

"Oh, you must have your gift back again," Joan urged. "This is a most precious keepsake. Why, see, the initials are engraved opposite as well."

But having said that and extended the locket so that her companion could see, Joan realized the initials were "J. C.," not "A. C."

Mistress Frances noticed this too. "Why, it's of my uncle, which explains how the locket came to be among his things." She said that Joan might have the locket after all, and might throw away the portrait inside, for she wanted no further part of her uncle or any images of him.

Joan took the locket and said, "He seems to have been a proper, handsome man."

"Ironically," Mistress Frances said, "the depiction you see there would have better served my father than my uncle."

"Why, how so?" Joan asked, interested in every aspect of Challoner family history.

"My father and uncle were born the very same hour," the young woman explained. "My mother said they were so much alike in stature and visage that had it not been for a deformity in my uncle, you could not have distinguished the one from the other."

"A deformity?" Joan searched the features of the likeness for some blemish she had overlooked. "Why, I see no deformity at all. Your uncle, for all his crimes, seems endowed with great beauty."

"My *father* was so endowed," Mistress Frances said proudly. "As for my uncle, the artist whose work you see here flattered, as artists often do, improving upon nature. Believe me, there was much to improve upon. My uncle suffered an accident of birth—a harelip that so disfigured his mouth that one could see from ragged teeth up to his swollen gums, giving him the fierce grimace that put to flight his enemies. But for that flaw, my father and he were cut of the same cloth. Except for their souls, which I pray to God were as different as night from day."

Mistress Frances now excused herself to change, leaving Joan with the locket to contemplate. Fascinated by the striking handsomeness of the face and intrigued by the incongruity of semblance and reality, she remembered Edward's infant son, a victim too of John Challoner's affliction.

At the same moment the material fact she had overlooked—the fact she could not have known before—took its proper place in the line of other facts she had been so long in finding.

Upon the return that evening of Thomas and Matthew, Joan had little opportunity to share her discovery with her husband, for the two men were no sooner through the door than supper was laid, and thereafter young Master Cooke so pressed upon Matthew to sing for the company that he could not refuse. He sang for nearly two hours, until he had gone practically from the first of Master Dowland's *Second Booke of Songs and Ayres* to the last, and still those at table called for more.

While Matthew sang, Joan listened with appreciation, but it was lessened by her eagerness to discuss the Challoner matter with him. Finally the evening came to an end and good-nights were said. Joan and Matthew went to their chamber and Joan told Matthew what she believed had really happened the day Sir John Challoner came home from Ireland.

Matthew listened, thought, and concurred. And in good time, for now he understood that the report he had intended for the Queen's approbation was only partly true, and being true in part, it was, by order of logic, false.

28

THEIR audience with the Queen was for nine o'clock, but they were not led into the Queen's apartment until nearly eleven and then were forced to wait in a drafty corridor until Cecil appeared to inform them that Her Majesty had been late in rising and would not see them in the Presence Chamber but in the Privy Chamber instead. There, Cecil warned, they should not be dismayed to find the Queen of England squat like a Mohammedan upon floor cushions, which she had taken to do of late, despite the contrary opinion of her physicians, who thought that way of sitting harmful to the bowels.

"Marry, you've come in good time," Cecil said good-humoredly. "It was the very devil to get the Queen to see you. I do believe she has forgotten entirely your mission, for she asked who Matthew Stock was and supposed you were the mayor of Cambridge who had sent her some strawberries last year because he heard she delighted in them."

"If Her Majesty is not well, perhaps we should come another time," Joan ventured to say, thinking how frail the old

Queen had appeared in their last interview and not wishing to cause her any distress.

"Believe me, now *is* the time," Cecil said adamantly. "The learned Dr. Dee has warned the Queen to beware of Whitehall, and even now she contemplates spending January in Richmond, the warmest of her palaces. No, now is the time, or not at all. It is here you saw her last; seeing you again in the same place may quicken her memory."

Cecil told them a gentleman usher would presently appear to show them inside. Joan waited with the Cookes and Edward Bastian, chatting quietly, while Matthew went into a corner to have private words with Cecil.

But when they were led into the Privy Chamber they found the Queen not on the floor cushions as reported but seated at the virginals, which she continued to play with considerable skill, Joan thought, for several minutes, until she became aware of Cecil's presence. "Ah, Robin," she said. "And these with you, we trust—"

"Matthew Stock and his wife, Joan; Master Thomas Cooke and Mistress Frances Cooke, whom you will remember as Mistress Frances Challoner; and Edward Bastian, Master Cooke's manservant."

The old Queen's face brightened as she recognized Mistress Frances, and Joan thought she saw a tear of happiness glisten in her eye. Then, aided by a gentleman who upon later introduction turned out to be Sir John Harington, the Queen's godson, the Queen went up to Mistress Frances and kissed her, saying, "God save you, Frances, whom we must henceforth call Mistress Cooke, and right welcome home again to London."

Joan noticed that the Queen limped and used a cane and seemed to be in great physical discomfort all the while. She was helped down upon the large floor cushions of which Cecil had spoken and sat very erect and cast her gaze about each one of them as though trying to fix in her memory who each was. Then suddenly it all seemed to come to her again. She asked her godson to bring her something from a desk standing in the corner.

She was given a letter, which turned out to have been written from Thorncombe by Cecil on the day following the wedding. She looked over the page and said,

"Oh yes, so Master Stock, you have done your duty, as it says here. Mistress Frances' life endangered—but saved by the hostler of the castle—"

"Edward Bastian, Majesty," Cecil said, indicating where Edward stood in the rear of the room. Joan thought Edward looked very handsome for the occasion. The Cookes had provided him with a new suit of clothes and he could almost have been taken for a gentleman.

The Queen asked that Edward be brought closer so she could have a good look at him. Edward approached, knelt, and was told to rise.

The Queen continued to comment on the letter.

"And the dead body of your late father, Arthur Challoner, discovered in a cave, and presumably murdered by your uncle. A crime most horrible and damnable too," she said, adjusting her red wig and scowling in general disapproval of homicide in all its forms. "The murderer, I take it, of Sir John, the same murderer being this fellow yonder's father, once a servant of the house?"

She peered suspiciously at Edward.

Cecil said, "But young Edward here was faithful, unlike his father."

"If it please, Your Majesty," Mistress Frances interjected. "Edward Bastian saved my life, stood between my death and his father's vengeance."

"Did he so?" the Queen said, subjecting Edward to another searching gaze. "Then he shall have our thanks for that as well as yours, for we told Sir Robert when you were gone unto Derbyshire that we would rather have lost an arm than see you come to harm."

Now the Queen turned her attention to Matthew.

"Master Stock, you have pleased us well in the matter and confirmed our better opinion of your qualifications. According to this report—"

"Which must be revised, Your Majesty," Matthew said.

"Revised?"

Matthew looked over at Cecil, whom he had informed earlier of Joan's new understanding of the case and who had given his permission that it be withheld until this moment. "The intelligence that Your Majesty has by way of Sir Robert's letter represents the best of our knowledge at the time it was written. Since then, new information has come to light—particularly as it regards the death of Sir John Challoner."

"Do you wish to say, Master Stock," the Queen exclaimed, "that this man's father was not the murderer of three persons and the attempted murderer of Mistress Frances?"

"I'faith, Your Majesty," Matthew said. "Hugh Bastian was in truth the perpetrator of the deaths of the two servants. He it was who also attempted the life of Mistress Frances, now Mistress Cooke, for in each case the same instrument was used and the same wounds inflicted. Yet until this hour we knew not why Hugh Bastian killed, but thought it ancient grievance come to boil or motiveless malignity, such as possess madmen. Now we understand there was cause more immediate. We also understand that Hugh Bastian did not drown Sir John but desired to protect him who did."

At this assertion there was a murmur in the room of interest and surprise. Joan looked at Mistress Frances, who looked at her husband, then at Edward, who stood very stiff and expressionless, although he had still not recovered from amazement at being where he was and in such great presence.

"Have you an accusation to make, Master Stock?" asked the Queen.

"I do."

"Make it, and pray God it's just, for there have been many false conclusions to this matter and I am more than ready to have the whole truth at last."

Matthew turned to Edward Bastian and pointed his finger at the young man's chest. "I accuse you, Edward Bastian, of murdering your lawful lord, Sir John Challoner, on the sixteenth day of the month of August, year of grace, 1601, and of designing to conceal your crime and shift the blame to another, namely your own father."

There was an awful stillness in the chamber when Matthew had finished and all eyes were turned to the accused man. During Matthew's words, Edward had continued to stand like a sentry on guard; now, Joan could see, his breathing was heavy, his shoulders had slumped. Slowly he sank into a kneeling position, with his head bowed as though he were already prepared for the headsman's ax.

"Is there ample evidence to support such a charge?" the Queen asked.

"We believe there is," Matthew answered. "Upon Sir Robert's recommendation we chose this moment to bring it forth, that Your Majesty might be judge of its merits and the degree of guilt of the accused."

"Then present the evidence straightway," the Queen said, "for I have little tolerance for more surprises or delays."

Matthew said, "Since this evidence was largely compiled by my wife, I let her speak."

The Queen turned to Joan and motioned for her to proceed.

Joan said, "The evidence is an empty chest found by me at the lake; Edward Bastian's own child, by adoption rather than nature, or so we now believe; and a likeness of Sir John Challoner, revealed to me only yesterday. By these facts we hope to show the true circumstances of Sir John's death as well as the depth of his depravity and to have these things confessed by him who executed the decree of justice upon the offender."

Now Cecil stepped forward and said to Edward, "Speak, Edward Bastian, speak truly, as you have not done in full until this present hour. You stand before your Queen, and God, too, is a witness to these proceedings. Save in Him, you will never find a more just judge of your inequities or a royal heart sooner to pardon. Now therefore speak the truth and the whole truth, so God help you."

Edward made no answer. Joan could see his mouth was

firmly set in defiance; he would submit to punishment but would not speak.

"Speak, sirrah," the Queen commanded. "If you have aught to respond to these charges, speak now, or I will order guards to bear you straightway to a more suitable place for your confession."

Joan heard the accused hostler emit a low groan, as though he were in terrible agony. He ran his fingers through his hair in a distracted manner and looked up at the Queen. Yet still he would not speak.

Joan said, "Edward, you trusted God to preserve you from a fall from the castle roof; trust God now. Make peace with Him and your conscience, that all wrongs may be known and set aright."

Another silence followed. At last Edward said, slowly and in an anguished voice,

"The day Sir John came home from Ireland, he came to my father's cottage where I lived with Brigid. He wanted to take up where he left off with her."

Joan said, "The child was *his*, wasn't it?—Sir John's bastard child, bearing the same deformity as he."

"It was," Edward said. "The devil was his father. Brigid had been a servant in the castle and the mating of the two was a rape, the lord of the manor taking his due, as he put it. But a child was conceived as a result of it. A child bearing his own curse so that all and sundry who saw it would know."

"That's why you tried to conceal the child's existence," Matthew said.

"Aye, I thought that it was better that no one knew about the child. Brigid loved it, loved it despite its father. And I loved her and the child, because it was a child of her body. But I hated him for his ruthlessness and his lust."

"For which you killed him," Cecil said.

Edward looked at the knight. He said, "I didn't intend it, Sir Robert, I swear before God. When Sir John came to the cottage he demanded to see the child, and when he saw it he swore vilely, first at the child and then at Brigid, whom he blamed for having borne it, and then for having let it live.

He ordered her back to the castle. He wanted her to be a servant again, for such purposes as I leave to your imagination, knowing his nature. He thought it was his right."

"But she refused," Joan prompted.

"Aye. She refused, as any decent woman would."

"What did Sir John do then?" the Queen asked.

"Why, he seized the child, told Brigid she should have it when he had her and not before. He threatened to drown it in the lake like an unwanted puppy."

"And so the chest was secured," Joan said.

"He put the child in it. He had brought it with him to the cottage, as though the damned creature knew that Brigid would have none of him, and he would take the child away.

"I followed him back to the castle, begging him to let me have the child to give to its mother again. He laughed in my face. He told me to go and shut my mouth about the child, and I told him if he would give it to me I would take the mother and the three of us would leave Derbyshire and he would never hear aught of us again."

"And he made what answer?" asked the Queen.

"Why, Your Majesty, he told me roundly he could not abide a puling, whining servant, no more than a misbegotten bastard. He called me churl and varlet and worse names I forbear to mention in this company."

"And for these provocations you killed your master?"

"For these things, Your Majesty, and as God is my witness, I would do it over again did the opportunity present itself. It happened this way. The rain had begun to fall, a filthy drizzle. He was by the lake, ready to push off in his shallop with the child confined in the chest and mewling, ignorant of his doom. I knew the price Sir John demanded for the child's salvation, and he knew I was not willing to pay it—nor was Brigid. I begged him not to be so cruel. I reminded him that the child was his own flesh and blood. But he confessed his was cursed blood indeed and challenged me to dispute with him that his face did not give ready evidence of the curse. I furnished him with a dozen reasons why what he undertook was an offense to God as well as man.

He laughed the more, pushed off, commending me to the devil. Whereupon, full of fury, I dashed into the water and seized the gunwale, swung the shallop round, and he, being caught unawares, lost his balance and fell overboard."

"It was then you drowned him," said the Queen.

"I saved the child, Your Majesty," Edward declared in a cold, steady voice of one no longer caring for his life. "I took the chest and carried the precious burden to shore, maugre his hail of curses and threats. The water where he fell was only shoulder-deep, you see. He was struggling to come to shore. Then his curses stopped. I turned to look. He had disappeared, gone under.

"I knew what had happened. It was one of those damnable holes and he had fallen into it. I confess I was tempted to let him drown and go to hell forthwith, thinking it was a fully satisfying judgment of God that he should have stepped into a hole in the middle of a good round curse, blaspheming God and Christ. But I couldn't do it, though I hated him. I put the child down on the shore and went back."

"To murder him," the Queen said.

"I had no murder in my heart, I swear it. Only a desire to save the child, to protect my wife, which having done, I was content to be on my way. But I went back, curse my fate, groped around in the dark water until I got a fistful of hair, and pulled him up half-drowned and choking. He had lost a leg in Ireland to the surgeon's knife and he wasn't the man he had been and knew it. That made him all the angrier, having had what he deemed his—the child, I mean—taken by such a one as I.

"I got him into the shallop again and pushed it toward the shore. The thought ran through my mind that he might give me thanks for saving his life, which showed the fool I was, for he no sooner came to himself but started another volley of curses and threats. Would to God he had drowned the first time. Would to God I had left him where I set my foot upon the shore with the child in my arms and my mind set on returning to Brigid. Let God judge me, I didn't go down into the lake to murder my master, but to save Brigid's child. Up to then Sir John had always done well by me, although he had ill-used my father. But his lust possessed him and drove him forward in evil. It was he who was bent on murder, not I. But I could not let him have the child; no, not if it meant my death.

"I realized that after what I had already done, I would be beaten at least, hanged at worst. What would have happened to Brigid then? Why, the devil would have been at her as before, that's what! I was done for, bereft of a decent choice. I had lifted my hand against my master, defied his will, caused him grave injury, committed a battery upon his person, as he worded it. I was completely in his power now, for such was the law. Gallows fodder for sure, he said, and I knew the child would be drowned all the same, for he was determined to do it. He hated the child because it was like him—that's the cruel sum."

"How exactly did Sir John die, then, if you saved him from drowning as you say?" the Queen asked.

"He died by my hand, Your Majesty. I don't deny that. He was sitting in his shallop, head down, still coughing and cursing, for he said he had swallowed half the lake and had been poisoned thereby. I took the blanket the child was wrapped in, soaked it twice its weight, and, making my way to where he was, pressed it over Sir John's face before he guessed at my intent. I held it there with all my strength. It took very little, to say true. Sir John wasn't the man he'd been. He struggled slightly. Then he sat very still, slumped over like a drowsing fisherman, the rain falling with such fury one could have believed the second deluge had come."

"At least you saved the child's life," Joan remarked when Edward paused in his account.

"I cast the empty chest out upon the water as far as I could throw and left Sir John where he sat, not caring what anyone might make of his death. I returned to the cottage with the child, told Brigid what necessity had driven me to perform, wept many a tear with her of regret, and then returned to the castle, where no one took my wet clothes amiss since all who had been out of doors were in such a state. When Cuth Fludd went in search of the master I went as his companion, feigned surprise when we found him dead, and grief, too, keeping silent about the rest. There was enough water in his belly that all thought he had drowned.''

At this point several comments were made by those present, including the Queen's godson, Sir John Harington, who swore it was the most piteous tale he had ever heard, and that if Master Shakespeare had been so fortunate to have been present, he would have at once made a fine tragedy thereof to rival *Titus Andronicus* or *Romeo and Juliet.*

But while these remarks were being made, Joan considered the justness of Edward's actions. She well understood the hostler's predicament, for had the facts of Sir John's death been known, Edward's claim of self-defense would have given him but a tenuous purchase on life. How much less secure would he have been with the truth as he had told it. The law could not forgive a servant's murder of his master. There had been no witnesses to Sir John's abduction of the child, the rape of the mother, his threats against them both and against Edward. Edward's confession would have been his death warrant, the jury's verdict a foregone conclusion. Edward had been right about having no choice—at least not a choice a decent man could make. He had been the victim of cruel circumstances—a figure of tragedy, as Sir John Harington had wittily said. Had Edward only been a prince rather than a lowly hostler.

But there was still more to be revealed, and it was the Queen who opened the door to it. "Tell me," she said, "did your father know what you had done?"

"I never told him directly, Your Majesty," Edward answered. "But he must have overheard me tell Brigid. And it was thus Aileen Mogaill's murder became a part of my misery. She had seen me quarreling with the master on the shore. Later she reckoned what it had meant, for when questioned by the coroner's jury, I claimed to have been at the stable and not set eyes on Sir John all the afternoon. She came to suspect that I had killed the master and she told me she would tell unless I gave her money, which I did for nearly a year for her silence's sake. My father must have learned about that, too, must have heard me tell Brigid what I had done, for I kept nothing from her. You must understand how my father hated Sir John, hated him for old wrongs and even unto madness for new ones. But he loved me out of his great, ailing heart and perplexed brain, and that, too, was a cause of these misfortunes, for he went about by stealth, whilst Brigid and I were unawares, righting wrongs done to us in a god-forbidden way. I didn't understand this at the time it was done. It was for me he killed Aileen. It was for me he killed Conroy, as he feared the Irishman sought my life or meant to take up where Aileen Mogaill left off in extracting money for his silence."

"And Mistress Frances," the Queen asked. "What had your father against her other than she was her uncle's heir?"

To this Edward had no answer, whereupon Cecil conjectured, "Perhaps at that point in his madness he was persuaded that because she *was* her uncle's heir she would wreak vengeance on his murderer."

The Queen said she thought Cecil's suggestion not implausible, and therefore the Queen, Cecil, and her godson discussed for a very long time the circumstances of the case, related principles of law, and how justice might be served. To Joan the learned conversation, including many Latin words and phrases beyond her ken, was all very edifying, but how she wished the Queen's verdict would come. They had been over an hour in the Privy Chamber, and standing all the while, except for Edward, who remained on his knees, and Joan was exhausted. She had wept much during Edward's confession and now she longed for resolution of the case and the chance to talk it all out with Matthew.

At long last, the Queen pronounced her judgment.

"The murder of a master by his servant, for whatever cause, cannot be countenanced by us. On this point, both man's law and God's concur. Yet neither can the murder of an innocent child be suffered, be it perpetrated by commoner or peer. Sir John's depravities have been proved. He was fratricide and lecher. It is most likely he would have executed his threat to kill his bastard—and perhaps even bury it with the body of his brother. Therefore''—the Queen took a deep breath, suggesting she herself was weary from the long morning's proceedings—''therefore, because we revere mercy as well as justice, and honor courage even as we punish treason, we pardon you, Edward Bastian, for your crime, and commend you to your new master and mistress for such advancement as seems suitable to them. You may go, we wish you well—and God keep you.''

29

EVEN as the Queen granted her pardon to Edward Bastian, Cecil was thinking about the man the hostler had killed—a prideful, degenerate knight who had murdered his own brother for his title and land and perhaps, too, for the unblemished countenance by which, in contrast, John Challoner seemed all the more deformed. Physically deformed himself, Cecil was not totally without understanding of Challoner's envy, yet Cecil had done no murders, held his lusts in check, and maintained his knightly honor and respect for the law. Which things Challoner had not, for what a parade of deadly sins marched across the pages of the baronet's history, now full blown. Challoner had not been the first lord to make his social power an opportunity for lechery and rape and cover it all with the veneer of respectability. Surely he would not be the last.

Cecil thought, too, of the innocent child. It had been Challoner's own, although by nature rather than law. An unnatural attempted murder of natural progeny, awful to contemplate. Cecil remembered the island crypt. Had Challoner really planned to entomb Brigid's baby there, disposing of it along with his own brother's bones, as the Queen had in her pardon of Edward Bastian speculated?

Arthur Challoner's remains had already been removed from the island. They had been taken for decent burial beneath the floor of St. Ann's in Buxton, where the baronial dignities stolen from him in life had now been restored in mortuary splendor. *Requiescat in pace.*

And finally Cecil thought about love and its awesome power. The love of Edward for Brigid O'Donnal; the love of Hugh Bastian for his son. A great thing and dangerous, love was. As all the old poets had said.

But now the Queen was dismissing the company, blessing them all, wishing them well. Fatigued as they were, she had decided the audience had gone on too long. Now Cecil wondered if and when his royal mistress would take up the question of Matthew Stock's reward, long overdue to Cecil's mind, and settle the wager.

Her Majesty was suffering from rheumatism and in a miserable mood. She seemed more interested in whether Cecil had partaken of the baths at Buxton and with what good result than in continuing the discussion of the Challoner murders, about which she roundly declared more than enough had been spoken that morning, what with Edward Bastian's long confession (splendid though it was!) and the philosophical debate that followed (relevant, but somewhat tedious after all!). It required, therefore, some effort on Cecil's part to bring the royal attention back to what was uppermost in his mind. Was a knighthood not appropriate for Matthew Stock, Cecil asked, given service rendered at Bartholomew Fair and now in Derbyshire?

The Queen gnawed upon her thumb and stared off vacantly into space. It was a while before she answered.

"A sum of money is sufficient, I think. There are too many knights in England already. Most are popinjays of no more desert than a dog and I regret dubbing them every day of my life. No, I am not prepared for Sir Matthew and Lady Joan, by your leave. As for Joan Stock, I like her as she is—a plain, simple woman equipped with a brain. The best of our English breed! Would all our peers were endowed with her judgment! As for the little ferret, Matthew Stock, I mean, I cannot see him with a knight's sword. He would be mocked by lesser men who resented his advancement—and that would please neither him nor me. He would be perfectly out of his element and no better a man for being so."

"And yet he did prove that Sir John was murdered, identified the murderer, discovered—"

"Tush, tush, Robin. You mean his *wife* did. You can't fool me. I can tell who unraveled that skein. Let us give credit where credit is due. Stock's sharp, but the wife is sharper."

Since Cecil could not dispute that point and seeing that the Queen's mind was set and no further remonstrations would serve, he politicly changed the subject. It was plain that it pleased Her Majesty to forget the twenty crowns she owed *him*, aside from what she may or may not have owed Master Stock.

Well, Cecil knew he could kiss the twenty crowns farewell. Thank God he was a rich man and could afford such trivial losses. Besides, who dared remind the Queen that she had forgotten?

Matthew and Joan were too eager to return to Chelmsford and take up their ordinary lives again to bewail the loss of a knighthood, for, as Joan pointed out, drawing from her seemingly inexhaustible store of proverbial wisdom, only a fool mourns the loss of what he never had.

Cecil had presented them with another purse on the Queen's behalf, guaranteed to cover any losses they had sustained by their absence from trade, and Thomas Cooke had given Matthew a fine sword of Spanish steel and an emerald ring, and of course Joan had still from Mistress Frances the gold locket that had proved the key to the entire Challoner mystery and was worth, she judged, a good fifty pounds sterling if it was worth a shilling.

Joan planned to remove the portrait of Sir John Challoner and burn it, for she declared she wanted no memento of the dishonorable baronet. She decided that in its place she would put a likeness of Elizabeth, their daughter, and wear it always next to her heart.

They made plans to leave London for Chelmsford at first light the next day and already had procured horses for that purpose when Thomas Cooke summoned Matthew for a private talk.

Joan waited nervously in their chamber for her husband's return, fearing a further delay threatened. It was nearly suppertime when Matthew appeared, the hesitant expression on his plain, square countenance of one who bears ill tidings.

"I pray you, husband," Joan said, not loath to speak her mind. "What was this urgent conversation you twain had?"

He returned her question with another. "How would it please you to spend Christmas in London?"

"I would rather spend Christmas in Chelmsford," she said without hesitation.

"Master Cooke has made me acquainted with certain difficulties at the Middle Temple," Matthew went on, as though she had already expressed her approval of the plan. "You see, he was impressed with our services at Thorncombe and had heard from Sir Robert and others at court about Bartholomew Fair."

"What difficulties? Are the young lawyers' revels become such riots that a country constable is needed to quell them?"

"Not exactly," Matthew said. "There have been several mysterious deaths—suicides, during the last month. Master Cooke fears there may be more. He desires that discreet inquiries be made, by a disinterested party."

"Disinterested party?" she exclaimed. "A fine lawyerly phrase *that*. I pray your brief association with Master Cooke has not corrupted your honest English beyond redemption. If these be suicides, as is supposed, then let inquiries be made to the victims themselves, for they would know best why they practice self-slaughter. I really don't understand you, Matthew. Pray God you gave no promise to our host! There are limits to a guest's gratitude, and have we not gone beyond ours? Let's home—to Chelmsford—as we planned."

"Well, it isn't as though *you* must stay, Joan."

But that concession, such as Joan regarded it, hardly pleased her either. "Great gods and little fishes, Matthew! You stay in London whilst I hie home to pass Christmas by myself and worry unto death about whatever mischief you've got yourself into?"

"There may be no danger at all. Master Cooke's suppositions may be groundless."

"Aye, as Mistress Frances' were, when she suspected her uncle had been murdered, the coroner's wise verdict to the contrary!"

"Joan—"

"Matthew! Pray credit me with what little brain God gave me. If Master Cooke wants you to inquire into suicides at the Middle Temple, I'll wager he thinks they're murders for good cause. Where there are murders done, there are murderers—a wretched breed notorious for keeping their works of evil to themselves and passing eager to send the nosy to an early grave for their pains. Master Cooke will just have to find someone else to solve these new enormities, if so they prove. Over a month we're now gone from our dear Chelmsford. The house will be a ruin, and heaven only knows how your business stands."

"Now, Joan—"

"Don't now-Joan me!"

"Joan!"

"Matthew, I shall be blunt, as is my fashion. You may stay here if you must, but I shall go home, if I have to walk the way. A pox upon all lawyers! Do they not stir up enough trouble in the courts with their quiddities and quibbles, suits and quittances, that they must murder one another and draw simple honest souls like ourselves into the stew!"

Matthew let Joan have her say and at length, when she had exhausted her store of objections, he said,

"Well, what do you think now?"

"I suppose Master Cooke provided you with all facts pertinent?"

"He did."

"And good and sufficient reasons why he thinks these suicides something worse?"

"Good and sufficient."

"But there has been no investigation by the authorities, I presume, else the London constabulary would have this charge?"

"The facts are dubious, as he reports them to me. The alleged murders seem to have no cause."

"In sum," she concluded, "it's another mystery—like Sir John's drowning. Murky incidents of such dubiousness as to appear self-slaughter."

"Exactly, although the manner of deaths is different."

She said, "Small compensation for this new broil."

She thought about it some more, these suicides at the Middle Temple. She looked at Matthew. His face wore that silly, knowing grin of his and it maddened her. She knew he would have his way despite her objections, for he knew her curiosity was as strong, indeed stronger, than his.

"Oh, very well, Matthew," she said at length. "You may accept the Cookes' invitation on our behalf."

And before he could budge from the spot, she added, "I have often heard of these Inns, as they are called, where our young students of the hoary law learn their litigious art, and I fain would see them for myself, even under these strange and dangerous circumstances."

His grin now full, Matthew went to do Joan's bidding, humming as he went a tune he had learned that day from an itinerant singer on Fleet Street and confident that no tale wanted its modicum of happiness wherein a merry tune was at its close.

About the Author

LEONARD TOURNEY teaches at the University of California, Santa Barbara. He is the author of THE BARTHOLOMEW FAIR MURDERS, LOW TREASON, THE PLAYERS' BOY IS DEAD, and FAMILIAR SPIRITS, all published by Ballantine Books.

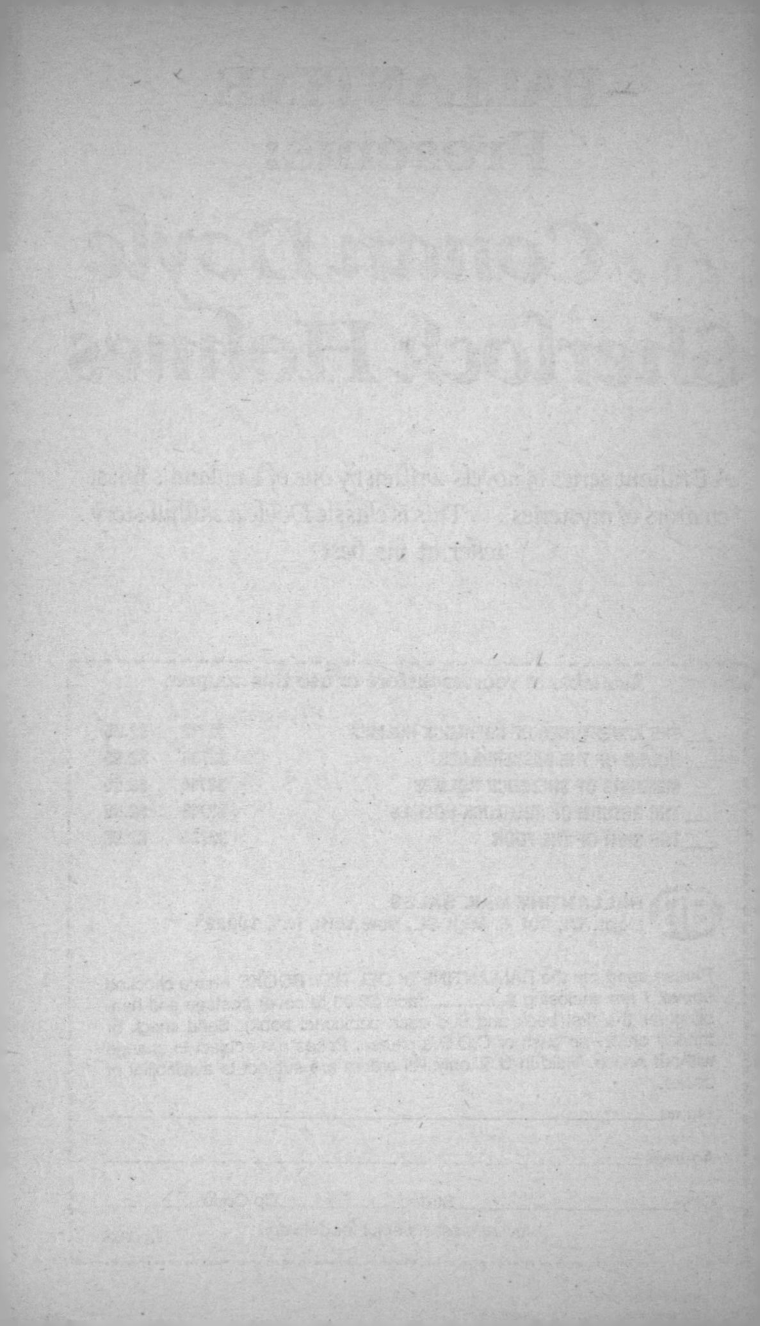